DUNE MESSIAH

"Complex, evocative, brilliant, it is all that DUNE was, and maybe a little more."

Galaxy Magazine

Frank Herbert was born in 1920 in Tacoma, Washington. He served in the U.S. Navy in World War II. He has worked as a photographer, television cameraman, oyster diver, lay analyst, and as a radio newsman. He was for many years a newspaperman in west coast cities from Los Angeles to Seattle, including more than ten years on the San Francisco *Examiner*. He lives with his family at the northeast corner of the northwest corner of the state of Washington. A project of his there is turning his six wooded acres into an ecological demonstration project to show how a high quality of life can be maintained with a minimum drain on the total energy system.

DUNE MESSIAH

FRANK HERBERT

BERKLEY BOOKS, NEW YORK

A shorter version of this book
appeared in Galaxy Magazine for
July-September, 1969, Copyright
© 1969 by Galaxy Publishing Corporation

DUNE MESSIAH

A Berkley Book / published by arrangement with
the author

PRINTING HISTORY
Berkley edition / September 1975
Forty-third printing / April 1983

ISBN: 0-425-06436-0

A BERKLEY BOOK ® TM 757,375

DUNE
MESSIAH

Q: What led you to take your particular approach to a
history of Muad'dib?

A: Why should I answer your questions?

Q: Because I will preserve your words.

A: Ahhh! The ultimate appeal to a historian!

Q: Will you cooperate then?

A: Why not? But you'll never understand what inspired
my Analysis of History. Never. You Priests have too
much at stake to...

Q: Try me.

A: Try you? Well, Again... why not? I was caught by the
shallowness of the common view of this planet which
arises from its popular name: Dune. Not Arrakis,
notice, but Dune. History is obsessed by Dune as
desert, as birthplace of the Fremen. Such history
concentrates on the customs which grew out of water
scarcity and the fact that Fremen led semi-nomadic
lives in stillsuits which recovered most of their body's
moisture.

Q: Are these things not true, then?

A: They are surface truth. As well ignore what lies beneath that surface as...as try to understand my birthplanet, Ix, without exploring how we derived our name from the fact that we are the ninth planet of our sun. No...no. It is not enough to see Dune as a place of savage storms. It is not enough to talk about the threat posed by the gigantic sandworms.

Q: But such things are crucial to the Arrakeen character!

A: Crucial? Of course. But they produce a one-view planet in the same way that Dune is a one-crop planet because it is the sole and exclusive source of the spice, melange.

Q: Yes. Let us hear you expand on the sacred spice.

A: Sacred! As with all things sacred, it gives with one hand and takes with the other. It extends life and allows the adept to foresee his future, but it ties him to a cruel addiction and marks his eyes as yours are marked: total blue without any white. Your eyes, your organs of *sight*, become one thing without contrast, a single view.

Q: Such heresy brought you to this cell!

A: I was brought to this cell by your Priests. As with all priests, you learned early to call the truth heresy.

Q: You are here because you dared to say that Paul Atreides lost something essential to his humanity before he could become Muad'dib.

A: Not to speak of his losing his father here in the Harkonnen war. Nor the death of Duncan Idaho, who sacrificed himself that Paul and the Lady Jessica could escape.

Q Your cynicism is duly noted.

A: Cynicism! That, no doubt is a greater crime than heresy. But, you see, I'm not really a cynic. I'm just an observer and commentator. I saw true nobility in Paul as he fled into the desert with his pregnant mother. Of course, she was a great asset as well as a burden.

Q: The flaw in your historians is that you'll never leave well enough alone. You see true nobility in the Holy Muad'dib, but you must append a cynical footnote. It's no wonder that the Bene Gesserit also denounce you.

A: You Priests do well to make common cause with the Bene Gesserit Sisterhood. They, too, survive by concealing what they do. But they cannot conceal the fact that the Lady Jessica was a Bene Gesserit-trained adept. You know she trained her son in the sisterhood's ways. My *crime* was to discuss this as a phenomenon, to expound upon their mental arts and their genetic program. You don't want attention called to the fact that Muad'dib was the Sisterhood's hoped for captive messiah, that he was their *kwisatz haderach* before he was your prophet.

Q: If I had any doubts about your death sentence, you have dispelled them.

A: I can only die once.

Q: There are deaths and there are deaths.

A: Beware lest you make a martyr of *me*. I do not think Muad'dib. . . . Tell me, does Muad'dib know what you do in these dungeons?

Q: We do not trouble the Holy Family with trivia.

A: (Laughter) And for this Paul Atreides fought his way to a niche among the Fremen! For this he learned to control and ride the sandworm! It was a mistake to answer your questions.

Q: But I will keep my promise to preserve your words.

A: Will you really? Then listen to me carefully, you Fremen degenerate, you Priest with no god except yourself! You have much to answer for. It was a Fremen ritual which gave Paul his first massive dose of melange, thereby opening him to visions of his futures. It was a Fremen ritual by which that same melange awakened the unborn Alia in the Lady Jessica's womb. Have you considered what it meant for Alia to be born into this universe fully cognitive, possessed of all her mother's memories and knowledge? No rape could be more terrifying.

Q: Without the sacred melange Muad'dib would not have become leader of all Fremen. Without her holy experience Alia would not be Alia.

A: Without your blind Fremen cruelty you would not be a priest. Ahhh, I know you Fremen. You think Muad'dib is yours because he mated with Chani, because he adopted Fremen customs. But he was an Atreides first and he was trained by a Bene Gesserit adept. He possessed disciplines totally unknown to you. You thought he brought you new organization and a new mission. He promised to transform your desert planet into a water-rich paradise. And while he dazzled you with such visions, he took your virginity!

Q: Such heresy does not change the fact that the Ecological Transformation of Dune proceeds apace.

A: And I committed the heresy of tracing the roots of that transformation, of exploring the consequences. That battle out there on the Plains of Arrakeen may have taught the universe that Fremen could defeat Imperial Sardaukar, but what else did it teach? When the stellar empire of the Corrino Family became a Fremen empire under Muad'dib, what else did the Empire become? Your Jihad only took twelve years, but what a lesson it taught. Now, the Empire understands the sham of Muad'dib's marriage to the Princess Irulan!

Q: You dare accuse Muad'dib of sham!

A: Though you kill me for it, it's not heresy. The Princess became his consort, not his mate. Chani, his little Fremen darling—she's his mate. Everyone knows this. Irulan was the key to a throne, nothing more.

Q: It's easy to see why those who conspire against Muad'dib use your Analysis of History as their rallying argument!

A: I'll not persuade you; I know that. But the argument of the conspiracy came before my Analysis. Twelve years of Muad'dib's Jihad created the argument. That's what united the ancient power groups and ignited the conspiracy against Muad'dib.

Such a rich store of myths enfolds Paul Muad'dib, the Mentat Emperor, and his sister, Alia, it is difficult to see the real persons behind these veils. But there were, after all, a man born Paul Atreides and a woman born Alia. Their flesh was subject to space and time. And even though their oracular powers placed them beyond the usual limits of time and space, they came from human stock. They experienced real events which left real traces upon a real universe. To understand them, it must be seen that their catastrophe was the catastrophe of all mankind. This work is dedicated, then, not to Muad'dib or his sister, but to their heirs—to all of us.

—Dedication in the Muad'dib Concordance as
  copied from The Tabla Memorium of the
  Mahdi Spirit Cult

Muad'dib's Imperial reign generated more historians than any other era in human history. Most of them argued a particular viewpoint, jealous and sectarian, but it says something about the peculiar impact of this man that he aroused such passions on so many diverse worlds.

Of course, he contained the ingredients of history, ideal and idealized. This man, born Paul Atreides in an ancient Great Family, received the deep *prana-bindu* training from the Lady Jessica, his Bene Gesserit mother, and had through this a superb control over muscles and nerves. But more than that, he was a *mentat*, an intellect whose capacities surpassed those of the religiously proscribed mechanical computers used by the ancients.

Above all else, Muad'dib was the *kwisatz haderach* which the Sisterhood's breeding program had sought across thousands of generations.

The kwisatz haderach, then, the one who could be "many places at once," this prophet, this man through whom the Bene Gesserit hoped to control human destiny—this man became Emperor Muad'dib and executed a marriage of convenience with a daughter of the Padishah Emperor he had defeated.

Think on the paradox, the failure implicit in this moment, for you surely have read other histories and know the surface facts. Muad'dib's wild Fremen did, indeed, overwhelm the Padishah Shaddam IV. They toppled the Sardaukar legions, the allied forces of the Great Houses, the Harkonnen armies and the mercenaries bought with money voted in the Landsraad. He brought the Spacing Guild to its knees and placed his own sister, Alia, on the religious throne the Bene Gesserit had thought their own.

He did all these things and more.

Muad'dib's Qizarate missionaries carried their religious war across space in a Jihad whose major impetus endured only twelve standard years, but in that time, religious colonialism brought all but a fraction of the human universe under one rule.

He did this because capture of Arrakis, that planet known more often as Dune, gave him a monopoly over the ultimate coin of the realm—the geriatric spice, melange, the poison that gave life.

Here was another ingredient of ideal history: a material whose psychic chemistry unraveled Time. Without melange, the Sisterhood's Reverend Mothers could not perform their feats of observation and human control. Without melange, the Guild's Steersmen could not navigate across space. Without melange, billions upon billions of Imperial citizens would die of addictive withdrawal.

Without melange, Paul-Muad'dib could not prophesy.

We know this moment of supreme power contained failure. There can be only one answer, that completely accurate and total prediction is lethal.

Other histories say Muad'dib was defeated by obvious plotters—the Guild, the Sisterhood and the scientific amoralists of the Bene Tleilex with their Face-Dancer disguises. Other histories point out the spies in Muad'dib's household. They make much of the Dune Tarot which clouded Muad'dib's powers of prophecy. Some show how Muad'dib was made to accept the services of a *ghola*, the flesh brought back from the dead and trained to destroy him. But certainly they must know this ghola was Duncan Idaho, the Atreides lieutenant who perished saving the life of the young Paul.

Yet, they delineate the Qizarate cabal guided by Korba the Panegyrist. They take us step by step through Korba's plan to make a martyr of Muad'dib and place the blame on Chani, the Fremen concubine.

How can any of this explain the facts as history has revealed them? They cannot. Only through the lethal nature of prophecy can we understand the failure of such enormous and far-seeing power.

Hopefully, other historians will learn something from this revelation.

—Analysis of History: Muad'dib
by Bronso of Ix

There exists no separation between gods and men; one blends softly casual into the other.
                                  —Proverbs of Muad'dib

Despite the murderous nature of the plot he hoped to devise, the thoughts of Scytale, the Tleilaxu Face Dancer, returned again and again to rueful compassion.

I shall regret causing death and misery to Muad'dib, he told himself.

He kept this benignity carefully hidden from his fellow conspirators. Such feelings told him, though, that he found it easier to identify with the victim than with the attackers—a thing characteristic of the Tleilaxu.

Scytale stood in bemused silence somewhat apart from the others. The argument about psychic poison had been going on for some time now. It was energetic and vehement, but polite in that blindly compulsive way adepts of the Great Schools always adopted for matters close to their dogma.

"When you think you have him skewered, right then you'll find him unwounded!"

That was the old Reverend Mother of the Bene Gesserit, Gaius Helen Mohiam, their hostess here on Wallach IX. She was a black-robed stick figure, a witch crone seated in a floater chair at Scytale's left. Her aba hood had been thrown back to expose a leathery face beneath silver hair. Deeply pocketed eyes stared out of skull-mask features.

They were using a *mirabhasa* language, honed phalange consonants and joined vowels. It was an instrument for conveying fine emotional subtleties. Edric, the Guild Steersman, replied to the Reverend Mother now with a vocal curtsy contained in a sneer—a lovely touch of disdainful politeness.

Scytale looked at the Guild envoy. Edric swam in a container of orange gas only a few paces away. His container sat in the center of the transparent dome which the Bene Gesserit had built for this meeting. The Guildsman was an elongated figure, vaguely humanoid with finned feet and hugely fanned membranous hands—a fish in a strange sea. His tank's vents emitted a pale orange cloud rich with the smell of the geriatric spice, melange.

"If we go on this way, we'll die of stupidity!"

That was the fourth person present—the *potential* member of the conspiracy—Princess Irulan, wife (*but not mate*, Scytale reminded himself) of their mutual foe. She stood at a corner of Edric's tank, a tall blond beauty, splendid in a robe of blue whale fur and matching hat. Gold buttons glittered at her ears. She carried herself with an aristocrat's hauteur, but something in the absorbed smoothness of her features betrayed the controls of her Bene Gesserit background.

Scytale's mind turned from nuances of language and faces to nuances of location. All around the dome lay hills mangy with melting snow which reflected mottled wet blueness from the small blue-white sun hanging at the meridian.

Why this particular place? Scytale wondered. The Bene Gesserit seldom did anything casually. Take the dome's open plan: a more conventional and confining space might've inflicted the Guildsman with claustrophobic nervousness. Inhibitions in his psyche were those of birth and life off-planet in open space.

To have built this place especially for Edric, though— what a sharp finger that pointed at his weakness.

What here, Scytale wondered, was aimed at me?

"Have you nothing to say for yourself, Scytale?" the Reverend Mother demanded.

"You wish to draw me into this fools' fight?" Scytale asked. "Very well. We're dealing with a potential messiah. You don't launch a frontal attack upon such a one. Martyrdom would defeat us."

They all stared at him.

"You think that's the only danger?" the Reverend Mother demanded, voice wheezing.

Scytale shrugged. He had chosen a bland, round-faced appearance for this meeting, jolly features and vapid full lips, the body of a bloated dumpling. It occurred to him now, as he studied his fellow conspirators, that he had made an ideal choice—out of instinct perhaps. He alone in this group could manipulate fleshly appearance across a wide spectrum of bodily shapes and features. He was the human chameleon, a Face Dancer, and the shape he wore now invited others to judge him too lightly.

"Well?" the Reverend Mother pressed.

"I was enjoying the silence," Scytale said. "Our hostilities are better left unvoiced."

The Reverend Mother drew back, and Scytale saw her reassessing him. They were all products of profound prana-bindu training, capable of muscle and nerve control that few humans ever achieved. But Scytale, a Face Dancer, had muscles and nerve linkages the others didn't even possess plus a special quality of *sympatico*, a mimic's insight with which he could put on the psyche of another as well as the other's appearance.

Scytale gave her enough time to complete the reassessment, said: "Poison!" He uttered the word with the atonals which said he alone understood its secret meaning.

The Guildsman stirred and ⸙ voice rolled from the glittering speaker globe which ⸱ ⸱ited a corner of his tank above Irulan. "We're discv⸱ ⸱ing *psychic* poison, not a physical one."

Scytale laughed. Mirabhasa laughter could flay an opponent and he held nothing back now.

Irulan smiled in appreciation, but the corners of the Reverend Mother's eyes revealed a faint hint of anger.

"Stop that!" Mohiam rasped.

Scytale stopped, but he had their attention now, Edric in a silent rage, the Reverend Mother alert in her anger, Irulan amused but puzzled.

"Our friend Edric suggests," Scytale said, "that a pair of Bene Gesserit witches trained in all their subtle ways have not learned the true uses of deception."

Mohiam turned to stare out at the cold hills of her Bene Gesserit homeworld. She was beginning to see the vital thing here, Scytale realized. That was good. Irulan, though, was another matter.

"Are you one of us or not, Scytale?" Edric asked. He stared out of tiny rodent eyes.

"My allegiance is not the issue," Scytale said. He kept his attention on Irulan. "You are wondering, Princess, if this was why you came all those parsecs, risked so much?"

She nodded agreement.

"Was it to bandy platitudes with a humanoid fish or dispute with a fat Tleilaxu Face Dancer?" Scytale asked.

She stepped away from Edric's tank, shaking her head in annoyance at the thick odor of melange.

Edric took this moment to pop a melange pill into his mouth. He ate the spice and breathed it and, no doubt, drank it, Scytale noted. Understandable, because the spice heightened a Steersman's prescience, gave him the power to guide a Guild heighliner across space at translight speeds. With spice awareness he found that line of the ship's future which avoided peril. Edric smelled another kind of peril now, but his crutch of prescience might not find it.

"I think it was a mistake for me to come here," Irulan said.

The Reverend Mother turned, opened her eyes, closed them, a curiously reptilian gesture.

Scytale shifted his gaze from Irulan to the tank, inviting the Princess to share his viewpoint. She would, Scytale knew, see Edric as a repellent figure: the bold stare, those monstrous feet and hands moving softly in the gas, the smoky swirling of orange eddies around him. She would wonder about his sex habits, thinking how odd it would be to mate with such a one. Even the field-force generator which recreated for Edric the weightlessness of space would set him apart from her now.

"Princess," Scytale said, "because of Edric here, your husband's oracular sight cannot stumble upon certain incidents, including this one ... presumably."

"Presumably," Irulan said.

Eyes closed, the Reverend Mother nodded. "The phenomenon of prescience is poorly understood even by its initiates," she said.

"I am a full Guild Navigator and have the Power," Edric said.

Again, the Reverend Mother opened her eyes. This time, she stared at the Face Dancer, eyes probing with that peculiar Bene Gesserit intensity. She was weighing minutiae.

"No, Reverend Mother," Scytale murmured, "I am not as simple as I appeared."

"We don't understand this Power of second sight," Irulan said. "There's a point. Edric says my husband cannot see, know or predict what happens within the sphere of a Navigator's influence. But how far does that influence extend?"

"There are people and things in our universe which I know only by their effects," Edric said, his fish mouth held in a thin line. "I know they have been here ...there...somewhere. As water creatures stir up the currents in their passage, so the prescient stir up Time. I have seen where your husband has been; never have I seen him nor the people who truly share his aims and loyalties. This is the concealment which an adept gives to those who are his."

"Irulan is not yours," Scytale said. And he looked sideways at the Princess.

"We all know why the conspiracy must be conducted only in my presence," Edric said.

Using the voice mode for describing a machine, Irulan said: "You have your uses, apparently."

She sees him now for what he is, Scytale thought. *Good!*

"The future is a thing to be shaped," Scytale said. "Hold that thought, Princess."

Irulan glanced at the Face Dancer.

"People who share Paul's aims and loyalties," she said. "Certain of his Fremen legionaries, then, wear his cloak. I have seen him prophesy for them, heard their cries of adulation for their Mahdi, their Muad'dib."

It has occurred to her, Scytale thought, *that she is on trial here, that a judgment remains to be made which could preserve her or destroy her. She sees the trap we set for her.*

Momentarily, Scytale's gaze locked with that of the Reverend Mother and he experienced the odd realization that they had shared this thought about Irulan. The Bene Gesserit, of course, had briefed their Princess, primed her with the *lie adroit.* But the moment always came when a Bene Gesserit must trust her own training and instincts.

"Princess, I know what it is you most desire from the Emperor," Edric said.

"Who does not know it?" Irulan asked.

"You wish to be the founding mother of the royal dynasty," Edric said, as though he had not heard her. "Unless you join us, that will never happen. Take my oracular word on it. The Emperor married you for political reasons, but you'll never share his bed."

"So the oracle is also a voyeur," Irulan sneered.

"The Emperor is more firmly wedded to his Fremen concubine than he is to you!" Edric snapped.

"And she gives him no heir," Irulan said.

"Reason is the first victim of strong emotion," Scytale murmured. He sensed the outpouring of Irulan's anger, saw his admonition take effect.

"She gives him no heir," Irulan said, her voice measuring out controlled calmness, "because I am secretly administering a contraceptive. Is that the sort of admission you wanted from me?"

"It'd not be a thing for the Emperor to discover," Edric said, smiling.

"I have lies ready for him," Irulan said. "He may have truthsense, but some lies are easier to believe than the truth."

"You must make the choice, Princess," Scytale said, "but understand what it is protects you."

"Paul is fair with me," she said. "I sit in his Council."

"In the twelve years you've been his Princess Consort," Edric asked, "has he shown you the slightest warmth?"

Irulan shook her head.

"He deposed your father with his infamous Fremen horde, married you to fix his claim to the throne, yet he has never crowned you Empress," Edric said.

"Edric tries to sway you with emotion, Princess," Scytale said. "Is that not interesting?"

She glanced at the Face Dancer, saw the bold smile on his features, answered it with raised eyebrows. She was fully aware now, Scytale saw, that if she left this conference under Edric's sway, part of their plot, these moments might be concealed from Paul's oracular vision.

If she withheld commitment, though...

"Does it seem to you, Princess," Scytale asked, "that Edric holds undue sway in our conspiracy?"

"I've already agreed," Edric said, "that I'll defer to the best judgment offered in our councils."

"And who chooses the best judgment?" Scytale asked.

"Do you wish the Princess to leave here without joining us?" Edric asked.

"He wishes her commitment to be a real one," the Reverend Mother growled. "There should be no trickery between us."

Irulan, Scytale saw, had relaxed into a thinking posture, hands concealed in the sleeves of her robe. She would be thinking now of the bait Edric had offered: *to found a royal dynasty!* She would be wondering what scheme the conspirators had provided to protect themselves from her. She would be weighing many things.

"Scytale," Irulan said presently, "it is said that you Tleilaxu have an odd system of honor: your victims must always have a means of escape."

"If they can but find it," Scytale agreed.

"Am I a victim?" Irulan asked.

A burst of laughter escaped Scytale.

The Reverend Mother snorted.

"Princess," Edric said, his voice softly persuasive, "you already are one of us, have no fear of that. Do you not spy upon the Imperial Household for your Bene Gesserit superiors?"

"Paul knows I report to my teachers," she said.

"But don't you give them the material for strong propaganda against your Emperor?" Edric asked.

Not "our" Emperor, Scytale noted. *"Your" Emperor. Irulan is too much the Bene Gesserit to miss that slip.*

"The question is one of powers and how they may be used," Scytale said, moving closer to the Guildsman's tank. "We of the Tleilaxu believe that in all the universe there is only the insatiable appetite of matter, that energy is the only true *solid*. And energy learns. Hear me well,

Princess: energy learns. This, we call power."

"You haven't convinced me we can defeat the Emperor," Irulan said.

"We haven't even convinced ourselves," Scytale said.

"Everywhere we turn," Irulan said, "his power confronts us. He's the kwisatz haderach, the one who can be many places at once. He's the Mahdi whose merest whim is absolute command to his Qizarate missionaries. He's the mentat whose computational mind surpasses the greatest ancient computers. He is Muad'dib whose orders to the Fremen legions depopulate planets. He possesses oracular vision which sees into the future. He has that gene pattern which we Bene Gesserits covet for—"

"We know his attributes," the Reverend Mother interrupted. "And we know the abomination, his sister Alia, possesses this gene pattern. But they're also humans, both of them. Thus, they have weaknesses."

"And where are those human weaknesses?" the Face Dancer asked. "Shall we search for them in the religious arm of his Jihad? Can the Emperor's Qizara be turned against him? What about the civil authority of the Great Houses? Can the Landsraad Congress do more than raise a verbal clamor?"

"I suggest the Combine Honnete Ober Advancer Mercantiles," Edric said, turning in his tank. "CHOAM is business and business follows profits."

"Or perhaps the Emperor's mother," Scytale said. "The Lady Jessica, I understand, remains on Caladan, but is in frequent communication with her son."

"That traitorous bitch," Mohiam said, voice level. "Would I might disown my own hands which trained her."

"Our conspiracy requires a lever," Scytale said.

"We are more than conspirators," the Reverend Mother countered.

"Ah, yes," Scytale agreed. "We are energetic and we learn quickly. This makes us the one true hope, the certain salvation of humankind." He spoke in the speech mode for absolute conviction, which was perhaps the ultimate sneer coming, as it did, from a Tleilaxu.

Only the Reverend Mother appeared to understand the subtlety. "Why?" she asked, directing the question at Scytale.

Before the Face Dancer could answer, Edric cleared his throat, said: "Let us not bandy philosophical nonsense. Every question can be boiled down to the one: 'Why is there anything?' Every religious, business and governmental question has the single derivative: 'Who will exercise the power?' Alliances, combines, complexes, they all chase mirages unless they go for the power. All else is nonsense, as most thinking beings come to realize."

Scytale shrugged, a gesture designed solely for the Reverend Mother. Edric had answered her question for him. The pontificating fool was their major weakness. To make sure the Reverend Mother understood, Scytale said: "Listening carefully to the teacher, one acquires an education."

The Reverend Mother nodded slowly.

"Princess," Edric said, "make your choice. You have been chosen as an instrument of destiny, the very finest..."

"Save your praise for those who can be swayed by it," Irulan said. "Earlier, you mentioned a ghost, a revenant with which we may contaminate the Emperor. Explain this."

"The Atreides will defeat himself!" Edric crowed.

"Stop talking riddles!" Irulan snapped. "What is this ghost?"

"A very unusual ghost," Edric said. "It has a body and a name. The body—that's the flesh of a renowned swordmaster known as Duncan Idaho. The name..."

"Idaho's dead," Irulan said. "Paul has mourned the loss often in my presence. He saw Idaho killed by my father's Sardaukar."

"Even in defeat," Edric said, "your father's Sardaukar did not abandon wisdom. Let us suppose a wise

Sardaukar commander recognized the swordmaster in a corpse his men had slain. What then? There exist uses for such flesh and training... if one acts swiftly."

"A Tleilaxu ghola," Irulan whispered, looking sideways at Scytale.

Scytale, observing her attention, exercised his Face-Dancer powers—shape flowing into shape, flesh moving and readjusting. Presently, a slender man stood before her. The face remained somewhat round, but darker and with slightly flattened features. High cheekbones formed shelves for eyes with definite epicanthic folds. The hair was black and unruly.

"A ghola of this appearance," Edric said, pointing to Scytale.

"Or merely another Face Dancer?" Irulan asked.

"No Face Dancer," Edric said. "A Face Dancer risks exposure under prolonged surveillance. No; let us assume that our wise Sardaukar commander had Idaho's corpse preserved for the axolotl tanks. Why not? This corpse held the flesh and nerves of one of the finest swordsmen in history, an adviser to the Atreides, a military genius. What a waste to lose all that training and ability when it might be revived as an instructor for the Sardaukar."

"I heard not a whisper of this and I was one of my father's confidantes," Irulan said.

"Ahh, but your father was a defeated man and within a few hours you had been sold to the new Emperor," Edric said.

"Was it done?" she demanded.

With a maddening air of complacency, Edric said: "Let us presume that our wise Sardaukar commander, knowing the need for speed, immediately sent the preserved flesh of Idaho to the Bene Tleilax. Let us suppose further that the commander and his men died before conveying this information to your father—who couldn't have made much use of it anyway. There would remain then a physical fact, a bit of flesh which had been sent off to the Tleilaxu. There was only one way for it to be sent, of course, on a heighliner. We of the Guild naturally know every cargo we transport. Learning of this one, would we not think it additional wisdom to purchase the ghola as a gift befitting an Emperor?"

"You've done it then," Irulan said.

Scytale, who had resumed his roly-poly first appearance, said: "As our long-winded friend indicates, we've done it."

"How has Idaho been conditioned?" Irulan asked.

"Idaho?" Edric asked, looking at the Tleilaxu. "Do you know of an Idaho, Scytale?"

"We sold you a creature called Hayt," Scytale said.

"Ah, yes—Hayt," Edric said. "Why did you sell him to us?"

"Because we once bred a kwisatz haderach of our own," Scytale said.

With a quick movement of her old head, the Reverend Mother looked up at him. "You didn't tell us that!" she accused.

"You didn't ask," Scytale said.

"How did you overcome your kwisatz haderach?" Irulan asked.

"A creature who has spent his life creating one particular representation of his selfdom will die rather than become the antithesis of that representation," Scytale said.

"I do not understand," Edric ventured.

"He killed himself," the Reverend Mother growled.

"Follow me well, Reverend Mother," Scytale warned, using a voice mode which said: You are not a sex object, have never been a sex object, cannot be a sex object.

The Tleilaxu waited for the blatant emphasis to sink in. She must not mistake his intent. Realization must pass through anger into awareness that the Tleilaxu certainly could not make such an accusation, knowing as he must the breeding requirements of the Sisterhood. His words, though, contained a gutter insult, completely out of character for a Tleilaxu.

Swiftly, using the mirabhasa placative mode, Edric tried to smooth over the moment. "Scytale, you told us you sold Hayt because you shared our desire on how to use him."

"Edric, you will remain silent until I give you permission to speak," Scytale said. And as the Guildsman started to protest, the Reverend Mother snapped: "Shut up, Edric!"

The Guildsman drew back into his tank in flailing agitation.

"Our own transient emotions aren't pertinent to a solution of the mutual problem," Scytale said. "They cloud reasoning because the only relevant emotion is the basic fear which brought us to this meeting."

"We understand," Irulan said, glancing at the Reverend Mother.

"You must see the dangerous limitations of our shield," Scytale said. "The oracle cannot chance upon what it cannot understand."

"You are devious, Scytale," Irulan said.

How devious she must not guess, Scytale thought. *When this is done, we will possess a kwisatz haderach we can control. These others will possess nothing.*

"What was the origin of your kwisatz haderach?" the Reverend Mother asked.

"We've dabbled in various pure essences," Scytale said. "Pure good and pure evil. A pure villain who delights only in creating pain and terror can be quite educational."

"The old Baron Harkonnen, our Emperor's grandfather, was he a Tleilaxu creation?" Irulan asked.

"Not one of ours," Scytale said. "But then nature often produces creations as deadly as ours. We merely produce them under conditions where we can study them."

"I will not be passed by and treated this way!" Edric protested. "Who is it hides this meeting from—"

"You see?" Scytale asked. "Whose best judgment conceals us? What judgment?"

"I wish to discuss our mode of giving Hayt to the

Emperor," Edric insisted. "It's my understanding that Hayt reflects the old morality that the Atreides learned on his birthworld. Hayt is supposed to make it easy for the Emperor to enlarge his moral nature, to delineate the positive-negative elements of life and religion."

Scytale smiled, passing a benign gaze over his companions. They were as he'd been led to expect. The old Reverend Mother wielded her emotions like a scythe. Irulan had been well trained for a task at which she had failed, a flawed Bene Gesserit creation. Edric was no more (and no less) than the magician's hand: he might conceal and distract. For now, Edric relapsed into sullen silence as the others ignored him.

"Do I understand that this Hayt is intended to poison Paul's psyche?" Irulan asked.

"More or less," Scytale said.

"And what of the Qizarate?" Irulan asked.

"It requires only the slightest shift in emphasis, a glissade of the emotions, to transform envy into enmity," Scytale said.

"And CHOAM?" Irulan asked.

"They will rally round profit," Scytale said.

"What of the other power groups?"

"One invokes the name of government," Scytale said. "We will annex the less powerful in the name of morality and progress. Our opposition will die of its own entanglements."

"Alia, too?"

"Hayt is a multi-purpose ghola," Scytale said. "The Emperor's sister is of an age when she can be distracted by a charming male designed for that purpose. She will be attracted by his maleness and by his abilities as a mentat."

Mohiam allowed her old eyes to go wide in surprise. "The ghola's a mentat? That's a dangerous move."

"To be accurate," Irulan said, "a mentat must have accurate data. What if Paul asks him to define the purpose behind our gift?"

"Hayt will tell the truth," Scytale said. "It makes no difference."

"So you leave an escape door open for Paul," Irulan said.

"A mentat!" Mohiam muttered.

Scytale glanced at the old Reverend Mother, seeing the ancient hates which colored her responses. From the days of the Butlerian Jihad when "thinking machines" had been wiped from most of the universe, computers had inspired distrust. Old emotions colored the human computer as well.

"I do not like the way you smile," Mohiam said abruptly, speaking in the truth mode as she glared up at Scytale.

In the same mode, Scytale said: "And I think less of what pleases you. But we must work together. We all see that." He glanced at the Guildsman. "Don't we, Edric?"

"You teach painful lessons," Edric said. "I presume you wished to make it plain that I must not assert myself against the combined judgments of my fellow conspirators."

"You see, he can be taught," Scytale said.

"I see other things as well," Edric growled. "The Atreides holds a monopoly on the spice. Without it I cannot probe the future. The Bene Gesserit lose their truthsense. We have stockpiles, but these are finite. Melange is a powerful coin."

"Our civilization has more than one coin," Scytale said. "Thus, the law of supply and demand fails."

"You think to steal the secret of it," Mohiam wheezed. "And him with a planet guarded by his mad Fremen!"

"The Fremen are civil, educated and ignorant," Scytale said. "They're not mad. They're trained to believe, not to know. Belief can be manipulated. Only knowledge is dangerous."

"But will I be left with something to father a royal dynasty?" Irulan asked.

They all heard the commitment in her voice, but only Edric smiled at it.

"Something," Scytale said. "Something."

"It means the end of this Atreides as a ruling force," Edric said.

"I should imagine that others less gifted as oracles have made that prediction," Scytale said. "For them, *mektub al mellah*, as the Fremen say."

"The thing was written with salt," Irulan translated.

As she spoke, Scytale recognized what the Bene Gesserit had arrayed here for him—a beautiful and intelligent female who could never be his. *Ah, well,* he thought, *perhaps I'll copy her for another.*

Every civilization must contend with an unconscious force which can block, betray or countermand almost any conscious intention of the collectivity.

—Tleilaxu Theorem (unproven)

Paul sat on the edge of his bed and began stripping off his desert boots. They smelled rancid from the lubricant which eased the action of the heel-powered pumps that drove his stillsuit. It was late. He had prolonged his nighttime walk and caused worry for those who loved him. Admittedly, the walks were dangerous, but it was a kind of danger he could recognize and meet immediately. Something compelling and attractive surrounded walking anonymously at night in the streets of Arrakeen.

He tossed the boots into the corner beneath the room's lone glowglobe, attacked the seal strips of his stillsuit.

Gods below, how tired he was! The tiredness stopped at his muscles, though, and left his mind seething. Watching the mundane activities of everyday life filled him with profound envy. Most of that nameless flowing life outside the walls of his Keep couldn't be shared by an Emperor—but . . . to walk down a public street without attracting attention: what a privilege! To pass by the clamoring of mendicant pilgrims, to hear a Fremen curse a shopkeeper: "You have damp hands!" . . .

Paul smiled at the memory, slipped out of his stillsuit.

He stood naked and oddly attuned to his world. Dune was a world of paradox now—a world under siege, yet the center of power. To come under siege, he decided, was the inevitable fate of power. He stared down at the green carpeting, feeling its rough texture against his soles.

The streets had been ankle deep in sand blown over the Shield Wall on the stratus wind. Foot traffic had churned it into choking dust which clogged stillsuit filters. He could smell the dust even now despite a blower cleaning at the portals of his Keep. It was an odor full of desert memories.

Other days . . . other dangers.

Compared to those other days, the peril in his lonely walks remained minor. But, putting on a stillsuit, he put on the desert. The suit with all its apparatus for reclaiming his body's moisture guided his thoughts in subtle ways, fixed his movements in a desert pattern. He became wild Fremen. More than a disguise, the suit made of him a stranger to his city self. In the stillsuit, he abandoned security and put on the old skills of violence. Pilgrims and townfolk passed him then with eyes downcast. They left the wild ones strictly alone out of prudence. If the desert had a face for city folk, it was a Fremen face concealed by a stillsuit's mouth-nose filters.

In truth, there existed now only the small danger that someone from the old *sietch* days might mark him by his walk, by his odor or by his eyes. Even then, the chances of meeting an enemy remained small.

A swish of door hangings and a wash of light broke his reverie. Chani entered bearing his coffee service on a platinum tray. Two slaved glowglobes followed her, darting to their positions: one at the head of their bed, one hovering beside her to light her work.

Chani moved with an ageless air of fragile power—so self-contained, so vulnerable. Something about the way she bent over the coffee service reminded him then of their first days. Her features remained darkly elfin, seemingly unmarked by their years—unless one examined the outer corners of her whiteless eyes, noting the lines there: "sandtracks," the Fremen of the desert called them.

Steam wafted from the pot as she lifted the lid by its Hagar emerald knob. He could tell the coffee wasn't yet ready by the way she replaced the lid. The pot—fluting silver female shape, pregnant—had come to him as a *ghanima*, a spoil of battle won when he'd slain the former owner in single combat. Jamis, that'd been the man's name...Jamis. What an odd immortality death had earned for Jamis. Knowing death to be inevitable, had Jamis carried that particular one in his hand?

Chani put out cups: blue pottery squatting like attendants beneath the immense pot. There were three cups: one for each drinker and one for all the former owners.

"It'll only be a moment," she said.

She looked at him then, and Paul wondered how he appeared in her eyes. Was he yet the exotic offworlder, slim and wiry but water-fat when compared to Fremen? Had he remained the Usul of his tribal name who'd taken her in "Freman *tau*" while they'd been fugitives in the desert?

Paul stared down at his own body: hard muscles, slender...a few more scars, but essentially the same despite twelve years as Emperor. Looking up, he glimpsed his face in a shelf mirror—blue-blue Fremen eyes, mark of spice addiction; a sharp Atreides nose. He looked the proper grandson for an Atreides who'd died in the bull ring creating a spectacle for his people.

Something the old man had said slipped then into Paul's mind: *"One who rules assumes irrevocable responsibility for the ruled. You are a husbandman. This demands, at times, a selfless act of love which may only be amusing to those you rule."*

People still remembered that old man with affection.

And what have I done for the Atreides name? Paul asked himself. *I've loosed the wolf among the sheep.*

For a moment, he contemplated all the death and violence going on in his mind.

"Into bed now!" Chani said in a sharp tone of command that Paul knew would've shocked his Imperial subjects.

He obeyed, lay back with his hands behind his head, letting himself be lulled by the pleasant familiarity of Chani's movements.

The room around them struck him suddenly with amusement. It was not at all what the populace must imagine as the Emperor's bedchamber. The yellow light of restless glowglobes moved the shadows in an array of colored glass jars on a shelf behind Chani. Paul named their contents silently—the dry ingredients of the desert pharmacopoeia, unguents, incense, mementos... a pinch of sand from Sietch Tabr, a lock of hair from their firstborn... long dead... twelve years dead... an innocent bystander killed in the battle that had made Paul Emperor.

The rich odor of spice-coffee filled the room. Paul inhaled, his glance falling on a yellow bowl beside the tray where Chani was preparing the coffee. The bowl held ground nuts. The inevitable poison-snooper mounted beneath the table waved its insect arms over the food. The snooper angered him. They'd never needed snoopers in the desert days!

"Coffee's ready," Chani said. "Are you hungry?"

His angry denial was drowned in the whistling scream of a spice lighter hurling itself spaceward from the field outside Arrakeen.

Chani saw his anger, though, poured their coffee, put a cup near his hand. She sat down on the foot of the bed, exposed his legs, began rubbing them where the muscles were knotted from walking in the stillsuit. Softly, with a casual air which did not deceive him, she said: "Let us discuss Irulan's desire for a child."

Paul's eyes snapped wide open. He studied Chani carefully. "Irulan's been back from Wallach less than two days," he said. "Has she been at you already?"

"We've not discussed her frustrations," Chani said.

Paul forced his mind to mental alertness, examined Chani in the harsh light of observational minutiae, the Bene Gesserit Way his mother had taught him in violation of her vows. It was a thing he didn't like doing with Chani. Part of her hold on him lay in the fact he so seldom needed his tension-building powers with her. Chani mostly avoided indiscreet questions. She maintained a Fremen sense of good manners. Hers were more often practical questions. What interested Chani were facts which bore on the position of her man—his strength in Council, the loyalty of his legions, the abilities and talents of his allies. Her memory held catalogs of names and cross-indexed details. She could rattle off the major weakness of every known enemy, the potential dispositions of opposing forces, battle plans of their military leaders, the tooling and production capacities of basic industries.

Why now, Paul wondered, did she ask about Irulan?

"I've troubled your mind," Chani said. "That wasn't my intention."

"What was your intention?"

She smiled shyly, meeting his gaze. "If you're angered, love, please don't hide it."

Paul sank back against the headboard. "Shall I put her away?" he asked. "Her use is limited now and I don't like the things I sense about her trip home to the Sisterhood."

"You'll not put her away," Chani said. She went on massaging his legs, spoke matter-of-factly: "You've said many times she's your contact with our enemies, that you can read their plans through her actions."

"Then why ask about her desire for a child?"

"I think it'd disconcert our enemies and put Irulan in a vulnerable position should you make her pregnant."

He read by the movements of her hands on his legs what that statement had cost her. A lump rose in his throat. Softly, he said: "Chani, beloved, I swore an oath never to take her into my bed. A child would give her too much power. Would you have her displace you?"

"I have no place."

"Not so, Sihaya, my desert springtime. What is this sudden concern for Irulan?"

"It's concern for you, not for her! If she carried an Atreides child, her friends would question her loyalties. The less trust our enemies place in her, the less use she is to them."

"A child for her could mean your death," Paul said. "You know the plotting in this place." A movement of his arm encompassed the Keep.

"You must have an heir!" she husked.

"Ahhh," he said.

So that was it: Chani had not produced a child for him. Someone else, then, must do it. Why not Irulan? That was the way Chani's mind worked. And it must be done in an act of love because all the Empire avowed strong taboos against artificial ways. Chani had come to a Fremen decision.

Paul studied her face in this new light. It was a face he knew better in some ways than his own. He had seen this face soft with passion, in the sweetness of sleep, awash in fears and angers and griefs.

He closed his eyes, and Chani came into his memories as a girl once more—veiled in springtime, singing, waking from sleep beside him—so perfect that the very vision of her consumed him. In his memory, she smiled . . . shyly at first, then strained against the vision as though she longed to escape.

Paul's mouth went dry. For a moment, his nostrils tasted the smoke of a devastated future and the voice of

another kind of vision commanding him to disengage...disengage...disengage. His prophetic visions
had been eavesdropping on eternity for such a long while,
catching snatches of foreign tongues, listening to stones
and to flesh not his own. Since the day of his first
encounter with terrible purpose, he had peered at the
future, hoping to find peace.

There existed a way, of course. He knew it by heart
without knowing the heart of it—a rote future, strict in its
instructions to him: disengage, disengage, disengage...

Paul opened his eyes, looked at the decision in Chani's
face. She had stopped massaging his legs, sat still
now—purest Fremen. Her features remained familiar
beneath the blue *nezhoni* scarf she often wore about her
hair in the privacy of their chambers. But the mask of
decision sat on her, an ancient and alien-to-him way of
thinking. Fremen women had shared their men for
thousands of years—not always in peace, but with a way
of making the fact nondestructive. Something mysteriously Fremen in this fashion had happened in Chani.

"You'll give me the only heir I want," he said.

"You've seen this?" she asked, making it obvious by her
emphasis that she referred to prescience.

As he had done many times, Paul wondered how he
could explain the delicacy of the oracle, the Timelines
without number which vision waved before him on an
undulating fabric. He sighed, remembered water lifted
from a river in the hollow of his hands—trembling,
draining. Memory drenched his face in it. How could he
drench himself in futures growing increasingly obscure
from the pressures of too many oracles?

"You've not *seen* it, then," Chani said.

That vision-future scarce any longer accessible to him
except at the expenditure of life-draining effort, what
could it show them except grief? Paul asked himself. He
felt that he occupied an inhospitable middle zone, a
wasted place where his emotions drifted, swayed, swept
outward in unchecked restlessness.

Chani covered his legs, said: "An heir to House Atreides, this is not something you leave to chance or one woman."

That was a thing his mother might've said, Paul thought. He wondered if the Lady Jessica had been in secret communication with Chani. His mother would think in terms of House Atreides. It was a pattern bred and conditioned into her by the Bene Gesserit, and would hold true even now when her powers were turned against the Sisterhood.

"You listened when Irulan came to me today," he accused.

"I listened." She spoke without looking at him.

Paul focused his memory on the encounter with Irulan. He'd let himself into the family salon, noted an unfinished robe on Chani's loom. There'd been an acrid wormsmell to the place, an evil odor which almost hid the underlying cinnamon bite of melange. Someone had spilled unchanged spice essence and left it to combine there with a spice-based rug. It had not been a felicitous combination. Spice essence had dissolved the rug. Oily marks lay congealed on the plastone floor where the rug had been. He'd thought to send for someone to clean away the mess, but Harah, Stilgar's wife and Chani's closest feminine friend, had slipped in to announce Irulan.

He'd been forced to conduct the interview in the presence of that evil smell, unable to escape a Fremen superstition that evil smells foretold disaster.

Harah withdrew as Irulan entered.

"Welcome," Paul said.

Irulan wore a robe of gray whale fur. She pulled it close, touched a hand to her hair. He could see her wondering at his mild tone. The angry words she'd obviously prepared for this meeting could be sensed leaving her mind in a welter of second thoughts.

"You came to report that the Sisterhood had lost its last vestige of morality," he said.

"Isn't it dangerous to be that ridiculous?" she asked.

"To be ridiculous and dangerous, a questionable alliance," he said. His renegade Bene Gesserit training detected her putting down an impulse to withdraw. The effort exposed a brief glimpse of underlying fear, and he saw she'd been assigned a task not to her liking.

"They expect a bit too much from a princess of the blood royal," he said.

Irulan grew very still and Paul became aware that she had locked herself into a viselike control. A heavy burden, indeed, he thought. And he wondered why prescient visions had given him no glimpse of this possible future.

Slowly, Irulan relaxed. There was no point in surrendering to fear, no point in retreat, she had decided.

"You've allowed the weather to fall into a very primitive pattern," she said, rubbing her arms through the robe. "It was dry and there was a sandstorm today. Are you never going to let it rain here?"

"You didn't come here to talk about the weather," Paul said. He felt that he had been submerged in double meanings. Was Irulan trying to tell him something which her training would not permit her to say openly? It seemed that way. He felt that he had been cast adrift suddenly and now must thrash his way back to some steady place.

"I must have a child," she said.

He shood his head from side to side.

"I must have my way!" she snapped. "If need be, I'll find another father for my child. I'll cuckold you and dare you to expose me."

"Cuckold me all you wish," he said, "but no child."

"How can you stop me?"

With a smile of upmost kindness, he said: "I'd have you garroted, if it came to that."

Shocked silence held her for a moment and Paul sensed Chani listened behind the heavy draperies into their private apartments.

"I am your wife," Irulan whispered.

"Let us not play these silly games," he said. "You play a part, no more. We both know who my wife is."

"And I am a convenience, nothing more," she said, voice heavy with bitterness.

"I have no wish to be cruel to you," he said.

"You chose me for this position."

"Not I," he said. "Fate chose you. Your father chose you. The Bene Gesserit chose you. The Guild chose you. And they have chosen you once more. For what have they chosen you, Irulan?"

"Why can't I have your child?"

"Because that's a role for which you weren't chosen."

"It's my right to bear the royal heir! My father was—"

"Your father was and is a beast. We both know he'd lost almost all touch with the humanity he was supposed to rule and protect."

"Was he hated less than you're hated?" she flared.

"A good question," he agreed, a sardonic smile touching the edges of his mouth.

"You say you've no wish to be cruel to me, yet..."

"And that's why I agree that you can take any lover you choose. But understand me well: take a lover, but bring no sour-fathered child into my household. I would deny such a child. I don't begrudge you any male alliance as long as you are discreet... and childless. I'd be silly to feel otherwise under the circumstances. But don't presume upon this license which I freely bestow. Where the throne is concerned, I control what blood is heir to it. The Bene Gesserit doesn't control this, nor does the Guild. This is one of the privileges I won when I smashed your father's Sardaukar legions out there on the Plain of Arrakeen."

"It's on your head, then," Irulan said. She whirled and swept out of the chamber.

Remembering the encounter now, Paul brought his awareness out of it and focused on Chani seated beside him on their bed. He could understand his ambivalent feelings about Irulan, understand Chani's Fremen decision. Under other circumstances Chani and Irulan might have been friends.

"What have you decided?" Chani asked.

"No child," he said.

Chani made the Fremen crysknife sign with the index finger and thumb of her right hand.

"It could come to that," he agreed.

"You don't think a child would solve anything with Irulan?" she asked.

"Only a fool would think that."

"I am not a fool, my love."

Anger possessed him. "I've never said you were! But this isn't some damned romantic novel we're discussing. That's a real princess down the hall. She was raised in all the nasty intrigues of an Imperial Court. Plotting is as natural to her as writing her stupid histories!"

"They are not stupid, love."

"Probably not." He brought his anger under control, took her hand in his. "Sorry. But that woman has many plots—plots within plots. Give in to one of her ambitions and you could advance another of them."

Her voice mild, Chani said: "Haven't I always said as much?"

"Yes, of course you have." He stared at her. "Then what are you really trying to say to me?"

She lay down beside him, placed her hand against his neck. "They have come to a decision on how to fight you," she said. "Irulan reeks of secret decisions."

Paul stroked her hair.

Chani had peeled away the dross.

Terrible purpose brushed him. It was a *coriolis* wind in his soul. It whistled through the framework of his being. His body knew things then never learned in consciousness.

"Chani, beloved," he whispered, "do you know what I'd spend to end the Jihad—to separate myself from the damnable godhead the Qizarate forces onto me?"

She trembled. "You have but to command it," she said.

"Oh, no. Even if I died now, my name would still lead them. When I think of the Atreides name tied to this religious butchery..."

"But you're the Emperor! You've—"

"I'm a figurehead. When godhead's given, that's the one thing the so-called god no longer controls." A bitter laugh shook him. He sensed the future looking back at him out of dynasties not even dreamed. He felt his being cast out, crying, unchained from the rings of fate—only his name continued. "I was chosen," he said. "Perhaps at birth...certainly before I had much say in it. I was chosen."

"Then un-choose," she said.

His arm tightened around her shoulder. "In time, beloved. Give me yet a little time."

Unshed tears burned his eyes.

"We should return to Sietch Tabr," Chani said. "There's too much to contend with in this tent of stone."

He nodded, his chin moving against the smooth fabric of the scarf which covered her hair. The soothing spice smell of her filled his nostrils.

Sietch. The ancient Chakobsa word absorbed him: a place of retreat and safety in a time of peril. Chani's suggestion made him long for vistas of open sand, for clean distances where one could see an enemy coming from a long way off.

"The tribes expect Muad'dib to return to them," she said. She lifted her head to look at him. "You belong to us."

"I belong to a vision," he whispered.

He thought then of the Jihad, of the gene mingling across parsecs and the vision which told him how he might end it. Should he pay the price? All the hatefulness would evaporate, dying as fires die—ember by ember. But...oh! The terrifying price!

I never wanted to be a god, he thought. *I wanted only to disappear like a jewel of trace dew caught by the morning. I wanted to escape the angels and the damned—alone...as though by an oversight.*

"Will we go back to the Sietch?" Chani pressed.

"Yes," he whispered. And he thought: *I must pay the price.*

Chani heaved a deep sigh, settled back against him.

I've loitered, he thought. And he saw how he'd been hemmed in by boundaries of love and the Jihad. And what was one life, no matter how beloved, against all the lives the Jihad was certain to take? Could single misery be weighed against the agony of multitudes?

"Love?" Chani said, questioning.

He put a hand against her lips.

I'll yield up myself, he thought. *I'll rush out while I yet have the strength, fly through a space a bird might not find.* It was a useless thought, and he knew it. The Jihad would follow his ghost.

What could he answer? he wondered. How explain when people taxed him with brutal foolishness? Who might understand?

I wanted only to look back and say: "There! There's an existence which couldn't hold me. See! I vanish! No restraint or net of human devising can trap me ever again. I renounce my religion! This glorious instant is mine! I'm free!"

What empty words!

"A big worm was seen below the Shield Wall yesterday," Chani said. "More than a hundred meters long, they say. Such big ones come rarely into this region any more. The water repels them, I suppose. They say this one came to summon Muad'dib home to his desert." She pinched his chest. "Don't laugh at me!"

"I'm not laughing."

Paul, caught by wonder at the persistent Fremen mythos, felt a heart constriction, a thing inflicted upon his lifeline: *adab,* the demanding memory. He recalled his childhood room on Caladan then...dark night in the stone chamber...a vision! It'd been one of his earliest prescient moments. He felt his mind dive into the vision, saw through a veiled cloud-memory (vision-within-vision) a line of Fremen, their robes trimmed with dust. They paraded past a gap in tall rocks. They carried a long, cloth-wrapped burden.

And Paul heard himself say in the vision: "It was

mostly sweet... but you were the sweetest of all..."

Adab released him.

"You're so quiet," Chani whispered. "What is it?"

Paul shuddered, sat up, face averted. "You're angry because I've been to the desert's edge," Chani said.

He shook his head without speaking.

"I only went because I want a child," Chani said.

Paul was unable to speak. He felt himself consumed by the raw power of that early vision. Terrible purpose! In that moment, his whole life was a limb shaken by the departure of a bird... and the bird was *chance*. Free will.

I succumbed to the lure of the oracle, he thought.

And he sensed that succumbing to this lure might be to fix himself upon a single-track life. Could it be, he wondered, that the oracle didn't *tell* the future? Could it be that the oracle *made* the future? Had he exposed his life to some web of underlying threads, trapped himself there in that long-ago awakening, victim of a spider-future which even now advanced upon him with terrifying jaws.

A Bene Gesserit axiom slipped into his mind: *To use raw power is to make yourself infinitely vulnerable to greater powers.*

"I know it angers you," Chani said, touching his arm. "It's true that the tribes have revived the old rites and the blood sacrifices, but I took no part in those."

Paul inhaled a deep, trembling breath. The torrent of his vision dissipated, became a deep, still place whose currents moved with absorbing power beyond his reach.

"Please," Chani begged. "I want a child, our child. Is that a terrible thing?"

Paul caressed her arm where she touched him, pulled away. He climbed from the bed, extinguished the glowglobes, crossed to the balcony window, opened the draperies. The deep desert could not intrude here except by its odors. A windowless wall climbed to the night sky across from him. Moonlight slanted down into an enclosed garden, sentinel trees and broad leaves, wet foliage. He could see a fish pond reflecting stars among the leaves, pockets of white floral brilliance in the shadows. Momentarily, he saw the garden through Fremen eyes: alien, menacing, dangerous in its waste of water.

He thought of the Water Sellers, their way destroyed by the lavish dispensing from his hands. They hated him. He'd slain the past. And there were others, even those who'd fought for the sols to buy precious water, who hated him for changing the old ways. As the ecological pattern dictated by Muad'dib remade the planet's landscape, human resistance increased. Was it not presumptuous, he wondered, to think he could make over an entire planet—everything growing where and how he told it to grow? Even if he succeeded, what of the universe waiting out there? Did it fear similar treatment?

Abruptly, he closed the draperies, sealed the ventilators. He turned toward Chani in the darkness, felt her waiting there. Her water rings tinkled like the almsbells of pilgrims. He groped his way to the sound, encountered her outstretched arms.

"Beloved," she whispered. "Have I troubled you?"

Her arms enclosed his future as they enclosed him.

"Not you," he said. "Oh . . . not you."

The advent of the Field Process shield and the lasgun with their explosive interaction, deadly to attacker and attacked, placed the current determinatives on weapons technology. We need not go into the special role of atomics. The fact that any Family in my Empire could so deploy its atomics as to destroy the planetary bases of fifty or more other Families causes some nervousness, true. But all of us possess precautionary plans for devastating retaliation. Guild and Landsraad contain the keys which hold this force in check, No, my concern goes to the development of humans as special weapons. Here is a virtually unlimited field which a few powers are developing.

—Muad'dib: Lecture to the War College
from The Stilgar Chronicle

The old man stood in his doorway peering out with blue-in-blue eyes. The eyes were veiled by that native suspicion all desert folk held for strangers. Bitter lines tortured the edges of his mouth where it could be seen through a fringe of white beard. He wore no stillsuit and it said much that he ignored this fact in the full knowledge of the moisture pouring from his house through the open door.

Scytale bowed, gave the greeting signal of the conspiracy.

From somewhere behind the old man came the sound of a rebec wailing through the atonal dissonance of *semuta* music. The old man's manner carried no drug dullness, an indication that semuta was the weakness of another. It seemed strange to Scytale, though, to find that sophisticated vice in this place.

"Greetings from afar," Scytale said, smiling through the flat-featured face he had chosen for this encounter. It occurred to him, then, that this old man might recognize the chosen face. Some of the older Fremen here on Dune had known Duncan Idaho.

The choice of features, which he had thought amusing, might have been a mistake, Scytale decided. But he dared not change the face out here. He cast nervous glances up and down the street. Would the old man never invite him inside?

"Did you know my son?" the old man asked.

That, at least, was one of the countersigns. Scytale made the proper response, all the time keeping his eyes alert for any suspicious circumstance in his surroundings. He did not like his position here. The street was a cul-de-sac ending in this house. The houses all around had been built for veterans of the Jihad. They formed a suburb of Arrakeen which stretched into the Imperial Basin past Tiemag. The walls which hemmed in this street presented blank faces of dun plasmeld broken by dark shadows of sealed doorways and, here and there, scrawled obscenities. Beside this very door someone had chalked a pronouncement that one Beris had brought back to Arrakis a loathsome disease which deprived him of his manhood.

"Do you come in partnership," the old man asked.

"Alone," Scytale said.

The old man cleared his throat, still hesitating in that maddening way.

Scytale cautioned himself to patience. Contact in this fashion carried its own dangers. Perhaps the old man knew some reason for carrying on this way. It was the proper hour, though. The pale sun stood almost directly overhead. People of this quarter remained sealed in their houses to sleep through the hot part of the day.

Was it the new neighbor who bothered the old man? Scytale wondered. The adjoining house, he knew, had been assigned to Otheym, once a member of Muad'dib's dreaded Fedaykin death commandos. And Bijaz, the catalyst-dwarf, waited with Otheym.

Scytale returned his gaze to the old man, noted the empty sleeve dangling from the left shoulder and the lack of a stillsuit. An air of command hung about this old man. He'd been no foot slogger in the Jihad.

"May I know the visitor's name?" the old man asked.

Scytale suppressed a sigh of relief. He was to be accepted, after all. "I am Zaal," he said, giving the name assigned him for this mission.

"I am Farok," the old man said, "once Bashar of the Ninth Legion in the Jihad. Does this mean anything to you?"

Scytale read menace in the words, said: "You were born in Sietch Tabr with allegiance to Stilgar."

Farok relaxed, stepped aside. "You are welcome in my house."

Scytale slipped past him into a shadowy atrium—blue tile floor, glittering designs worked in crystal on the walls. Beyond the atrium was a covered courtyard. Light admitted by translucent filters spread an opalescence as silvery as the white-night of First Moon. The street door grated into its moisture seals behind him.

"We were a noble people," Farok said, leading the way toward the courtyard. "We were not of the cast-out. We lived in no *graben* village . . . such as this! We had a proper sietch in the Shield Wall above Habbanya Ridge. One worm could carry us into Kedem, the inner desert."

"Not like this," Scytale agreed, realizing now what had brought Farok into the conspiracy. The Fremen longed for the old days and the old ways.

They entered the courtyard.

Farok struggled with an intense dislike for his visitor, Scytale realized. Fremen distrusted eyes that were not the total blue of the Ibad. Offworlders, Fremen said, had unfocused eyes which saw things they were not supposed to see.

The semuta music had stopped at their entrance. It was replaced now by the strum of a baliset, first a nine-scale chord, then the clear notes of a song which was popular on the Naraj worlds.

As his eyes adjusted to the light, Scytale saw a youth sitting cross-legged on a low divan beneath arches to his right. The youth's eyes were empty sockets. With that uncanny facility of the blind, he began singing the moment Scytale focused on him. The voice was high and sweet:

> "A wind has blown the land away
> And blown the sky away
> And all the men!
> Who is this wind?
> The trees stand unbent,
> Drinking where men drank.
> I've known too many worlds,
> Too many men,
> Too many trees,
> Too many winds."

Those were not the original words of the song, Scytale noted. Farok led him away from the youth and under the arches on the opposite side, indicated cushions scattered over the tile floor. The tile was worked into designs of sea creatures.

"There is a cushion once occupied in sietch by

Muad'dib," Farok said, indicating a round, black mound. "It is yours now."

"I am in your debt," Scytale said, sinking to the black mound. He smiled. Farok displayed wisdom. A sage spoke of loyalty even while listening to songs of hidden meaning and words with secret messages. Who could deny the terrifying powers of the tyrant Emperor?

Inserting his words across the song without breaking the meter, Farok said: "Does my son's music disturb you?"

Scytale gestured to a cushion facing him, put his back against a cool pillar. "I enjoy music."

"My son lost his eyes in the conquest of Naraj," Farok said. "He was nursed there and should have stayed. No woman of the people will have him thus. I find it curious, though, to know I have grandchildren on Naraj that I may never see. Do you know the Naraj worlds, Zaal?"

"In my youth, I toured there with a troupe of my fellow Face Dancers," Scytale said.

"You are a Face Dancer, then," Farok said. "I had wondered at your features. They reminded me of a man I knew here once."

"Duncan Idaho?"

"That one, yes. A swordmaster in the Emperor's pay."

"He was killed, so it is said."

"So it is said," Farok agreed. "Are you truly a man, then? I've heard stories about Face Dancers that . . ." He shrugged.

"We are Jadacha hermaphrodites," Scytale said, "either sex at will. For the present, I am a man."

Farok pursed his lips in thought, then: "May I call for refreshments? Do you desire water? Iced fruit?"

"Talk will suffice," Scytale said.

"The guest's wish is a command," Farok said, settling to the cushion which faced Scytale.

"Blessed is Abu d' Dhur, Father of the Indefinite Roads of Time," Scytale said. And he thought: *There! I've told him straight out that I come from a Guild Steersman and wear the Steersman's conconcealment.*

"Thrice blessed," Farok said, folding his hands into his lap in the ritual clasp. They were old, heavily veined hands.

"An object seen from a distance betrays only its principle," Scytale said, revealing that he wished to discuss the Emperor's fortress Keep.

"That which is dark and evil may be seen for evil at any distance," Farok said, advising delay.

Why? Scytale wondered. But he said: "How did your son lose his eyes?"

"The Naraj defenders used a stone burner," Farok said. "My son was too close. Cursed atomics! Even the stone burner should be outlawed."

"It skirts the intent of the law," Scytale agreed. And he thought: *A stone burner on Naraj! We weren't told of that. Why does this old man speak of stone burners here?*

"I offered to buy Tleilaxu eyes for him from your masters," Farok said. "But there's a story in the legions that Tleilaxu eyes enslave their users. My son told me that such eyes are metal and he is flesh, that such a union must be sinful."

"The principle of an object must fit its original intent," Scytale said, trying to turn the conversation back to the information he sought.

Farok's lips went thin, but he nodded. "Speak openly of what you wish," he said. "We must put our trust in your steersman."

"Have you ever entered the Imperial Keep?" Scytale asked.

"I was there for the feast celebrating the Molitor victory. It was cold in all that stone despite the best Ixian space heaters. We slept on the terrace of Alia's Fane the night before. He has trees in there, you know—trees from many worlds. We Bashars were dressed in our finest green robes and had our tables set apart. We ate and drank too much. I was disgusted with some of the things I saw. The walking wounded came, dragging themselves along on their crutches. I do not think our Muad'dib knows how many men he has maimed."

"You objected to the feast?" Scytale asked, speaking from a knowledge of the Fremen orgies which were ignited by spice-beer.

"It was not like the mingling of our souls in the sietch," Farok said. "There was no tau. For entertainment, the troups had slave girls, and the men shared the stories of their battles and their wounds."

"So you were inside that great pile of stone," Scytale said.

"Muad'dib came out to us on the terrace," Farok said. "'Good fortune to us all,' he said. The greeting drill of the desert in that place!"

"Do you know the location of his private apartments?" Scytale asked.

"Deep inside," Farok said. "Somewhere deep inside. I am told he and Chani live a nomadic life and that all within the walls of their Keep. Out to the Great Hall he comes for the public audiences. He has reception halls and formal meeting places, a whole wing for his personal guard, places for the ceremonies and an inner section for communications. There is a room far beneath his fortress, I am told, where he keeps a stunted worm surrounded by a water moat with which to poison it. Here is where he reads the future."

Myth all tangled up with facts, Scytale thought.

"The apparatus of government accompanies him everywhere," Farok grumbled. "Clerks and attendants and attendants for the attendants. He trusts only the ones such as Stilgar who were very close to him in the old days."

"Not you," Scytale said.

"I think he has forgotten my existence," Farok said.

"How does he come and go when he leaves that building?" Scytale asked.

"He has a tiny 'thopter landing which juts from an inner wall," Farok said. "I am told Muad'dib will not permit another to handle the controls for a landing there. It requires an approach, so it is said, where the slightest miscalculation would plunge him down a sheer cliff of wall into one of his accursed gardens."

Scytale nodded. This, most likely, was true. Such an aerial entry to the Emperor's quarters would carry a certain measure of security. The Atreides were superb pilots all.

"He uses men to carry his *distrans* messages," Farok said. "It demeans men to implant wave translators in them. A man's voice should be his own to command. It should not carry another man's message hidden within its sounds."

Scytale shrugged. All great powers used the distrans in this age. One could never tell what obstacle might be placed between sender and addressee. The distrans defied political cryptology because it relied on subtle distortions of natural sound patterns which could be scrambled with enormous intricacy.

"Even his tax officials use this method," Farok complained. "In my day, the distrans was implanted only in the lower animals."

But revenue information must be kept secret, Scytale thought. *More than one government has fallen because people discovered the real extent of official wealth.*

"How do the Fremen cohorts feel now about Muad'dib's Jihad?" Scytale asked. "Do they object to making a god out of their Emperor?"

"Most of them don't even consider this," Farok said. "They think of the Jihad the way I thought of it—most of them. It is a source of strange experiences, adventure, wealth. This graben hovel in which I live"—Farok gestured at the courtyard—"it cost sixty lidas of spice. Ninety kontars! There was a time when I could not even imagine such riches." He shook his head.

Across the courtyard, the blind youth took up the notes of a love ballad on his baliset.

Ninety kontars, Scytale thought. *How strange. Great*

*riches, certainly. Farok's hovel would be a palace on
many another world, but all things were relative—even
the kontar. Did Farok, for example, know whence came
his measure for this weight of spice? Did he ever think to
himself that one and a half kontar once limited a camel
load? Not likely. Farok might never even have heard of a
camel or of the Golden Age of Earth.*

His words oddly in rhythm to the melody of his son's
baliset, Farok said: "I owned a crysknife, water rings to
ten liters, my own lance which had been my father's a
coffee service, a bottle made of red glass older than any
memory in my sietch. I had my own share of our spice, but
no money. I was rich and did not know it. Two wives I
had: one plain and dear to me, the other stupid and
obstinate, but with form and face of an angel. I was a
Fremen Naib, a rider of worms, master of the leviathan
and of the sand."

The youth across the courtyard picked up the beat of
his melody.

"I knew many things without the need to think about
them," Farok said. "I knew there was water far beneath
our sand, held there in bondage by the Little Makers. I
knew that my ancestors sacrificed virgins to Shai-
hulud . . . before Liet-Kynes made us stop. I had seen the
jewels in the mouth of a worm. My soul had four gates
and I knew them all."

He fell silent, musing.

"Then the Atreides came with his witch mother,"
Scytale said.

"The Atreides came," Farok agreed. "The one we
named *Usul* in our sietch, his private name among us. Our
Muad'dib, our Mahdi! And when he called for the Jihad,
I was one of those who asked: 'Why should I go to fight
there? I have no relatives there.' But other men
went—young men, friends, companions of my childhood.
When they returned, they spoke of wizardry, of the power
in this Atreides *savior*. He fought our enemy, the
Harkonnen. Liet-Kynes, who had promised us a paradise

upon our planet, blessed him. It was said this Atreides came to change our world and our universe, that he was the man to make the golden flower blossom in the night."

Farok held up his hands, examined the palms. "Men pointed to First Moon and said: 'His soul is there.' Thus, he was called Muad'dib. I did not understand all this."

He lowered his hands, stared across the courtyard at his son. "I had no thoughts in my head. There were thoughts only in my heart and my belly and my loins."

Again, the tempo of the background music increased.

"Do you know why I enlisted in the Jihad?" The old eyes stared hard at Scytale. "I heard there was a thing called a sea. It is very hard to believe in a sea when you have lived only here among our dunes. We have no seas. Men of Dune had never known a sea. We had our windtraps. We collected water for the great change Liet-Kynes promised us . . . this great change Muad'dib is bringing with a wave of his hand. I could imagine a *qanat,* water flowing across the land in a canal. From this, my mind could picture a river. But a sea?"

Farok gazed at the translucent cover of his courtyard as though trying to probe into the universe beyond. "A sea," he said, voice low. "It was too much for my mind to picture. Yet, men I knew said they had seen this marvel. I thought they lied, but I had to know for myself. It was for this reason that I enlisted."

The youth struck a loud final chord on the baliset, took up a new song with an oddly undulating rhythm.

"Did you find your sea?" Scytale asked.

Farok remained silent and Scytale thought the old man had not heard. The baliset music rose around them and fell like a tidal movement. Farok breathed to its rhythm.

"There was a sunset," Farok said presently. "One of the elder artists might have painted such a sunset. It had red in it the color of the glass in my bottle. There was gold . . . blue. It was on the world they call Enfeil, the one where I led my legion to victory. We came out of a mountain pass where the air was sick with water. I could scarcely breathe it. And there below me was the thing my friends had told me about: water as far as I could see and farther. We marched down to it. I waded out into it and drank. It was bitter and made me ill. But the wonder of it has never left me."

Scytale found himself sharing the old Fremen's awe.

"I immersed myself in that sea," Farok said, looking down at the water creatures worked into the tiles of his floor. "One man sank beneath that water . . . another man arose from it. I felt that I could remember a past which had never been. I stared around me with eyes which could accept anything . . . anything at all. I saw a body in the water—one of the defenders we had slain. There was a log nearby supported on that water, a piece of a great tree. I can close my eyes now and see that log. It was black on one end from a fire. And there was a piece of cloth in that water—no more than a yellow rag . . . torn, dirty. I looked at all these things and I understood why they had come to this place. It was for me to see them."

Farok turned slowly, stared into Scytale's eyes. "The universe is unfinished, you know," he said.

This one is garrulous, but deep, Scytale thought. And he said: "I can see it made a profound impression on you."

"You are a Tleilaxu," Farok said. "You have seen many seas. I have seen only this one, yet I know a thing about seas which you do not."

Scytale found himself in the grip of an odd feeling of disquiet.

"The Mother of Chaos was born in a sea," Farok said. "A Qizara Tafwid stood nearby when I came dripping from that water. He had not entered the sea. He stood on the sand . . . it was wet sand . . . with some of my men who shared his fear. He watched me with eyes that knew I had learned something which was denied to him. I had become a sea creature and I frightened him. The sea healed me of the Jihad and I think he saw this."

Scytale realized that somewhere in this recital the music had stopped. He found it disturbing that he could not place the instant when the baliset had fallen silent.

As though it were relevant to what he'd been recounting, Farok said: "Every gate is guarded. There's no way into the Emperor's fortress."

"That's its weakness," Scytale said.

Farok stretched his neck upward, peering.

"There's a way in," Scytale explained. "The fact that most men—including, we may hope, the Emperor—believe otherwise . . . that's to our advantage." He rubbed his lips, feeling the strangeness fo the visage he'd chosen. The musician's silence bothered him. Did it mean Farok's son was through transmitting? That had been the way of it, naturally: The message condensed and transmitted within the music. It had been impressed upon Scytale's own neutral system, there to be triggered at the proper moment by the distrans embedded in his adrenal cortex. If it was ended, he had become a container of unknown words. He was a vessel sloshing with data: every cell of the conspiracy here on Arrakis, every name, every contact phrase—all the vital information.

With this information, they could brave Arrakis, capture a sandworm, begin the culture of melange somewhere beyond Muad'dib's writ. They could break the monopoly as they broke Muad'dib. They could do many things with this information.

"We have the woman here," Farok said. "Do you wish to see her now?"

"I've seen her," Scytale said. "I've studied her with care. Where is she?"

Farok snapped his fingers.

The youth took up his rebec, drew the bow across it. Semuta music wailed from the strings. As though drawn by the sound, a young woman in a blue robe emerged from a doorway behind the musician. Narcotic dullness filled her eyes which were the total blue of the Ibad. She was a Fremen, addicted to the spice, and now caught by an offworld vice. Her awareness lay deep within the semuta, lost somewhere and riding the ecstasy of the music.

"Otheym's daughter," Farok said. "My son gave her the narcotic in the hope of winning a woman of the People for himself despite his blindness. As you can see, his victory is empty. Semuta has taken what he hoped to gain."

"Her father doesn't know?" Scytale asked.

"She doesn't even know," Farok said. "My son supplies false memories with which she accounts to herself for her visits. She thinks herself in love with him. This is what her family believes. They are outraged because he is not a complete man, but they won't interfere, of course."

The music trailed away to silence.

At a gesture from the musician, the young woman seated herself beside him, bent close to listen as he murmured to her.

"What will you do with her?" Farok asked.

Once more, Scytale studied the courtyard. "Who else is in this house?" he asked.

"We are all here now," Farok said. "You've not told me what you'll do with the woman. It is my son who wishes to know."

As though about to answer, Scytale extended his right arm. From the sleeve of his robe, a glistening needle darted, embedded itself in Farok's neck. There was no outcry, no change of posture. Farok would be dead in a minute, but he sat unmoving, frozen by the dart's poison.

Slowly, Scytale climbed to his feet, crossed to the blind musician. The youth was still murmuring to the young woman when the dart whipped into him.

Scytale took the young woman's arm, urged her gently to her feet, shifted his own appearance before she looked at him. She came erect, focused on him.

"What is it, Farok?" she asked.

"My son is tired and must rest," Scytale said. "Come. We'll go out the back way."

"We had such a nice talk," she said. "I think I've convinced him to get Tleilaxu eyes. It'd make a man of him again."

"Haven't I said it many times?" Scytale asked, urging her into a rear chamber.

His voice, he noted with pride, matched his features precisely. It unmistakably was the voice of the old Fremen, who certainly was dead by this time.

Scytale sighed. It had been done with sympathy, he told himself, and the victims certainly had known their peril. Now, the young woman would have to be given her chance.

Empires do not suffer emptiness of purpose at the time of their creation. It is when they have become established that aims are lost and replaced by vague ritual.

—Words of Muad'dib
by Princess Irulan.

It was going to be a bad session, this meeting of the Imperial Council, Alia realized. She sensed contention gathering force, storing up energy—the way Irulan refused to look at Chani, Stilgar's nervous shuffling of papers, the scowls Paul directed at Korba the Qizara.

She seated herself at the end of the golden council table so she could look out the balcony windows at the dusty light of the afternoon.

Korba, interrupted by her entrance, went on with something he'd been saying to Paul. "What I mean, m'Lord, is that there aren't as many gods as once there were."

Alia laughed, throwing her head back. The movement dropped the black hood of her aba robe. Her features lay exposed—blue-in-blue "spice eyes," her mother's oval face beneath a cap of bronze hair, small nose, mouth wide and generous.

Korba's cheeks went almost the color of his orange robe. He glared at Alia, an angry gnome, bald and fuming.

"Do you know what's being said about your brother?" he demanded.

"I know what's being said about your Qizarate," Alia countered. "You're not divines, you're god's spies."

Korba glanced at Paul for support, said: "We are sent by the writ of Muad'dib, that He shall know the truth of His people and they shall know the truth of Him."

"Spies," Alia said.

Korba pursed his lips in injured silence.

Paul looked at his sister, wondering why she provoked Korba. Abruptly, he saw that Alia had passed into womanhood, beautiful with the first blazing innocence of youth. He found himself surprised that he hadn't noticed it until this moment. She was fifteen—almost sixteen, a Reverend Mother without motherhood, virgin priestess, object of fearful veneration for the superstitious masses—Alia of the Knife.

"This is not the time or place for your sister's levity," Irulan said.

Paul ignored her, nodded to Korba. "The square's full of pilgrims. Go out and lead their prayer."

"But they expect *you*, m'Lord," Korba said.

"Put on your turban," Paul said. "They'll never know at this distance."

Irulan smothered irritation at being ignored, watched Korba arise to obey. She'd had the sudden disquieting thought that Edric might not hide her actions from Alia. *What do we really know of the sister?* she wondered.

Chani, hands tightly clasped in her lap, glanced across the table at Stilgar, her uncle, Paul's Minister of State. Did the old Fremen Naib ever long for the simpler life of his desert sietch? she wondered. Stilgar's black hair, she noted, had begun to gray at the edges, but his eyes beneath heavy brows remained far-seeing. It was the eagle stare of the wild, and his beard still carried the catchtube indentation of life in a stillsuit.

Made nervous by Chani's attention, Stilgar looked around the Council Chamber. His gaze fell on the balcony window and Korba standing outside. Korba raised outstretched arms for the benediction and a trick of the afternoon sun cast a red halo onto the window behind him. For a moment, Stilgar saw the Court Qizara as a figure crucified on a fiery fiery wheel. Korba lowered his arms, destroyed the illusion, but Stilgar remained shaken by it. His thoughts went in angry frustration to the fawning supplicants waiting in the Audience Hall, and to the hateful pomp which surrounded Muad'dib's throne.

Convening with the Emperor, one hoped for a fault in him, to find mistakes, Stilgar thought. He felt this might be sacrilege, but wanted it anyway.

Distant crowd murmuring entered the chamber as Korba returned. The balcony door thumped into its seals behind him, shutting off the sound.

Paul's gaze followed the Qizara. Korba took his seat at Paul's left, dark features composed, eyes glazed by fanaticism. He'd enjoyed that moment of religious power.

"The spirit presence has been invoked," he said.

"Thank the lord for that," Alia said.

Korba's lips went white.

Again, Paul studied his sister, wondered at her motives. Her innocence masked deception, he told himself. She'd come out of the same Bene Gesserit breeding program as he had. What had the kwisatz haderach genetics produced in her? There was always that mysterious difference: she'd been an embryo in the womb when her mother had survived the raw melange poison.

Mother and unborn daughter had become Reverend
Mothers simultaneously. But simultaneity didn't carry
identity.

Of the experience, Alia said that in one terrifying
instant she had awakened to consciousness, her memory
absorbing the uncounted other-lives which her mother
was assimilating.

"I became my mother and all the others," she said. "I
was unformed, unborn, but I became an old woman then
and there."

Sensing his thoughts on her, Alia smiled at Paul. His
expression softened. *How could anyone react to Korba
with other than cynical humor?* he asked himself. *What is
more ridiculous than a Death Commando transformed
into a priest?*

Stilgar tapped his papers. "If my liege permits," he
said. "These are matters urgent and dire."

"The Tupile Treaty?" Paul asked.

"The Guild maintains that we must sign this treaty
without knowing the precise location of the Tupile
Entente," Stilgar said. "They've some support from
Landsraad delegates."

"What pressures have you brought to bear?" Irulan
asked.

"Those pressures which my Emperor has designated
for this enterprise," Stilgar said. The stiff formality of his
reply contained all his disapproval of the Princess
Consort.

"My Lord and husband," Irulan said, turning to Paul,
forcing him to acknowledge her.

Emphasizing the titular difference in front of Chani,
Paul thought, *is a weakness.* In such moments, he shared
Stiliar's dislike for Irulan, but sympathy tempered his
emotions. What was Irulan but a Bene Gesserit pawn?

"Yes?" Paul said.

Irulan stared at him. "If you withheld their melange..."

Chani shook her head in dissent.

"We tread with caution," Paul said. "Tupile remains the place of sanctuary for defeated Great Houses. It symbolizes a last resort, a final place of safety for all our subjects. Exposing the sanctuary makes it vulnerable."

"If they can hide people they can hide other things," Stilgar rumbled. "An army, perhaps, or the beginnings of melange culture which—"

"You don't back people into a corner," Alia said. "Not if you want them to remain peaceful." Ruefully, she saw that she'd been drawn into the contention which she'd foreseen.

"So we've spent ten years of negotiation for nothing," Irulan said.

"None of my brother's actions is for nothing," Alia said.

Irulan picked up a scribe, gripped it with white-knuckled intensity. Paul saw her marshal emotional control in the Bene Gesserit way: the penetrating inward stare, deep breathing. He could almost hear her repeating the litany. Presently, she said: "What have we gained?"

"We've kept the Guild off balance," Chani said.

"We want to avoid a showdown confrontation with our enemies," Alia said. "We have no special desire to kill them. There's enough butchery going on under the Atreides banner."

She feels it, too, Paul thought. Strange, what a sense of compelling responsibility they both felt for that brawling, idolatrous universe with its ecstasies of tranquility and wild motion. *Must we protect them from themselves?* he wondered. *They play with nothingness every moment— empty lives, empty words. They ask too much of me.* His throat felt tight and full. How many moments would he lose? What sons? What dreams? Was it worth the price his vision had revealed? Who would ask the living of some far distant future, who would say to them: "But for Muad'dib, you would not be here."

"Denying them their melange would solve nothing," Chani said. "So the Guild's navigators would lose their ability to see into timespace. Your Sisters of the Bene Gesserit would lose their truthsense. Some people might die before their time. Communication would break down. Who could be blamed?"

"They wouldn't let it come to that," Irulan said.

"Wouldn't they?" Chani asked. "Why not? Who could blame the Guild? They'd be helpless, demonstrably so."

"We'll sign the treaty as it stands," Paul said.

"M'Lord," Stilgar said, concentrating on his hands, "there is a question in our minds."

"Yes?" Paul gave the old Fremen his full attention.

"You have certain...powers," Stilgar said. "Can you not locate the Entente despite the Guild?"

Powers! Paul thought. Stilgar couldn't just say: *"You're prescient. Can't you trace a path in the future that leads to Tupile?"*

Paul looked at the golden surface of the table. Always the same problem: How could he express the limits of the inexpressible? Should he speak of fragmentation, the natural destiny of all power? How could someone who'd never experienced the spice change of prescience conceive an awareness containing no localized spacetime, no personal image-vector nor associated sensory captives?

He looked at Alia, found her attention on Irulan. Alia sensed his movement, glanced at him, nodded toward Irulan. Ahhh, yes: any answer they gave would find its way into one of Irulan's special reports to the Bene Gesserit. They never gave up seeking an answer to their kwisatz haderach.

Stilgar, though, deserved an answer of some kind. For that matter, so did Irulan.

"The uninitiated try to conceive of prescience as obeying a *Natural Law*," Paul said. He steepled his hands in front of him. "But it'd be just as correct to say it's heaven speaking to us, that being able to read the future is a harmonious act of man's being. In other words, prediction is a natural consequence in the wave of the present. It wears the guise of nature, you see. But such

powers cannot be used from an attitude that prestates
aims and purposes. Does a chip caught in the wave say
where it's going? There's no cause and effect in the oracle.
Causes become occasions of convections and con-
fluences, places where the currents meet. Accepting
prescience, you fill your being with concepts repugnant to
the intellect. Your intellectual consciousness, therefore,
rejects them. In rejecting, intellect becomes a part of the
processes, and is subjugated."

"You cannot do it?" Stilgar asked.

"Were I to seek Tupile with prescience," Paul said,
speaking directly to Irulan, "this might hide Tupile."

"Chaos!" Irulan protested. "It has no . . . no
. . . consistency."

"I did say it obeys no Natural Law," Paul said.

"Then there are limits to what you can see or do with
your powers?" Irulan asked.

Before Paul could answer, Alia said: "Dear Irulan,
prescience has no limits. Not consistent? Consistency isn't
a necessary aspect of the universe."

"But he said . . ."

"How can my brother give you explicit information
about the limits of something which has no limits? The
boundaries escape the intellect."

That was a nasty thing for Alia to do, Paul thought. It
would alarm Irulan, who had such a careful consciousness, so dependent upon values derived from precise
limits. His gaze went to Korba, who sat in a pose of
religious reverie—*listening with the soul.* How could the
Qizarate use this exchange? More religious mystery?
Something to evoke awe? No doubt.

"Then you'll sign the treaty in its present form?" Stilgar
asked.

Paul smiled. The issue of the oracle, by Stilgar's
judgment, had been closed. Stilgar aimed only at victory,
not at discovering truth. Peace, justice and a sound
coinage—these anchored Stilgar's universe. He wanted
something visible and real—a signature on a treaty.

"I'll sign it," Paul said.

Stilgar took up a fresh folder. "The latest communication from our field commanders in Sector Ixian speaks of agitation for a constitution." The old Fremen glanced at Chani, who shrugged.

Irulan, who had closed her eyes and put both hands to her forehead in mnemonic impressment, opened her eyes, studied Paul intently.

"The Ixian Confederacy offers submission," Stilgar said, "but their negotiators question the amount of the Imperial Tax which they—"

"They want a legal limit to my Imperial will," Paul said. "Who would govern me, the Landsraad or CHOAM?"

Stilgar removed from the folder a note on *instroy* paper. "One of our agents sent this memorandum from a caucus of the CHOAM minority." He read the cipher in a flat voice: "The Throne must be stopped in its attempt at a power monopoly. We must tell the truth about the Atreides, how he maneuvers behind the triple sham of Landsraad legislation, religious sanction and bureaucratic efficiency." He pushed the note back into the folder.

"A constitution," Chani murmured.

Paul glanced at her, back to Stilgar. *Thus the Jihad falters,* Paul thought, *but not soon enough to save me.* The thought produced emotional tensions. He remembered his earliest visions of the Jihad-to-be, the terror and revulsion he'd experienced. Now, of course, he knew visions of greater terrors. He had lived with the real violence. He had seen his Fremen, charged with mystical strength, sweep all before them in the religious war. The Jihad gained a new perspective. It was finite, of course, a brief spasm when measured against eternity, but beyond lay horrors to overshadow anything in the past.

All in my name, Paul thought.

"Perhaps they could be given the *form* of a constitution," Chani suggested. "It needn't be actual."

"Deceit *is* a tool of statecraft," Irulan agreed.

"There are limits to power, as those who put their hopes in a constitution always discover," Paul said.

Korba straightened from his reverent pose. "M'Lord?"

"Yes?" And Paul thought, *Here now! Here's one who may harbor secret sympathies for an imagined rule of Law.*

"We could begin with a religious constitution," Korba said, "something for the faithful who—"

"No!" Paul snapped. "We will make this an Order in Council. Are you recording this, Irulan?"

"Yes, m'Lord," Irulan said, voice frigid with dislike for the menial role he forced upon her.

"Constitutions become the ultimate tyranny," Paul said. "They're ogranized power on such a scale as to be overwhelming. The constitution is social power mobilized and it has no conscience. It can crush the highest and the lowest, removing all dignity and individuality. It has an unstable balance point and no limitations. I, however, have limitations. In my desire to provide an ultimate protection for my people, I forbid a constitution. Order in Council, this date, etcetera, etcetera."

"What of the Ixian concern about the tax, m'Lord?" Stilgar asked.

Paul forced his attention away from the brooding, angry look on Korba's face, said: "You've a proposal, Stil?"

"We must have control of taxes, Sire."

"Our price to the Guild for my signature on the Tupile Treaty," Paul said, "is the submission of the Ixian Confederacy to our tax. The Confederacy cannot trade without Guild transport. They'll pay."

"Very good, m'Lord." Stilgar produced another folder, cleared his throat. "The Qizarate's report on Salusa Secundus. Irulan's father has been putting his legions through landing maneuvers."

Irulan found something of interest in the palm of her left hand. A pulse throbbed at her neck.

"Irulan," Paul asked, "do you persist in arguing that

your father's one legion is nothing more than a toy?"

"What could he do with only one legion?" she asked. She stared at him out of slitted eyes.

"He could get himself killed," Chani said.

Paul nodded. "And I'd be blamed."

"I know a few commanders in the Jihad," Alia said, "who'd pounce if they learned of this."

"But it's only his police force!" Irulan protested.

"Then they have no need for landing maneuvers," Paul said. "I suggest that your next little note to your father contain a frank and direct discussion of my views about his delicate position."

She lowered her gaze. "Yes, m'Lord. I hope that will be the end of it. My father would make a good martyr."

"Mmmmmm," Paul said. "My sister wouldn't send a message to those commanders she mentioned unless I ordered it."

"An attack on my father carries dangers other than the obvious military ones," Irulan said. "People are beginning to look back on his reign with a certain nostalgia."

"You'll go too far one day," Chani said in her deadly serious Fremen voice.

"Enough!" Paul ordered.

He weighed Irulan's revelation about public nostalgia—ah, now! that'd carried a note of truth. Once more, Irulan had proved her worth.

"The Bene Gesserit send a formal supplication," Stilgar said, presenting another folder. "They wish to consult you about the preservation of your bloodline."

Chani glanced sideways at the folder as though it contained a deadly device.

"Send the Sisterhood the usual excuses," Paul said.

"Must we?" Irulan demanded.

"Perhaps... this is the time to discuss it," Chani said.

Paul shook his head sharply. They couldn't know that this was part of the price he had not yet decided to pay.

But Chani wasn't to be stopped. "I have been to the prayer wall of Sietch Tabr where I was born," she said. "I have submitted to doctors. I have knelt in the desert and sent my thoughts into the depths where dwells Shaihulud. Yet"—she shrugged—"nothing avails."

Science and superstition, all have failed her, Paul thought. *Do I fail her, too, by not telling her what bearing an heir to House Atreides will precipitate?* He looked up to find an expression of pity in Alia's eyes. The idea of pity from his sister repelled him. Had she, too, seen that terrifying future?

"My Lord must know the dangers to his realm when he has no heir," Irulan said, using her Bene Gesserit powers of voice with an oily persuasiveness. "These things are naturally difficult to discuss, but they must be brought into the open. An Emperor is more than a man. His figure leads the realm. Should he die without an heir, civil strife must follow. As you love your people, you cannot leave them thus?"

Paul pushed himself away from the table, strode to the balcony windows. A wind was flattening the smoke of the city's fires out there. The sky presented a darkening silver-blue softened by the evening fall of dust from the Shield Wall. He stared southward at the escarpment which protected his northern lands from the coriolis wind, and he wondered why his own peace of mind could find no such shield.

The Council sat silently waiting behind him, aware of how close to rage he was.

Paul sensed time rushing upon him. He tried to force himself into a tranquility of many balances where he might shape a new future.

Disengage...disengage...disengage, he thought. What would happen if he took Chani, just picked up and left with her, sought sanctuary on Tupile? His name would remain behind. The Jihad would find new and more terrible centers upon which to turn. He'd be blamed for that, too. He felt suddenly fearful that in reaching for any new thing he might let fall what was most precious, that even the slightest noise from him might send the universe crashing back, receding until he never could recapture any piece of it.

Below him, the square had become the setting for a band of pilgrims in the green and white of the hajj. They wended their way like a disjointed snake behind a striding Arrakeen guide. They reminded Paul that his reception hall would be packed with supplicants by now. Pilgrims! Their exercise in homelessness had become a disgusting source of wealth for his Imperium. The hajj filled the spaceways with religious tramps. They came and they came and they came.

How did I set this in motion? he asked himself.

It had, of course, set itself in motion. It was in the genes which might labor for centuries to achieve this brief spasm.

Driven by that deepest religious instinct, the people came, seeking their resurrection. The pilgrimage ended here—"Arrakis, the place of rebirth, the place to die."

Snide old Fremen said he wanted the pilgrims for their water.

What was it the pilgrims really sought? Paul wondered. They said they came to a holy place. But they must know the universe contained no Eden-source, no Tupile for the soul. They called Arrakis the place of the unknown where all mysteries were explained. This was a link between their universe and the next. And the frightening thing was that they appeared to go away satisfied.

What do they find here? Paul asked himself.

Often in their religious ecstasy, they filled the streets with screeching like some odd aviary. In fact, the Fremen called them "passage birds." And the few who died here were "winged souls."

With a sigh, Paul thought how each new planet his legions subjugated opened new sources of pilgrims. They came out of gratitude for "the peace of Muad'dib."

Everywhere there is peace, Paul thought. *Everywhere . . . except in the heart of Muad'dib.*

He felt that some element of himself lay immersed in frosty hoar-darkness without end. His prescient power had tampered with the image of the universe held by all mankind. He had shaken the safe cosmos and replaced security with his Jihad. He had out-fought and out-thought and out-predicted the universe of men, but a certainty filled him that this universe still eluded him.

This planet beneath him which he had commanded be remade from desert into a water-rich paradise, it was alive. It had a pulse as dynamic as that of any human. It fought him, resisted, slipped away from his commands . . .

A hand crept into Paul's. He looked down to see Chani peering up at him, concern in her eyes. Those eyes drank him, and she whispered: "Please, love, do not battle with your ruh-self." An outpouring of emotion swept upward from her hand, buoyed him.

"Sihaya," he whispered.

"We must go to the desert soon," she said in a low voice.

He squeezed her hand, released it, returned to the table where he remained standing.

Chani took her seat.

Irulan stared at the papers in front of Stilgar, her mouth a tight line.

"Irulan proposes herself as mother of the Imperial heir," Paul said. He glanced at Chani, back to Irulan, who refused to meet his gaze. "We all know she holds no love for me."

Irulan went very still.

"I know the political arguments," Paul said. "It's the human arguments which concern me. I think if the Princess Consort were not bound by the commands of the Bene Gesserit, if she did not seek this out of desires for personal power, my reaction might be very different. As matters stand, though, I reject this proposal."

Irulan took a deep, shaky breath.

Paul, resuming his seat, thought he had never seen her under such poor control. Leaning toward her, he said: "Irulan, I am truly sorry."

She lifted her chin, a look of pure fury in her eyes. "I don't want your pity!" she hissed. And turning to Stilgar:

"Is there more that's urgent and dire?"

Holding his gaze firmly on Paul, Stilgar said: "One more matter, m'Lord. The Guild again proposes a formal embassy here on Arrakis."

"One of the deep-space kind?" Korba asked, his voice full of fanatic loathing.

"Presumably," Stilgar said.

"A matter to be considered with the utmost care, m'Lord," Korba warned. "The Council of Naibs would not like it, an actual Guildsman here on Arrakis. They contaminate the very ground they touch."

"They live in tanks and don't touch the ground," Paul said, letting his voice reveal irritation.

"The Naibs might take matters into their own hands, m'Lord," Korba said.

Paul glared at him.

"They are Fremen, after all, m'Lord," Korba insisted. "We well remember how the Guild brought those who oppressed us. We have not forgotten the way they blackmailed a spice ransom from us to keep our secrets from our enemies. They drained us of every—"

"Enough!" Paul snapped. "Do you think *I* have forgotten?"

As though he had just awakened to the import of his own words, Korba stuttered unintelligibly, then: "M'lord, forgive me. I did not mean to imply you are not Fremen. I did not..."

"They'll send a Steersman," Paul said. "It isn't likely a Steersman would come here if he could see danger in it."

Her mouth dry with sudden fear, Irulan said: "You've...*seen* a Steersman come here?"

"Of course I haven't *seen* a Steersman," Paul said, mimicking her tone. "But I can see where one's been and where one's going. Let them send us a Steersman. Perhaps I have a use for such a one."

"So ordered," Stilgar said.

And Irulan, hiding a smile behind her hand, thought: *It's true then. Our Emperor cannot see a Steersman. They are mutually blind. The conspiracy is hidden.*

"Once more the drama begins."

—The Emperor Paul Muad'dib
on his ascension to the Lion Throne

Alia peered down from her spy window into the great reception hall to watch the advance of the Guild entourage.

The sharply silver light of noon poured through clerestory windows onto a floor worked in green, blue and eggshell tiles to simulate a bayou with water plants and, here and there, a splash of exotic color to indicate bird or animal.

Guildsmen moved across the tile pattern like hunters stalking their prey in a strange jungle. They formed a moving design of gray robes, black robes, orange robes—all arrayed in a deceptively random way around the transparent tank where the Steersman-Ambassador swam in his orange gas. The tank slid on its supporting field, towed by two gray-robed attendants, like a rectangular ship being warped into its dock.

Directly beneath her, Paul sat on the Lion Throne on its raised dais. He wore the new formal crown with its fish and fist emblems. The jeweled golden robes of state covered his body. The shimmering of a personal shield surrounded him. Two wings of bodyguards fanned out on both sides along the dais and down the steps. Stilgar stood two steps below Paul's right hand in a white robe with a yellow rope for a belt.

Sibling empathy told her that Paul seethed with the same agitation she was experiencing, although she doubted another could detect it. His attention remained on an orange-robed attendant whose blindly staring metal eyes looked neither to right nor to left. This attendant walked at the right front corner of the Ambassador's troupe like a military outrider. A rather flat face beneath curly black hair, such of his figure as could be seen beneath the orange robe, every gesture shouted a familiar identity.

It was Duncan Idaho.

It could not be Duncan Idaho, yet it was.

Captive memories absorbed in the womb during the moment of her mother's spice change identified this man for Alia by a rihani decipherment which cut through all camouflage. Paul was seeing him, she knew, out of countless personal experiences, out of gratitudes and youthful sharing.

It was Duncan.

Alia shuddered. There could be only one answer: this was a Tleilaxu ghola, a being reconstructed from the dead flesh of the original. That original had perished saving Paul. This could only be a product of the axolotl tanks.

The ghola walked with the cock-footed alertness of a master swordsman. He came to a halt as the Ambassador's tank glided to a stop ten paces from the steps of the dais.

In the Bene Gesserit way she could not escape, Alia read Paul's disquiet. He no longer looked at the figure out of his past. Not looking, his whole being stared. Muscles strained against restrictions as he nodded to the Guild Ambassador, said: "I am told your name is Edric. We welcome you to our Court in the hope this will bring new understanding between us."

The Steersman assumed a sybaritic reclining pose in his orange gas, popped a melange capsule into his mouth before meeting Paul's gaze. The tiny transducer orbiting a corner of the Guildsman's tank reproduced a coughing sound, then the rasping, uninvolved voice: "I abase myself before my Emperor and beg leave to present my credentials and offer a small gift."

An aide passed a scroll up to Stilgar, who studied it, scowling, then nodded to Paul. Both Stilgar and Paul turned then toward the ghola standing patiently below the dais.

"Indeed my Emperor has discerned the gift," Edric said.

"We are pleased to accept your credentials," Paul said. "Explain the gift."

Edric rolled in the tank, bringing his attention to bear on the ghola. "This is a man called Hayt," he said, spelling the name. "According to our investigators, he has a most curious history. He was killed here on Arrakis...a grievous head-wound which required many months of regrowth. The body was sold to the Bene Tleilax as that of a master swordsman, an adept of the Ginaz School. It came to our attention that this must be Duncan Idaho, the trusted retainer of your household. We bought him as a gift befitting an Emperor." Edric peered up at Paul. "Is it not Idaho, Sire?"

Restraint and caution gripped Paul's voice. "He has the aspect of Idaho."

Does Paul see something I don't? Alia wondered. *No! It's Duncan!*

The man called Hayt stood impassively, metal eyes fixed straight ahead, body relaxed. No sign escaped him to indicate he knew himself to be the object of discussion.

"According to our best knowledge, it's Idaho," Edric said.

"He's called Hayt now," Paul said. "A curious name."

"Sire, there's no divining how or why the Tleilaxu bestow names," Edric said. "But names can be changed. The Tleilaxu name is of little importance."

This is a Tleilaxu thing, Paul thought. *There's the problem.* The Bene Tleilax held little attachment to phenomenal nature. Good and evil carried strange meanings in their philosophy. What might they have incorporated in Idaho's flesh—out of design or whim?

Paul glanced at Stilgar, noted the Fremen's superstitious awe. It was an emotion echoed all through his Fremen guard. Stilgar's mind would be speculating about the loathsome habits of Guildsmen, of Tleilaxu and of gholas.

Turning toward the ghola, Paul said: "Hayt, is that your only name?"

A serene smile spread over the ghola's dark features. The metal eyes lifted, centered on Paul, but maintained their mechanical stare. "That is how I am called, my Lord: Hayt."

In her dark spy hole, Alia trembled. It was Idaho's voice, a quality of sound so precise she sensed its imprint upon her cells.

"May it please my Lord," the ghola added, "if I say his voice gives me pleasure. This is a sign, say the Bene Tleilax, that I have heard the voice . . . before."

"But you don't know this for sure," Paul said.

"I know nothing of my past for sure, my Lord. It was explained that I can have no memory of my former life. All that remains from before is the pattern set by the genes. There are, however, niches into which once-familiar things may fit. There are voices, places, foods, faces, sounds, actions—a sword in my hand, the controls of a 'thopter . . ."

Noting how intently the Guildsmen watched this

exchange, Paul asked: "Do you understand that you're a gift?"

"It was explained to me, my Lord."

Paul sat back, hands resting on the arms of the throne. *What debt do I owe Duncan's flesh?* he wondered. *The man died saving my life. But this is not Idaho, this is a ghola.* Yet, here were body and mind which had taught Paul to fly a 'thopter as though the wings grew from his own shoulders. Paul knew he could not pick up a sword without leaning on the harsh education Idaho had given him. A ghola. This was flesh full of false impressions, easily misread. Old associations would persist. *Duncan Idaho.* It wasn't so much a mask the ghola wore as it was a loose, concealing garment of personality which moved in a way different from whatever the Tleilaxu had hidden here.

"How might you serve us?" Paul asked.

"In any way my Lord's wishes and my capabilities agree."

Alia, watching from her vantage point, was touched by the ghola's air of diffidence. She detected nothing feigned. Something ultimately innocent shone from the new Duncan Idaho. The original had been worldly, devil-may-care. But this flesh had been cleansed of all that. It was a pure surface upon which the Tleilaxu had written . . . what?

She sensed the hidden perils in this gift then. This was a Tleilaxu thing. The Tleilaxu displayed a disturbing lack of inhibitions in what they created. Unbridled curiosity might guide their actions. They boasted they could make *anything* from the proper human raw material—devils or saints. They sold killer-mentats. They'd produced a killer medic, overcoming the Suk inhibitions against the taking of human life to do it. Their wares included willing menials, pliant sex toys for any whim, soldiers, generals, philosophers, even an occasional moralist.

Paul stirred, looked at Edric. "How has this *gift* been trained?" he asked.

"If it please my Lord," Edric said, "it amused the Tleilaxu to train this ghola as a mentat and philosopher of the Zensunni. Thus, they sought to increase his abilities with the sword."

"Did they succeed?"

"I do not know, my Lord."

Paul weighed the answer. Truthsense told him Edric sincerely believed the ghola to be Idaho. But there was more. The waters of Time through which this oracular Steersman moved suggested dangers without revealing them. *Hayt*. The Tleilaxu name spoke of peril. Paul felt himself tempted to reject the gift. Even as he felt the temptation, he knew he couldn't choose that way. This flesh made demands on House Atreides—a fact the enemy well knew.

"Zensunni philosopher," Paul mused, once more looking at the ghola. "You've examined your own role and motives?"

"I approach my service in an attitude of humility, Sire. I am a cleansed mind washed free of the imperatives from my human past."

"Would you prefer we called you Hayt or Duncan Idaho?"

"My Lord may call me what he wishes, for I am not a name."

"But do you *enjoy* the name Duncan Idaho?"

"I think that was my name, Sire. It fits within me. Yet... it stirs up curious responses. One's name, I think, must carry much that's unpleasant along with the pleasant."

"What gives you the most pleasure?" Paul asked.

Unexpectedly, the ghola laughed, said: "Looking for signs in others which reveal my former self."

"Do you see such signs here?"

"Oh, yes, my Lord. Your man Stilgar there is caught between suspicion and admiration. He was friend to my former self, but this ghola flesh repels him. You, my Lord, admired the man I was... and you trusted him."

"Cleansed mind," Paul said. "How can a cleansed mind put itself in bondage to us?"

"Bondage, my Lord? The cleansed mind makes decisions in the presence of unknowns and without cause and effect. Is this bondage?"

Paul scowled. It was a Zensunni saying, cryptic, apt—immersed in a creed which denied objective function in all mental activity. *Without cause and effect!* Such thoughts shocked the mind. *Unknowns?* Unknowns lay in every decision, even in the oracular vision.

"You'd prefer we called you Duncan Idaho?" Paul asked.

"We live by differences, my Lord. Choose a name for me."

"Let your Tleilaxu name stand," Paul said. "Hayt—there's a name inspires caution."

Hayt bowed, moved back one step.

And Alia wondered: *How did he know the interview was over? I knew it because I know my brother. But there was no sign a stranger could read. Did the Duncan Idaho in him know?*

Paul turned toward the Ambassador, said: "Quarters have been set aside for your embassy. It is our desire to have a private consultation with you at the earliest opportunity. We will send for you. Let us inform you further, before you hear it from an inaccurate source, that a Reverend Mother of the Sisterhood, Gaius Helen Mohiam, has been removed from the heighliner which brought you. It was done at our command. Her presence on your ship will be an item in our talks."

A wave of Paul's left hand dismissed the envoy. "Hayt," Paul said, "stay here."

The Ambassador's attendants backed away, towing the tank. Edric became orange motion in orange gas—eyes, a mouth, gently waving limbs.

Paul watched until the last Guildsman was gone, the great doors swinging closed behind them.

I've done it now, Paul thought. *I've accepted the ghola.*

The Tleilaxu creation was bait, no doubt of it. Very likely the old hag of a Reverend Mother played the same role. But it was the time of the tarot which he'd forecast in an early vision. The damnable tarot! It muddied the waters of Time until the prescient strained to detect moments but an hour off. Many a fish took the bait and escaped, he reminded himself. And the tarot worked for him as well as against him. What he could not see, others might not detect as well.

The ghola stood, head cocked to one side, waiting.

Stilgar moved across the steps, hid the ghola from Paul's view. In Chakobsa, the hunting language of their sietch days, Stilgar said: "That creature in the tank gives me the shudders, Sire, but this *gift!* Send it away!"

In the same tongue, Paul said: "I cannot."

"Idaho's dead," Stilgar argued. "This isn't Idaho. Let me take its water for the tribe."

"The ghola is my problem, Stil. Your problem is our prisoner. I want the Reverend Mother guarded most carefully by the men I trained to resist the wiles of Voice."

"I like this not, Sire."

"I'll be cautious, Stil. See that you are, too."

"Very well, Sire." Stilgar stepped down to the floor of the hall, passed close to Hayt, sniffed him and strode out.

Evil can be detected by its smell, Paul thought. Stilgar had planted the green and white Atreides banner on a dozen worlds, but remained superstitious Fremen, proof against any sophistication.

Paul studied the gift.

"Duncan, Duncan," he whispered. "What have they done to you?"

"They gave me life, m'Lord," Hayt said.

"But why were you trained and given to us?" Paul asked.

Hayt pursed his lips, then: "They intend me to destroy you."

The statement's candor shook Paul. But then, how else could a Zensunni-mentat respond? Even in a ghola, a mentat could speak no less than the truth, especially out of Zensunni inner calm. This was a human computer, mind and nervous system fitted to the tasks relegated long ago to hated mechanical devices. To condition him also as a Zensunni meant a double ration of honesty... unless the Tleilaxu had built something even more odd into this flesh.

Why, for example, the mechanical eyes? Tleilaxu boasted their metal eyes improved on the original. Strange, then, that more Tleilaxu didn't wear them out of choice.

Paul glanced up at Alia's spy hole, longed for her presence and advice, for counsel not clouded by feelings of responsibility and debt.

Once more, he looked at the ghola. This was no frivolous gift. It gave honest answers to dangerous questions.

It makes no difference that I know this is a weapon to be used against me, Paul thought.

"What should I do to protect myself from you?" Paul asked. It was direct speech, no royal "we," but a question as he might have put it to the old Duncan Idaho.

"Send me away, m'Lord."

Paul shook his head from side to side. "How are you to destroy me?"

Hayt looked at the guards, who'd moved closer to Paul after Stilgar's departure. He turned, cast his gaze around the hall, brought his metal eyes back to bear on Paul, nodded.

"This is a place where a man draws away from people," Hayt said. "It speaks of such power that one can contemplate it comfortably only in the remembrance that all things are finite. Did my Lord's oracular powers plot his course into this place?"

Paul drummed his fingers against the throne's arms. The mentat sought data, but the question disturbed him. "I came to this position by strong decisions... not always out of my other... abilities."

"Strong decisions," Hayt said. "These temper a man's life. One can take the temper from fine metal by heating it and allowing it to cool without quenching."

"Do you divert me with Zensunni prattle?" Paul asked.

"Zensunni has other avenues to explore, Sire, than diversion and display."

Paul wet his lips with his tongue, drew in a deep breath, set his own thoughts into the counterbalance poise of the mentat. Negative answers arose around him. It wasn't expected that he'd go haring after the ghola to the exclusion of other duties. No, that wasn't it. Why a *Zensunni*-mentat? Philosophy . . . words . . . contemplation . . . inward searching . . . He felt the weakness of his data.

"We need more data," he muttered.

"The facts needed by a mentat do not brush off onto one as you might gather pollen on your robe while passing through a field of flowers," Hayt said. "One chooses his pollen carefully, examines it under powerful amplification."

"You must teach me this Zensunni way with rhetoric," Paul said.

The metallic eyes glittered at him for a moment, then: "M'Lord, perhaps that's what was intended."

To blunt my will with words and ideas? Paul wondered.

"Ideas are most to feared when they become actions," Paul said.

"Send me away, Sire," Hayt said, and it was Duncan Idaho's voice full of concern for "the young master."

Paul felt trapped by that voice. He couldn't send that voice away, even when it came from a ghola. "You will stay," he said, "and we'll both exercise caution."

Hayt bowed in submission.

Paul glanced up at the spy hole, eyes pleading for Alia to take this *gift* off his hands and ferret out its secrets. Gholas were ghosts to frighten children. He'd never thought to know one. To know this one, he had to set himself above all compassion . . . and he wasn't certain he could do it. *Duncan... Duncan...* Where was Idaho in this shaped-to-measure flesh? It wasn't flesh... it was a shroud in fleshly shape! Idaho lay dead forever on the floor of an Arrakeen cavern. His ghost stared out of metal eyes. Two beings stood side by side in this revenant flesh. One was a threat with its force and nature hidden behind unique veils.

Closing his eyes, Paul allowed old visions to sift through his awareness. He sensed the spirits of love and hate spouting there in a rolling sea from which no rock lifted above the chaos. No place at all from which to survey turmoil.

Why has no vision shown me this new Duncan Idaho? he asked himself. *What concealed Time from an oracle? Other oracles, obviously.*

Paul opened his eyes, asked: "Hayt, do you have the power of prescience?"

"No, m'Lord."

Sincerity spoke in that voice. It was possible the ghola didn't know he possessed this ability, of course. But that'd hamper his working as a mentat. What was the hidden design?

Old visions surged around Paul. Would he have to choose the terrible way? Distorted Time hinted at this ghola in that hideous future. Would that way close in upon him no matter what he did?

Disengage... disengage... disengage...

The thought tolled in his mind.

In her position above Paul, Alia sat with chin cupped in left hand, stared down at the ghola. A magnetic attraction about this Hayt reached up to her. Tleilaxu restoration had given him youth, an innocent intensity which called out to her. She'd understood Paul's unspoken plea. When oracles failed, one turned to real spies and physical powers. She wondered, though, at her own eagerness to accept this challenge. She felt a positive desire to be near this *new* man, perhaps to touch him.

He's a danger to both of us, she thought.

Truth suffers from too much analysis.

—Ancient Fremen Saying

"Reverend Mother, I shudder to see you in such circumstances," Irulan said.

She stood just inside the cell door, measuring the various capacities of the room in her Bene Gesserit way. It was a three-meter cube carved with cutterays from the veined brown rock beneath Paul's Keep. For furnishings, it contained one flimsy basket chair occupied now by the Reverend Mother Gaius Helen Mohiam, a pallet with a brown cover upon which had been spread a deck of the new Dune Tarot cards, a metered water tap above a reclamation basin, a Fremen privy with moisture seals. It was all sparse, primitive. Yellow light came from anchored and caged glowglobes at the four corners of the ceiling.

"You've sent word to the Lady Jessica?" the Reverend Mother asked.

"Yes, but I don't expect her to lift one finger against her firstborn," Irulan said. She glanced at the cards. They spoke of the powerful turning their backs on supplicants. The card of the Great Worm lay beneath Desolate Sand. Patience was counseled. *Did one require the tarot to see this?* she asked herself.

A guard stood outside watching them through a metaglass window in the door. Irulan knew there'd be other monitors on this encounter. She had put in much thought and planning before daring to come here. To have stayed away carried its own perils, though.

The Reverend Mother had been engaged in *prajna* meditation interspersed with examinations of the tarot. Despite a feeling that she would never leave Arrakis alive, she had achieved a measure of calm through this. One's oracular powers might be small, but muddy water was muddy water. And there was always the Litany Against Fear.

She had yet to assimilate the import of the actions which had precipitated her into this cell. Dark suspicions brooded in her mind (and the tarot hinted at confirmations). Was it possible the Guild had planned this?

A yellow-robed Qizara, head shaved for a turban, beady eyes of total blue in a bland round face, skin leathered by the wind and sun of Arrakis, had awaited her on the heighliner's reception bridge. He had looked up from a bulb of spice-coffee being served by an obsequious steward, studied her a moment, put down the coffee bulb.

"You are the Reverend Mother Gaius Helen Mohiam?"

To replay those words in her mind was to bring that moment alive in the memory. Her throat had constricted with an unmanageable spasm of fear. How had one of the Emperor's minions learned of her presence on the heighliner?

"It came to our attention that you were aboard," the

Qizara said. "Have you forgotten that you are denied permission to set foot on the holy planet?"

"I am not on Arrakis," she said. "I'm a passenger on a Guild heighliner in free space."

"There is no such thing as free space, Madame."

She read hate mingled with profound suspicion in his tone.

"Muad'dib rules everywhere," he said.

"Arrakis is not my destination," she insisted.

"Arrakis is the destination of everyone," he said. And she feared for a moment that he would launch into a recital of the mystical itinerary which pilgrims followed. (This very ship had carried thousands of them.)

But the Qizara had pulled a golden amulet from beneath his robe, kissed it, touched it to his forehead and placed it to his right ear, listened. Presently, he restored the amulet to its hidden place.

"You are ordered to gather your luggage and accompany me to Arrakis."

"But I have business elsewhere!"

In that moment, she suspected Guild perfidy...or exposure through some transcendent power of the Emperor or his sister. Perhaps the Steersman did not conceal the conspiracy, after all. The abomination, Alia, certainly possessed the abilities of a Bene Gesserit Reverend Mother. What happened when those powers were coupled with the forces which worked in her brother?

"At once!" the Qizara snapped.

Everything in her cried out against setting foot once more on that accursed desert planet. Here was where the Lady Jessica had turned against the Sisterhood. Here was where they'd lost Paul Atreides, the kwisatz haderach they'd sought through long generations of careful breeding.

"At once," she agreed.

"There's little time," the Qizara said. "When the Emperor commands, all his subjects obey."

So the order had come from Paul!

She thought of protesting to the heighliner's Naviga-tor-Commander, but the futility of such a gesture stopped her. What could the Guild do?

"The Emperor has said I must die if I set foot on Dune," she said, making a last desperate effort. "You spoke of this yourself. You are condemning me if you take me down there."

"Say no more," the Qizara ordered. "The thing is ordained."

That was how they always spoke of Imperial commands, she knew. *Ordained!* The holy ruler whose eyes could pierce the future had spoken. What must be must be. He had seen it, had He not?

With the sick feeling that she was caught in a web of her own spinning, she had turned to obey.

And the web had become a cell which Irulan could visit. She saw that Irulan had aged somewhat since their meeting on Wallach IX. New lines of worry spread from the corners of her eyes. Well . . . time to see if this Sister of the Bene Gesserit could obey her vows.

"I've had worse quarters," the Reverend Mother said. "Do you come from the Emperor?" And she allowed her fingers to move as though in agitation.

Irulan read the moving fingers and her own fingers flashed an answer as she spoke, saying: "No—I came as soon as I heard you were here."

"Won't the Emperor be angry?" the Reverend Mother asked. Again, her fingers moved: imperative, pressing, demanding.

"Let him be angry. You were my teacher in the Sisterhood, just as you were the teacher of his own mother. Does he think I will turn my back on you as she has done?" And Irulan's finger-talk made excuses, begged.

The Reverend Mother sighed. On the surface, it was the sigh of a prisoner bemoaning her fate, but inwardly she felt the response as a comment on Irulan. It was futile to hope the Atreides Emperor's precious gene pattern could be preserved through this instrument. No matter her beauty, this Princess was flawed. Under that veneer of sexual attraction lived a whining shrew more interested in words than in actions. Irulan was still a Bene Gesserit, though, and the Sisterhood reserved certain techniques to use on some of its weaker vessels as insurance that vital instructions would be carried out.

Beneath small talk about a softer pallet, better food, the Reverend Mother brought up her arsenal of persuasion and gave her orders: the brother-sister crossbreeding must be explored. (Irulan almost broke at receiving this command.)

"I must have my chance!" Irulan's fingers pleaded.

"You've had your chance," the Reverend Mother countered. And she was explicit in her instructions: Was the Emperor ever angry with his concubine? His unique powers must make him lonely. To whom could he speak in any hope of being understood? To the sister, obviously. She shared this loneliness. The depth of their communion must be exploited. Opportunities must be created to throw them together in privacy. Intimate encounters must be arranged. The possibility of eliminating the concubine must be explored. Grief dissolved traditional barriers.

Irulan protested. If Chani were killed, suspicion would fasten immediately upon the Princess-Consort. Besides, there were other problems. Chani had fastened upon an ancient Fremen diet supposed to promote fertility and the diet eliminated all opportunity for administering the contraceptive drugs. Lifting the suppressives would make Chani even more fertile.

The Reverend Mother was outraged and concealed it with difficulty while her fingers flashed their demands. Why had this information not been conveyed at the beginning of their conversation? How could Irulan be that stupid? If Chani conceived and bore a son, the

Emperor would declare the child his heir!

Irulan protested that she understood the dangers, but the genes might not be totally lost.

Damn such stupidity! the Reverend Mother raged. Who knew what suppressions and genetic entanglements Chani might introduce from her wild Fremen strain? The Sisterhood must have only the pure line! And an heir would renew Paul's ambitions, spur him to new efforts in consolidating his Empire. The conspiracy could not afford such a setback.

Defensively, Irulan wanted to know how she could have prevented Chani from trying this diet?

But the Reverend Mother was in no mood for excuses. Irulan received explicit instructions now to meet this new threat. If Chani conceived, an abortifact must be introduced into her food or drink. Either that, or she must be killed. An heir to the throne from that source must be prevented at all costs.

An abortifact would be as dangerous as an open attack on the concubine, Irulan objected. She trembled at the thought of trying to kill Chani.

Was Irulan deterred by danger? The Reverend Mother wanted to know, her finger-talk conveying deep scorn.

Angered, Irulan signaled that she knew her value as an agent in the royal household. Did the conspiracy wish to waste such a valuable agent? Was she to be thrown away? In what other way could they keep this close a watch on the Emperor? Or had they introduced another agent into the household? Was that it? Was she to be used now, desperately, and for the last time?

In a war, all values acquired new relationships, the Reverend Mother countered. Their greatest peril was that House Atreides should secure itself with an Imperial line. The Sisterhood could not take such a risk. This went far beyond the danger to the Atreides genetic pattern. Let Paul anchor his family to the throne and the Sisterhood could look forward to centuries of disruption for its programs.

Irulan understood the argument, but she couldn't escape the thought that a decision had been made to spend the Princess-Consort for something of great value. Was there something she should know about the ghola? Irulan ventured.

The Reverend Mother wanted to know if Irulan thought the Sisterhood composed of fools. When had they ever failed to tell Irulan all she *should* know?

It was no answer, but an admission of concealment, Irulan saw. It said she would be told no more than she needed to know.

How could they be certain the ghola was capable of destroying the Emperor? Irulan asked.

She could just as well have asked if melange were capable of destruction, the Reverend Mother countered.

It was a rebuke with a subtle message, Irulan realized. The Bene Gesserit "whip that instructs" informed her that she should have understood long ago this similarity between the spice and the ghola. Melange was valuable, but it exacted a price—addiction. It added years to a life—decades for some—but it was still just another way to die.

The ghola was something of deadly value.

The obvious way to prevent an unwanted birth was to kill the prospective mother before conception, the Reverend Mother signaled, returning to the attack.

Of course, Irulan thought. *If you decide to spend a certain sum, get as much for it as you can.*

The Reverend Mother's eyes, dark with the blue brilliance of her melange addiction, stared up at Irulan, measuring, waiting, observing minutiae.

She reads me clearly, Irulan thought with dismay. *She trained me and observed me in that training. She knows I realize what decision has been taken here. She only observes now to see how I will take this knowledge. Well, I will take it as a Bene Gesserit and a princess.*

Irulan managed a smile, pulled herself erect, thought of the evocative opening passage of the Litany Against Fear:

"I must not fear. Fear is the mind-killer. Fear is the little-death that brings total obliteration. I will face my fear . . ."

When calmness had returned, she thought: *Let them spend me. I will show them what a princess is worth. Perhaps I'll buy them more than they expected.*

After a few more empty vocalizations to bind off the interview, Irulan departed.

When she had gone, the Reverend Mother returned to her tarot cards, laying them out in the fire-eddy pattern. Immediately, she got the Kwisatz Haderach of the Major Arcana and the card lay coupled with the Eight of Ships: the sibyl hoodwinked and betrayed. These were not cards of good omen: they spoke of concealed resources for her enemies.

She turned away from the cards, sat in agitation, wondering if Irulan might yet destroy them.

The Fremen see her as the Earth Figure, a demi-goddess whose special charge is to protect the tribes through her powers of violence. She is Reverend Mother to their Reverend Mothers. To pilgrims who seek her out with demands that she restore virility or make the barren fruitful, she is a form of antimentat. She feeds on that proof that the "analytic" has limits. She represents ultimate tension. She is the virgin-harlot—witty, vulgar, cruel, as destructive in her whims as a coriolis storm.

—St. Alia of the Knife
as taken from The Irulan Report

Alia stood like a black-robed sentinel figure on the south platform of her temple, the Fane of the Oracle which Paul's Fremen cohorts had built for her against a wall of his stronghold.

She hated this part of her life, but knew no way to

evade the temple without bringing down destruction upon them all. The pilgrims (damn them!) grew more numerous every day. The temple's lower porch was crowded with them. Vendors moved among the pilgrims, and there were minor sorcerers, haruspices, diviners, all working their trade in pitiful imitation of Paul Muad'dib and his sister.

Red and green packages containing the new Dune Tarot were prominent among the vendors' wares, Alia saw. She wondered about the tarot. Who was feeding this device into the Arrakeen market? Why had the tarot sprung to prominence at this particular time and place? Was it to muddy Time? Spice addiction always conveyed some sensitivity to prediction. Fremen were notoriously fey. Was it an accident that so many of them dabbled in portents and omens here and now? She decided to seek an answer at the first opportunity.

There was a wind from the southeast, a small leftover wind blunted by the scarp of the Shield Wall which loomed high in these northern reaches. The rim glowed orange through a thin dust haze underlighted by the late afternoon sun. It was a hot wind against her cheeks and it made her homesick for the sand, for the security of open spaces.

The last of the day's mob began descending the broad greenstone steps of the lower porch, singly and in groups, a few pausing to stare at the keepsakes and holy amulets on the street vendors' racks, some consulting one last minor sorcerer. Pilgrims, supplicants, townfolk, Fremen, vendors closing up for the day—they formed a straggling line that trailed off into the palm-lined avenue which led to the heart of the city.

Alia's eyes picked out the Fremen, marking the frozen looks of superstitious awe on their faces, the half-wild way they kept their distance from the others. They were her strength and her peril. They still captured giant worms for transport, for sport and for sacrifice. They resented the offworld pilgrims, barely tolerated the townfolk of graben and *pan*, hated the cynicism they saw in the street vendors. One did not jostle a wild Fremen, even in a mob such as the ones which swarmed to Alia's Fane. There were no knifings in the Sacred Precincts, but bodies had been found . . . later.

The departing swarm had stirred up dust. The flinty odor came to Alia's nostrils, ignited another pang of longing for the open *bled*. Her sense of the past, she realized, had been sharpened by the coming of the ghola. There'd been much pleasure in those untrammeled days before her brother had mounted the throne—time for joking, time for small things, time to enjoy a cool morning or a sunset, time . . . time . . . time . . . Even danger had been good in those days—clean danger from known sources. No need then to strain the limits of prescience, to peer through murky veils for frustrating glimpses of the future.

Wild Fremen said it well: "Four things cannot be hidden—love, smoke, a pillar of fire and a man striding across the open bled."

With an abrupt feeling of revulsion, Alia retreated from the platform into the shadows of the Fane, strode along the balcony which looked down into the glistening opalescence of her Hall of Oracles. Sand on the tiles rasped beneath her feet. *Supplicants always tracked sand into the Sacred Chambers!* She ignored attendants, guards, postulants, the Qizarate's omnipresent priest-sycophants, plunged into the spiral passage which twisted upward to her private quarters. There, amidst divans, deep rugs, tent hangings and mementos of the desert, she dismissed the Fremen amazons Stilgar had assigned as her personal guardians. *Watchdogs, more likely!* When they had gone, muttering and objecting, but more fearful of her than they were of Stilgar, she stripped off her robe, leaving only the sheathed crysknife on its thong around her neck, strewed garments behind as she made for the bath.

He was near, she knew—that shadow-figure of a man

she could sense in her future, but could not see. It angered her that no power of prescience could put flesh on that figure. He could be sensed only at unexpected moments while she scanned the lives of others. Or she came upon a smoky outline in solitary darkness when innocence lay coupled with desire. He stood just beyond an unfixed horizon, and she felt that if she strained her talents to an unexpected intensity she might see him. He was *there*—a constant assault on her awareness: fierce, dangerous, immoral.

Moist warm air surrounded her in the tub. Here was a habit she had learned from the memory-entities of the uncounted Reverend Mothers who were strung out in her awareness like pearls on a glowing necklace. Water, warm water in a sunken tub, accepted her skin as she slid into it. Green tiles with figures of red fish worked into a sea pattern surrounded the water. Such an abundance of water occupied this space that a Fremen of old would have been outraged to see it used merely for washing human flesh.

He was near.

It was lust in tension with chastity, she thought. Her flesh desired a mate. Sex held no casual mystery for a Reverend Mother who had presided at the sietch orgies. The *tau* awareness of her *other-selves* could supply any detail her curiosity required. This feeling of nearness could be nothing other than flesh reaching for flesh.

Need for action fought lethargy in the warm water.

Abruptly, Alia climbed dripping from the bath, strode wet and naked into the training chamber which adjoined her bedroom. The chamber, oblong and skylighted, contained the gross and subtle instruments which toned a Bene Gesserit adept into ultimate physical and mental awareness/preparedness. There were mnemonic amplifiers, digit mills from Ix to strengthen and sensitize fingers and toes, odor synthesizers, tactility sensitizers, temperature gradient fields, pattern betrayers to prevent her falling into detectable habits, alpha-wave-response trainers, blink-synchronizers to tone abilities in light/dark/ spectrum analysis...

In ten-centimeter letters along one wall, written by her own hand in mnemonic paint, stood the key reminder from the Bene Gesserit Creed:

"Before us, all methods of learning were tainted by instinct. We learned how to learn. Before us, instinct-ridden researchers possessed a limited attention span—often no longer than a single lifetime. Projects stretching across fifty or more lifetimes never occurred to them. The concept of total muscle/nerve training had not entered awareness."

As she moved into the training room, Alia caught her own reflection multiplied thousands of times in the crystal prisms of a fencing mirror swinging in the heart of a target dummy. She saw the long sword waiting on its brackets against the target, and she thought: *Yes! I'll work myself to exhaustion—drain the flesh and clear the mind.*

The sword felt right in her hand. She slipped the crysknife from its sheath at her neck, held it sinister, tapped the activating stud with the sword tip. Resistance came alive as the aura of the target shield built up, pushing her weapon slowly and firmly away.

Prisms glittered. The target slipped to her left.

Alia followed with the tip of the long blade, thinking as she often did that the thing could almost be alive. But it was only servomotors and complex reflector circuits designed to lure the eyes away from danger, to confuse and teach. It was an instrument geared to react as she reacted, an anti-self which moved as she moved, balancing light on its prisms, shifting its target, offering its counter-blade.

Many blades appeared to lunge at her from the prisms, but only one was real. She countered the real one, slipped the sword past shield resistance to tap the target. A marker light came alive: red and glistening among the prisms... more distraction.

Again the thing attacked, moving at one-marker speed

now, just a bit faster than it had at the beginning.

She parried and, against all caution, moved into the danger zone, scored with the crysknife.

Two lights glowed from the prisms.

Again, the thing increased speed, moving out on its rollers, drawn like a magnet to the motions of her body and the tip of her sword.

Attack—parry—counter.

Attack—parry—counter . . .

She had four lights alive in there now, and the thing was becoming more dangerous, moving faster with each light, offering more areas of confusion.

Five lights.

Sweat glistened on her naked skin. She existed now in a universe whose dimensions were outlined by the threatening blade, the target, bare feet against the practice floor, senses/nerves/muscles—motion against motion.

Attack—parry—counter.

Six lights . . . seven . . .

Eight!

She had never before risked eight.

In a recess of her mind there grew a sense of urgency, a crying out against such wildness as this. The instrument of prisms and target could not think, feel caution or remorse. And it carried a real blade. To go against less defeated the purpose of such training. That attacking blade could maim and it could kill. But the finest swordsmen in the Imperium never went against more than seven lights.

Nine!

Alia experienced a sense of supreme exaltation. Attacking blade and target became blurs among blurs. She felt that the sword in her hand had come alive. She was an anti-target. She did not move the blade; it moved her.

Ten!

Eleven!

Something flashed past her shoulder, slowed at the

shield aura around the target, slid through and tripped the deactivating stud. The lights darkened. Prisms and target twisted their way to stillness.

Alia whirled, angered by the intrusion, but her reaction was thrown into tension by awareness of the supreme ability which had hurled that knife. It had been a throw timed to exquisite nicety—just fast enough to get through the shield zone and not too fast to be deflected.

And it had touched a one-millimeter spot within an eleven-light target.

Alia found her own emotions and tensions running down in a manner not unlike that of the target dummy. She was not at all surprised to see who had thrown the knife.

Paul stood just inside the training room doorway, Stilgar three steps behind him. Her brother's eyes were squinted in anger.

Alia, growing conscious of her nudity, thought to cover herself, found the idea amusing. What the eyes had seen could not be erased. Slowly, she replaced the crysknife in its sheath at her neck.

"I might've known," she said.

"I presume you know how dangerous that was," Paul said. He took his time reading the reactions on her face and body: the flush of her exertions coloring her skin, the wet fullness of her lips. There was a disquieting femaleness about her that he had never considered in his sister. He found it odd that he could look at a person who was this close to him and no longer recognize her in the identity framework which had seemed so fixed and familiar.

"That was madness," Stilgar rasped, coming up to stand beside Paul.

The words were angry, but Alia heard awe in his voice, saw it in his eyes.

"Eleven lights," Paul said, shaking his head.

"I'd have made it twelve if you hadn't interfered," she said. She began to pale under his close regard, added:

"And why do the damned things have that many lights if we're not supposed to try for them?"

"A Bene Gesserit should ask the reasoning behind an open-ended system?" Paul asked.

"I suppose you never tried for more than seven!" she said, anger returning. His attentive posture began to annoy her.

"Just once," Paul said. "Gurney Halleck caught me on ten. My punishment was sufficiently embarrassing that I won't tell you what he did. And speaking of embarrassment..."

"Next time, perhaps you'll have yourselves announced," she said. She brushed past Paul into the bedroom, found a loose gray robe, slipped into it, began brushing her hair before a wall mirror. She felt sweaty, sad, a post-coitum kind of sadness that left her with a desire to bathe once more...and to sleep. "Why're you here?" she asked.

"My Lord," Stilgar said. There was an odd inflection in his voice that brought Alia around to stare at him.

"We're here at Irulan's suggestion," Paul said, "as strange as that may seem. She believes, and information in Stil's possession appears to confirm it, that our enemies are about to make a major try for—"

"My Lord!" Stilgar said, his voice sharper.

As her brother turned, questioning, Alia continued to look at the old Fremen Naib. Something about him now made her intensely aware that he was one of the primitives. Stilgar believed in a supernatural world very near him. It spoke to him in a simple pagan tongue dispelling all doubts. The natural universe in which he stood was fierce, unstoppable, and it lacked the common morality of the Imperium.

"Yes, Stil," Paul said. "Do you want to tell her why we came?"

"This isn't the time to talk of why we came," Stilgar said.

"What's wrong, Stil?"

Stilgar continued to stare at Alia. "Sire, are you blind?"

Paul turned back to his sister, a feeling of unease beginning to fill him. Of all his aides, only Stilgar dared speak to him in that tone, but even Stilgar measured the occasion by its need.

"This one must have a mate!" Stilgar blurted. "There'll be trouble if she's not wed, and that soon."

Alia whirled away, her face suddenly hot. *How did he touch me?* she wondered. Bene Gesserit self-control had been powerless to prevent her reaction. How had Stilgar done that? He hadn't the power of the Voice. She felt dismayed and angry.

"Listen to the great Stilgar!" Alia said, keeping her back to them, aware of a shrewish quality in her voice and unable to hide it. "Advice to maidens from Stilgar, the Fremen!"

"As I love you both, I must speak," Stilgar said, a profound dignity in his tone. "I did not become a chieftain among the Fremen by being blind to what moves men and women together. One needs no mysterious powers for this."

Paul weighed Stilgar's meaning, reviewed what they had seen here and his own undeniable male reaction to his own sister. Yes—there'd been a ruttish air about Alia, something wildly wanton. What had made her enter the practice floor in the nude? And risking her life in that foolhardy way! Eleven lights in the fencing prisms! That brainless automaton loomed in his mind with all the aspects of an ancient horror creature. Its possession was the shibboleth of this age, but it carried also the taint of old immorality. Once, they'd been guided by an artificial intelligence, computer brains. The Butlerian Jihad had ended that, but it hadn't ended the aura of aristocratic vice which enclosed such things.

Stilgar was right, of course. They must find a mate for Alia.

"I will see to it," Paul said. "Alia and I will discuss this later—privately."

Alia turned around, focused on Paul. Knowing how his mind worked, she realized she'd been the subject of a mentat decision, uncounted bits falling together in that human-computer analysis. There was an inexorable quality to this realization—a movement like the movement of planets. It carried something of the order of the universe in it, inevitable and terrifying.

"Sire," Stilgar said, "perhaps we'd—"

"Not now!" Paul snapped. "We've other problems at the moment."

Aware that she dared not try to match logic with her brother, Alia put the past few moments aside, Bene Gesserit fashion, said: "Irulan sent you?" She found herself experiencing menace in that thought.

"Indirectly," Paul said. "The information she gives us confirms our suspicion that the Guild is about to try for a sandworm."

"They'll try to capture a small one and attempt to start the spice cycle on some other world," Stilgar said. "It means they've found a world they consider suitable."

"It means they have Fremen accomplices!" Alia argued. "No offworlder could capture a worm!"

"That goes without saying," Stilgar said.

"No, it doesn't," Alia said. She was outraged by such obtuseness. "Paul, certainly you . . ."

"The rot is setting in," Paul said. "We've known that for quite some time. "I've never *seen* this other world, though, and that bothers me. If they—"

"*That* bothers you?" Alia demanded. "It means only that they've clouded its location with Steersmen the way they hide their sanctuaries."

Stilgar opened his mouth, closed it without speaking. He had the overwhelming sensation that his idols had admitted blasphemous weakness.

Paul, sensing Stilgar's disquiet, said: "We've an immediate problem! I want your opinion, Alia. Stilgar suggests we expand our patrols in the open bled and reinforce the sietch watch. It's just possible we could spot a landing party and prevent the—"

"With a Steersman guiding them?" Alia asked.

"They *are* desperate, aren't they?" Paul agreed. "*That* is why I'm here."

"What've they *seen* that we haven't?" Alia asked.

"Precisely."

Alia nodded, remembering her thoughts about the new Dune Tarot. Quickly, she recounted her fears.

"Throwing a blanket over us," Paul said.

"With adequate patrols," Stilgar ventured, "we might prevent the—"

"We prevent nothing . . . forever," Alia said. She didn't like the *feel* of the way Stilgar's mind was working now. He had narrowed his scope, eliminated obvious essentials. This was not the Stilgar she remembered.

"We must count on their getting a worm," Paul said. "Whether they can start the melange cycle on another planet is a different question. They'll need more than a worm."

Stilgar looked from brother to sister. Out of ecological thinking that had been ground into him by sietch life, he grasped their meaning. A captive worm couldn't live except within a bit of Arrakis—sand plankton, Little Makers and all. The Guild's problem was large, but not impossible. His own growing uncertainty lay in a different area.

"Then your visions do not detect the Guild at its work?" he asked.

"Damnation!" Paul exploded.

Alia studied Stilgar, sensing the savage sideshow of ideas taking place in his mind. He was hung on a rack of enchantment. Magic! Magic! To glimpse the future was to steal terrifying fire from a sacred flame. It held the attraction of ultimate peril, souls ventured and lost. One brought back from the formless, dangerous distances something with form and power. But Stilgar was beginning to sense other forces, perhaps greater powers beyond that unknown horizon. His Queen Witch and

Sorcerer Friend betrayed dangerous weaknesses.

"Stilgar," Alia said, fighting to hold him, "you stand in a valley between dunes. I stand on the crest. I see where you do not see. And, among other things, I see mountains which conceal the distances."

"There are things hidden from you," Stilgar said. "This you've always said."

"All power is limited," Alia said.

"And danger may come from behind the mountains," Stilgar said.

"It's *something* on that order," Alia said.

Stilgar nodded, his gaze fastened on Paul's face. "But whatever comes from behind the mountains must cross the dunes."

The most dangerous game in the universe is to govern from an oracular base. We do not consider ourselves wise enough or brave enough to play that game. The measures detailed here for regulation in lesser matters are as near as we dare venture to the brink of government. For our purposes, we borrow a definition from the Bene Gesserit and we consider the various worlds as gene pools, sources of teachings and teachers, sources of the possible. Our goal is not to rule, but to tap these gene pools, to learn, and to free ourselves from all restraints imposed by dependency and government.

—"The Orgy as a Tool of Statecraft,"
Chapter Three of The Steersman's Guild

"Is that where your father died?" Edric asked, sending a beam pointer from his tank to a jeweled marker on one of the relief maps adorning a wall of Paul's reception salon.

"That's the shrine of his skull," Paul said. "My father died a prisoner on a Harkonnen frigate in the sink below us."

"Oh, yes: I recall the story now," Edric said. "Something about killing the old Baron Harkonnen, his mortal enemy." Hoping he didn't betray too much of the terror which small enclosures such as this room imposed upon him, Edric rolled over in the orange gas, directed his gaze at Paul, who sat alone on a long divan of striped gray and black.

"My sister killed the Baron," Paul said, voice and manner dry, "just before the battle of Arrakeen."

And why, he wondered, did the Guild man-fish reopen old wounds in this place and at this time?

The Steersman appeared to be fighting a losing battle to contain his nervous energies. Gone were the languid fish motions of their earlier encounter. Edric's tiny eyes jerked here...there, questing and measuring. The one attendant who had accompanied him in here stood apart near the line of houseguards ranging the end wall at Paul's left. The attendant worried Paul—hulking, thick-necked, blunt and vacant face. The man had entered the salon, nudging Edric's tank along on its supporting field, walking with a strangler's gait, arms akimbo.

Scytale, Edric had called him. *Scytale, an aide.*

The aide's surface shouted stupidity, but the eyes betrayed him. They laughed at everything they saw.

"Your concubine appeared to enjoy the performance of the Face Dancers," Edric said. "It pleases me that I could provide that small entertainment. I particularly enjoyed her reaction to seeing her own features simultaneously repeated by the whole troupe."

"Isn't there a warning against Guildsmen bearing gifts?" Paul asked.

And he thought of the performance out there in the Great Hall. The dancers had entered in the costumes and guise of the Dune Tarot, flinging themselves about in seemingly random patterns that devolved into fire eddies and ancient prognostic designs. Then had come the rulers—a parade of kings and emperors like faces on coins, formal and stiff in outline, but curiously fluid. And the jokes: a copy of Paul's own face and body, Chani repeated across the floor of the Hall, even Stilgar, who had grunted and shuddered while others laughed.

"But our gifts have the kindest intent," Edric protested.

"How kindly can you be?" Paul asked. "The ghola you gave us believes he was designed to destroy us."

"Destroy you, Sire?" Edric asked, all bland attention. "Can one destroy a god?"

Stilgar, entering on the last words, stopped, glared at the guards. They were much farther from Paul than he liked. Angrily he motioned them closer.

"It's all right, Stil," Paul said, lifting a hand. "Just a friendly discussion. Why don't you move the Ambassador's tank over by the end of my divan?"

Stilgar, weighing the order, saw that it would put the Steersman's tank between Paul and the hulking aide, much too close to Paul, but...

"It's all right, Stil," Paul repeated, and he gave the private hand-signal which made the order an imperative.

Moving with obvious reluctance, Stilgar pushed the tank closer to Paul. He didn't like the feel of the container or the heavily perfumed smell of melange around it. He took up a position at the corner of the tank beneath the orbiting device through which the Steersman spoke.

"To kill a god," Paul said. "That's very interesting. But who says I'm a god?"

"Those who worship you," Edric said, glancing pointedly at Stilgar.

"Is this what you believe?" Paul asked.

"What I believe is of no moment, Sire," Edric said. "It seems to most observers, however, that you conspire to make a god of yourself. And one might ask if that is something any mortal can do... safely?"

Paul studied the Guildsman. Repellent creature, but perceptive. It was a question Paul had asked himself time and again. But he had seen enough alternate Timelines to know of worse possibilities than accepting godhead for himself. Much worse. These were not, however, the normal avenues for a Steersman to probe. Curious. Why had that question been asked? What could Edric hope to gain by such effrontery? Paul's thoughts went *flick* (the association of Tleilaxu would be behind this move)—*flick* (the Jihad's recent Sembou victory would bear on Edric's action)—*flick* (various Bene Gesserit credos showed themselves here) *flick* ...

A process involving thousands of information bits poured flickering through his computational awareness. It required perhaps three seconds.

"Does a Steersman question the guidelines of prescience?" Paul asked, putting Edric on the weakest ground.

This disturbed the Steersman, but he covered well, coming up with what sounded like a long aphorism: "No man of intelligence questions the fact of prescience, Sire. Oracular vision has been known to men since most ancient times. It has a way of entangling us when we least suspect. Luckily, there are other forces in our universe."

"Greater than prescience?" Paul asked, pressing him.

"If prescience alone existed and did everything, Sire, it would annihilate itself. Nothing but prescience? Where could it be applied except to its own degenerating movements?"

"There's always the human situation," Paul agreed.

"A precarious thing at best," Edric said, "without confusing it by hallucinations."

"Are my visions no more than hallucinations?" Paul asked, mock sadness in his voice. "Or do you imply that my worshippers hallucinate?"

Stilgar, sensing the mounting tensions, moved a step nearer Paul, fixed his attention on the Guildsman reclining in the tank.

"You twist my words, Sire," Edric protested. An odd sense of violence lay suspended in the words.

Violence here? Paul wondered. *They wouldn't dare!*

Unless (and he glanced at his guards) *the forces which protected him were to be used in replacing him.*

"But you accuse me of conspiring to make a god of myself," Paul said, pitching his voice that only Edric and Stilgar might hear. "Conspire?"

"A poor choice of words, perhaps, my Lord," Edric said.

"But significant," Paul said. "It says you expect the worst of me."

Edric arched his neck, stared sideways at Stilgar with a look of apprehension. "People always expect the worst of the rich and powerful, Sire. It is said one can always tell an aristocrat: he reveals only those of his vices which will make him popular."

A tremor passed across Stilgar's face.

Paul looked up at the movement, sensing the thoughts and angers whispering in Stilgar's mind. How dared this Guildsman talk thus to Muad'dib?

"You're not joking, of course," Paul said.

"Joking, Sire?"

Paul grew aware of dryness in his mouth. He felt that there were too many people in this room, that the air he breathed had passed through too many lungs. The taint of melange from Edric's tank felt threatening.

"Who might my accomplices be in such a conspiracy?" Paul asked presently. "Do you nominate the Qizarate?"

Edric's shrug stirred the orange gas around his head. He no longer appeared concerned by Stilgar, although the Fremen continued to glare at him.

"Are you suggesting that my missionaries of the Holy Orders, *all of them,* are preaching subtle falsehood?" Paul insisted.

"It could be a question of self-interest and sincerity," Edric said.

Stilgar put a hand to the crysknife beneath his robe.

Paul shook his head, said: "Then you accuse me of insincerity."

"I'm not sure that *accuse* is the proper word, Sire."

The boldness of this creature! Paul thought. And he said: "Accused or not, you're saying my bishops and I are no better than power-hungry brigands."

"Power-hungry, Sire?" Again, Edric looked at Stilgar. "Power tends to isolate those who hold too much of it. Eventually, they lose touch with reality...and fall."

"M'Lord," Stilgar growled, "you've had men executed for less!"

"Men, yes," Paul agreed. "But this is a Guild Ambassador."

"He accuses you of an unholy fraud!" Stilgar said.

"His thinking interests me, Stil," Paul said. "Contain your anger and remain alert."

"As Muad'dib commands."

"Tell me, Steersman," Paul said, "how could we maintain this hypothetical fraud over such enormous distances of space and time without the means to watch every missionary, to examine every nuance in every Qizarate priory and temple?"

"What is time to you?" Edric asked.

Stilgar frowned in obvious puzzlement. And he thought: *Muad'dib has often said he sees past the veils of time. What is the Guildsman really saying?*

"Wouldn't the structure of such a fraud begin to show holes?" Paul asked. "Significant disagreements, schisms ...doubts, confessions of guilt—surely fraud could not suppress all these."

"What religion and self-interest cannot hide, governments can," Edric said.

"Are you testing the limits of my tolerance?" Paul asked.

"Do my arguments lack all merit?" Edric countered.

Does he want us to kill him? Paul wondered. *Is Edric offering himself as a sacrifice?*

"I prefer the cynical view," Paul said, testing. "You obviously are trained in all the lying tricks of statecraft, the double meanings and the power words. Language is nothing more than a weapon to you and, thus, you test my armor."

"The cynical view," Edric said, a smile stretching his mouth. "And rulers are notoriously cynical where religions are concerned. Religion, too, is a weapon. What manner of weapon is religion when it becomes the government?"

Paul felt himself go inwardly still, a profound caution gripping him. To whom was Edric speaking? Damnable clever words, heavy with manipulation leverages—that undertone of comfortable humor, the unspoken air of shared secrets: his manner said he and Paul were two sophisticates, men of a wider universe who understood things not granted common folk. With a feeling of shock, Paul realized that he had not been the main target for all this rhetoric. This affliction visited upon the court had been speaking for the benefit of others—speaking to Stilgar, to the household guards . . . perhaps even to the hulking aide.

"Religious *mana* was thrust upon me," Paul said. "I did not seek it." And he thought: *There! Let this man-fish think himself victorious in our battle of words!*

"Then why have you not disavowed it, Sire?" Edric asked.

"Because of my sister Alia," Paul said, watching Edric carefully. "She is a goddess. Let me urge caution where Alia is concerned lest she strike you dead with her glance."

A gloating smile began forming on Edric's mouth, was replaced by a look of shock.

"I am deadly serious," Paul said, watching the shock spread, seeing Stilgar nod.

In a bleak voice, Edric said: "You have mauled my confidence in you, Sire. And no doubt that was your intent."

"Do not be certain you know my intent," Paul said, and he signaled Stilgar that the audience was at an end.

To Stilgar's questioning gesture asking if Edric were to be assassinated, Paul gave a negative hand-sign, amplified it with an imperative lest Stilgar take matters into his own hands.

Scytale, Edric's aide, moved to the rear corner of the tank, nudged it toward the door. When he came opposite Paul, he stopped, turned that laughing gaze on Paul, said: "If my Lord permits?"

"Yes, what is it?" Paul asked, noting how Stilgar moved close in answer to the implied menace from this man.

"Some say," Scytale said, "that people cling to Imperial leadership because space is infinite. They feel lonely without a unifying symbol. For a lonely people, the Emperor is a definite place. They can turn toward him and say: 'See, there He is. He makes us one.' Perhaps religion serves the same purpose, m'Lord."

Scytale nodded pleasantly, gave Edric's tank another nudge. They moved out of the salon, Edric supine in his tank, eyes closed. The Steersman appeared spent, all his nervous energies exhausted.

Paul stared after the shambling figure of Scytale, wondering at the man's words. A peculiar fellow, that Scytale, he thought. While he was speaking, he had radiated a feeling of many people—as though his entire genetic inheritance lay exposed on his skin.

"That was odd," Stilgar said, speaking to no one in particular.

Paul arose from the divan as a guard closed the door behind Edric and the escort.

"Odd," Stilgar repeated. A vein throbbed at his temple.

Paul dimmed the salon's lights, moved to a window which opened onto an angled cliff of his Keep. Lights glittered far below—pigmy movement. A work gang moved down there bringing giant plasmeld blocks to repair a facade of Alia's temple which had been damaged by a freak twisting of a sandblast wind.

"That was a foolish thing, Usul, inviting that creature into these chambers," Stilgar said.

Usul, Paul thought. *My sietch name. Stilgar reminds*

me that he ruled over me once, that he saved me from the desert.

"Why did you do it?" Stilgar asked, speaking from close behind Paul.

"Data," Paul said. "I need more data."

"Is it not dangerous to try meeting this threat *only* as a mentat?"

That was perceptive, Paul thought.

Mentat computation remained finite. You couldn't say something boundless within the boundaries of any language. Mentat abilities had their uses, though. He said as much now, daring Stilgar to refute his argument.

"There's always something outside," Stilgar said. "Some things best *kept* outside."

"Or inside," Paul said. And he accepted for a moment his own oracular/mentat summation. Outside, yes. And inside: here lay the true horror. How could he protect himself from himself? They certainly were setting him up to destroy himself, but this was a position hemmed in by even more terrifying possibilities.

His reverie was broken by the sound of rapid footsteps. The figure of Korba the Qizara surged through the doorway backlighted by the brilliant illumination in the hallways. He entered as though hurled by an unseen force and came to an almost immediate halt when he encountered the salon's gloom. His hands appeared to be full of shigawire reels. They glittered in the light from the hall, strange little round jewels that were extinguished as a guardsman's hand came into view, closed the door.

"Is that you, m'Lord?" Korba asked, peering into the shadows.

"What is it?" Stilgar asked.

"Stilgar?"

"We're both here. What is it?"

"I'm disturbed by this reception for the Guildsman."

"Disturbed?" Paul asked.

"The people say, m'Lord, that you honor our enemies."

"Is that all?" Paul said. "Are those the reels I asked you

to bring earlier?" He indicated the shigawire orbs in Korba's hands.

"Reels...oh! Yes, m'Lord. These are the histories. Will you view them here?"

"I've viewed them. I want them for Stilgar here."

"For me?" Stilgar asked. He felt resentment grow at what he interpreted as caprice on Paul's part. Histories! Stilgar had sought out Paul earlier to discuss the logistics computations for the Zabulon conquest. The Guild Ambassador's presence had intervened. And now— Korba with histories!

"How much history do you know?" Paul mused aloud, studying the shadowy figure beside him.

"M'Lord, I can name every world our people touched in their migrations. I know the reaches of Imperial..."

"The Golden Age of Earth, have you ever studied that?"

"Earth? Golden Age?" Stilgar was irritated and puzzled. Why would Paul wish to discuss myths from the dawn of time? Stilgar's mind still felt crammed with Zabulon data—computations from the staff mentats: two hundred and five attack frigates with thirty legions, support battalions, pacification cadres, Qizarate missionaries...the food requirements (he had the figures right here in his mind) and melange...weaponry, uniforms, medals...urns for the ashes of the dead...the number of specialists—men to produce raw materials of propaganda, clerks, accountants...spies...and spies upon the spies...

"I brought the pulse-synchronizer attachment, also, m'Lord," Korba ventured. He obviously sensed the tensions building between Paul and Stilgar and was disturbed by them.

Stilgar shook his head from side to side. *Pulse-synchronizer?* Why would Paul wish him to use a mnemonic flutter-system on a shigawire projector? Why scan for specific data in histories? This was mentat work! As usual, Stilgar found he couldn't escape a deep suspicion at the thought of using a projector and attachments. The thing always immersed him in disturbing sensations, an overwhelming shower of data which his mind sorted out later, surprising him with information he had not known he possessed.

"Sire, I came with the Zabulon computations," Stilgar said.

"Dehydrate the Zabulon computations!" Paul snapped, using the obscene Fremen term which meant that here was moisture no man could demean himself by touching.

"M'Lord!"

"Stilgar," Paul said, "you urgently need a sense of balance which can come only from an understanding of long-term effects. What little information we have about the old times, the pittance of data which the Butlerians left us, Korba has brought it for you. Start with the Genghis Khan."

"Ghengis...Khan? Was he of the Sardaukar, m'-Lord?"

"Oh, long before that. He killed...perhaps four million."

"He must've had formidable weaponry to kill that many, Sire. Lasbeams, perhaps, or..."

"He didn't kill them himself, Stil. He killed the way I kill, by sending out his legions. There's another emperor I want you to note in passing—a Hitler. He killed more than six million. Pretty good for those days."

"Killed...by his legions?" Stilgar asked.

"Yes."

"Not very impressive statistics, m'Lord."

"Very good, Stil." Paul glanced at the reels in Korba's hands. Korba stood with them as though he wished he could drop them and flee. "Statistics: at a conservative estimate, I've killed sixty-one billion, sterilized ninety planets, completely demoralized five hundred others. I've wiped out the followers of forty religions which had existed since—"

"Unbelievers!" Korba protested. "Unbelievers all!"

"No," Paul said. "Believers."

"My Liege makes a joke," Korba said, voice trembling. "The Jihad has brought ten thousand worlds into the shining light of—"

"Into the darkness," Paul said. "We'll be a hundred generations recovering from Muad'dib's Jihad. I find it hard to imagine that anyone will ever surpass this." A barking laugh erupted from his throat.

"What amuses Muad'dib?" Stilgar asked.

"I am not amused. I merely had a sudden vision of the Emperor Hitler asying something similar. No doubt he did."

"No other ruler ever had your powers," Korba argued. "Who would dare challenge you? Your legions control the known universe and all the—"

"The legions control," Paul said. "I wonder if they know this?"

"You control your legions, Sire," Stilgar interrupted, and it was obvious from the tone of his voice that he suddenly felt his own position in that chain of command, his own hand guiding all that power.

Having set Stilgar's thoughts in motion along the track he wanted, Paul turned his full attention to Korba, said: "Put the reels here on the divan." As Korba obeyed, Paul said: "How goes the reception, Korba? Does my sister have everything well in hand?"

"Yes, m'Lord." Korba's tone was wary. "And Chani watches from the spy hole. She suspects there may be Sardaukar in the Guild entourage."

"No doubt she's correct," Paul said. "The jackals gather."

"Bannerjee," Stilgar said, naming the chief of Paul's Security detail, "was worried earlier that some of them might try to penetrate the private areas of the Keep."

"Have they?"

"Not yet."

"But there was some confusion in the formal gardens," Korba said.

"What sort of confusion?" Stilgar demanded.

Paul nodded.

"Strangers coming and going," Korba said, "trampling the plants, whispered conversations—I heard reports of some disturbing remarks."

"Such as?" Paul asked.

"Is this the way our taxes are spent? I'm told the Ambassador himself asked that question."

"I don't find that surprising," Paul said. "Were there many strangers in the gardens?"

"Dozens, m'Lord."

"Bannerjee stationed picked troopers at the vulnerable doors, m'Lord," Stilgar said. He turned as he spoke, allowing the salon's single remaining light to illuminate half his face. The peculiar lighting, the face, all touched a node of memory in Paul's mind—something from the desert. Paul didn't bother bringing it to full recall, his attention being focused on how Stilgar had pulled back mentally. The Fremen had a tight-skinned forehead which mirrored almost every thought flickering across his mind. He was suspicious now, profoundly suspicious of his Emperor's odd behavior.

"I don't like the intrusion into the gardens," Paul said. "Courtesy to guests is one thing, and the formal necessities of greeting an envoy, but this..."

"I'll see to removing them," Korba said. "Immediately."

"Wait!" Paul ordered as Korba started to turn.

In the abrupt stillness of the moment, Stilgar edged himself into a position where he could study Paul's face. It was deftly done. Paul admired the way of it, an achievement devoid of any forwardness. It was a Fremen thing: slyness touched by respect for another's privacy, a movement of necessity.

"What time is it?" Paul asked.

"Almost midnight, Sire," Korba said.

"Korba, I think you may be my finest creation," Paul said.

"Sire!" There was injury in Korba's voice.

"Do you feel awe of me?" Paul asked.

"You are Paul-Muad'dib who was Usul in our sietch," Korba said. "You know my devotion to—"

"Have you ever felt like an apostle?" Paul asked.

Korba obviously misunderstood the words, but correctly interpreted the tone. "My Emperor knows I have a clean conscience!"

"Shai-hulud save us," Paul murmured.

The questioning silence of the moment was broken by the sound of someone whistling as he walked down the outer hall. The whistling was stilled by a guardsman's barked command as it came opposite the door.

"Korba, I think you may survive all this," Paul said. And he read the growing light of understanding on Stilgar's face.

"The strangers in the gardens, Sire?" Stilgar asked.

"Ahh, yes," Paul said. "Have Bannerjee put them out, Stil. Korba will assist."

"Me, Sire?" Korba betrayed deep disquiet.

"Some of my friends have forgotten they once were Fremen," Paul said, speaking to Korba, but designing his words for Stilgar. "You will mark down the ones Chani identifies as Sardaukar and you will have them killed. Do it yourself. I want it done quietly and without undue disturbance. We must keep in mind that there's more to religion and government than approving treaties and sermons."

"I obey the orders of Muad'dib," Korba whispered.

"The Zabulon computations?" Stilgar asked.

"Tomorrow," Paul said. "And when the strangers are removed from the gardens, announce that the reception is ended. The party's over, Stil."

"I understand, m'Lord."

"I'm sure you do," Paul said.

Here lies a toppled god—
His fall was not a small one.
We did but build his pedestal,
A narrow and a tall one.

—Tleilaxu Epigram

Alia crouched, resting elbows on knees, chin on fists, stared at the body on the dune—a few bones and some tattered flesh that once had been a young woman. The hands, the head, most of the upper torso were gone—eaten by the coriolis wind. The sand all around bore the tracks of her brother's medics and questors. They were gone now, all excepting the mortuary attendants who stood to one side with Hayt, the ghola, waiting for her to finish her mysterious perusal of what had been written here.

A wheat-colored sky enfolded the scene in the glaucous light common to midafternoon for these latitudes.

The body had been discovered several hours earlier by a low-flying courier whose instruments had detected a faint water trace where none should be. His call had brought the experts. And they had learned—what? That this had been a woman of about twenty years, Fremen, addicted to semuta...and she had died here in the crucible of the desert from the effects of a subtle poison of Tleilaxu origin.

To die in the desert was a common enough occurrence. But a Fremen addicted to semuta, this was such a rarity that Paul had sent her to examine the scene in the ways their mother had taught them.

Alia felt that she had accomplished nothing here except to cast her own aura of mystery about a scene that was already mysterious enough. She heard the ghola's feet stir the sand, looked at him. His attention rested momentarily upon the escort 'thopters circling overhead like a flock of ravens.

Beware of the Guild bearing gifts, Alia thought.

The mortuary 'thopter and her own craft stood on the sand near a rock outcropping behind the ghola. Focusing on the grounded 'thopters filled Alia with a craving to be airborne and away from here.

But Paul had thought she might see something here which others would miss. She squirmed in her stillsuit. It felt raspingly unfamiliar after all the suitless months of city life. She studied the ghola, wondering if he might know something important about this peculiar death. A lock of his black-goat hair, she saw, had escaped his stillsuit hood. She sensed her hand longing to tuck that hair back into place.

As though lured by this thought, his gleaming gray metal eyes turned toward her. The eyes set her trembling and she tore her gaze away from him.

A Fremen woman had died here from a poison called "the throat of hell."

A Fremen addicted to semuta.

She shared Paul's disquiet at this conjunction.

The mortuary attendants waited patiently. This corpse contained not enough water for them to salvage. They felt no need to hurry. And they'd believe that Alia, through some glyptic art, was reading a strange truth in these remains.

No strange truth came to her.

There was only a distant feeling of anger deep within her at the obvious thoughts in the attendants' minds. It was a product of the damned religious mystery. She and her brother could not be *people*. They had to be something more. The Bene Gesserit had seen to that by manipulating Atreides ancestry. Their mother had contributed to it by thrusting them onto the path of witchery.

And Paul perpetuated the difference.

The Reverend Mothers encapsulated in Alia's memories stirred restlessly, provoking adab flashes of thought: *"Peace, Little One! You are what you are. There are compensations."*

Compensations!

She summoned the ghola with a gesture.

He stopped beside her, attentive, patient.

"What do you see in this?" she asked.

"We may never learn who it was died here," he said. "The head, the teeth are gone. The hands... Unlikely such a one had a genetic record somewhere to which her cells could be matched."

"Tleilaxu poison," she said. "What do you make of that?"

"Many people buy such poisons."

"True enough. And this flesh is too far gone to be regrown as was done with your body."

"Even if you could trust the Tleilaxu to do it," he said.

She nodded, stood. "You will fly me back to the city now."

When they were airborne and pointed north, she said:

"You fly exactly as Duncan Idaho did."

He cast a speculative glance at her. "Others have told me this."

"What are you thinking now?" she asked.

"Many things."

"Stop dodging my question, damn you!"

"Which question?"

She glared at him.

He saw the glare, shrugged.

How like Duncan Idaho, that gesture, she thought. Accusingly, her voice thick and with a catch in it, she said: "I merely wanted your reactions voiced to play my own thoughts against them. That young woman's death bothers me."

"I was not thinking about that."

"What were you thinking about?"

"About the strange emotions I feel when people speak of the one I may have been."

"May have been?"

"The Tleilaxu are very clever."

"Not that clever. You were Duncan Idaho."

"Very likely. It's the prime computation."

"So you get emotional?"

"To a degree. I feel eagerness. I'm uneasy. There's a tendency to tremble and I must devote effort to controlling it. I get . . . flashes of imagery."

"What imagery?"

"It's too rapid to recognize. Flashes. Spasms . . . almost memories."

"Aren't you curious about such memories?"

"Of course. Curiosity urges me forward, but I move against a heavy reluctance. I think: 'What if I'm not the one they believe me to be?' I don't like that thought."

"And this is all you were thinking?"

"You know better than that, Alia."

How dare he use my given name? She felt anger rise and go down beneath the memory of the way he'd spoken: softly throbbing undertones, casual male confidence. A muscle twitched along her jaw. She clenched her teeth.

"Isn't that El Kuds down there?" he asked, dipping a wing briefly, causing a sudden flurry in their escort.

She looked down at their shadows rippling across the promontory above Harg Pass, at the cliff and the rock pyramid containing the skull of her father. *El Kuds—the Holy Place.*

"That's the Holy Place," she said.

"I must visit that place one day," he said. "Nearness to your father's remains may bring memories I can capture."

She saw suddenly how strong must be this need to know who he'd been. It was a central compulsion with him. She looked back at the rocks, the cliff with its base sloping into a dry beach and a sea of sand—cinnamon rock lifting from the dunes like a ship breasting waves.

"Circle back," she said.

"The escort..."

"They'll follow. Swing under them."

He obeyed.

"Do you truly serve my brother?" she asked, when he was on the new course, the escort following.

"I serve the Atreides," he said, his tone formal.

And she saw his right hand lift, fall—almost the old salute of Caladan. A pensive look came over his face. She watched him peer down at the rock pyramid.

"What bothers you?" she asked.

His lips moved. A voice emerged, brittle, tight: "He was...he was..." A tear slid down his cheek.

Alia found herself stilled by Fremen awe. He gave water to the dead! Compulsively, she touched a finger to his cheek, felt the tear.

"Duncan," she whispered.

He appeared locked to the 'thopter's controls, gaze fastened to the tomb below.

She raised her voice: "Duncan!"

He swallowed, shook his head, looked at her, the metal eyes glistening. "I...felt...an arm...on my shoulders," he whispered. "I felt it! An arm." His throat worked. "It was...a friend. It was...my friend."

"Who?"

"I don't know. I think it was...I don't know."

The call light began flashing in front of Alia, their escort captain wanting to know why they returned to the desert. She took the microphone, explained that they had paid a brief homage to her father's tomb. The captain reminded her that it was late.

"We will go to Arrakeen now," she said, replacing the microphone.

Hayt took a deep breath, banked their 'thopter around to the north.

"It was my father's arm you felt, wasn't it?" she asked.

"Perhaps."

His voice was that of the mentat computing probabilities, and she saw he had regained his composure.

"Are you aware of how I know my father?" she asked.

"I have some idea."

"Let me make it clear," she said. Briefly, she explained how she had awakened to Reverend Mother awareness before birth, a terrified fetus with the knowledge of countless lives embedded in her nerve cells—and all this after the death of her father.

"I know my father as my mother knew him," she said. "In every last detail of every experience she shared with him. In a way, I am my mother. I have all her memories up to the moment when she drank the Water of Life and entered the trance of transmigration."

"Your brother explained something of this."

"He did? Why?"

"I asked."

"Why?"

"A mentat requires data."

"Oh." She looked down at the flat expanse of the Shield Wall—tortured rock, pits and crevices.

He saw the direction of her gaze, said: "A very exposed place, that down there."

"But an easy place to hide," she said. She looked at him. "It reminds me of a human mind ... with all its concealments."

"Ahhh," he said.

"Ahhh? What does that mean—ahhh?" She was suddenly angry with him and the reason for it escaped her.

"You'd like to know what my mind conceals," he said. It was a statement, not a question.

"How do you know I haven't exposed you for what you are by my powers of prescience?" she demanded.

"Have you?" He seemed genuinely curious.

"No!"

"Sibyls have limits," he said.

He appeared to be amused and this reduced Alia's anger. "Amused? Have you no respect for my powers?" she asked. The question sounded weakly argumentative even to her own ears.

"I respect your omens and portents perhaps more than you think," he said. "I was in the audience for your Morning Ritual."

"And what does that signify?"

"You've great ability with symbols," he said, keeping his attention on the 'thopter's controls. "That's a Bene Gesserit thing, I'd say. But, as with many witches, you've become careless of your powers."

She felt a spasm of fear, blared: "How dare you?"

"I dare much more than my makers anticipated," he said. "Because of that rare fact, I remain with your brother."

Alia studied the steel balls which were his eyes: no human expression there. The stillsuit hood concealed the line of his jaw. His mouth remained firm, though. Great strength in it ... and determination. His words had carried a reassuring intensity. "... dare much more ..." That was a thing Duncan Idaho might have said. Had the Tleilaxu fashioned their ghola better than they knew—or was this mere sham, part of his conditioning?

"Explain yourself, ghola," she commanded.

"Know thyself, is that thy commandment?" he asked.

Again, she felt that he was amused. "Don't bandy words with me, you...you *thing!*" she said. She put a hand to the crysknife in its throat sheath. "Why were you given to my brother?"

"Your brother tells me that you watched the presentation," he said. "You've heard me answer that question for him."

"Answer it again...for me!"

"I am intended to destroy him."

"Is that the mentat speaking?"

"You know the answer to that without asking," he chided. "And you know, as well, that such a gift wasn't necessary. Your brother already was destroying himself quite adequately."

She weighed these words, her hand remaining on the haft of her knife. A tricky answer, but there was sincerity in the voice.

"Then why such a gift?" she probed.

"It may have amused the Tleilaxu. And, it is true, that the Guild asked for me as a gift."

"Why?"

"Same answer."

"How am I careless of my powers?"

"How are you employing them?" he countered.

His question slashed through to her own misgivings. She took her hand away from the knife, asked: "Why do you say my brother was destroying himself?"

"Oh, come now, child! Where are these vaunted powers? Have you no ability to reason?"

Controlling anger, she said: "Reason *for* me, mentat."

"Very well." He glanced around at their escort, returned his attention to their course. The plain of Arrakeen was beginning to show beyond the northern rim of the Shield Wall. The pattern of the pan and graben villages remained indistinct beneath a dust pall, but the distant gleam of Arrakeen could be discerned.

"Symptoms," he said. "Your brother keeps an official Panegyrist who—"

"Who was a gift of the Fremen Naibs!"

"An odd gift from friends," he said. "Why would they surround him with flattery and servility? Have you really listened to this Panegyrist? *'The people are illuminated by Muad'dib. The Umma Regent, our Emperor, came out of darkness to shine resplendently upon all men. He is our Sire. He is precious water from an endless fountain. He spills joy for all the universe to drink,'* Pah!"

Speaking softly, Alia said: "If I but repeated your words for our Fremen escort, they'd hack you into bird feed."

"Then tell them."

"My brother rules by the natural law of heaven!"

"You don't believe that, so why say it?"

"How do you know what I believe?" She experienced trembling that no Bene Gesserit powers could control. This ghola was having an effect she hadn't anticipated.

"You commanded me to reason as a mentat," he reminded her.

"No mentat knows what I believe!" She took two deep, shuddering breaths. "How dare you judge us?"

"Judge you? I don't judge."

"You've no idea how we were taught!"

"Both of you were taught to govern," he said. "You were conditioned to an overweening thirst for power. You were imbued with a shrewd grasp of politics and a deep understanding for the uses of war and ritual. Natural law? What natural law? That myth haunts human history. Haunts! It's a ghost. It's insubstantial, unreal. Is your Jihad a natural law?"

"Mentat jabber," she sneered.

"I'm a servant of the Atreides and I speak with candor," he said.

"Servant? We've no servants; only disciples."

"And I am a disciple of awareness," he said. "Understand that, child, and you—"

"Don't call me child!" she snapped. She slipped her crysknife half out of its sheath.

"I stand corrected." He glanced at her, smiled, returned

his attention to piloting the 'thopter. The cliffsided structure of the Atreides Keep could be made out now, dominating the northern suburbs of Arrakeen. "You are something ancient in flesh that is little more than a child," he said. "And the flesh is disturbed by its new womanhood."

"I don't know why I listen to you," she growled, but she let the crysknife fall back into its sheath, wiped her palm on her robe. The palm, wet with perspiration, disturbed her sense of Fremen frugality. Such a waste of the body's moisture!

"You listen because you know I'm devoted to your brother," he said. "My actions are clear and easily understood."

"Nothing about you is clear and easily understood. You're the most complex creature I've ever seen. How do I know what the Tleilaxu built into you?"

"By mistake or intent," he said, "they gave me freedom to mold myself."

"You retreat into Zensunni parables," she accused. "The wise man molds himself—the fool lives only to die." Her voice was heavy with mimicry. "Disciple of awareness!"

"Men cannot separate means and enlightenment," he said.

"You speak riddles!"

"I speak to the opening mind."

"I'm going to repeat all this to Paul."

"He's heard most of it already."

She found herself overwhelmed by curiosity. "How is it you're still alive . . . and free? What did he say?"

"He laughed. And he said, 'People don't want a bookkeeper for an Emperor; they want a master, someone who'll protect them from change.' But he agreed that destruction of his Empire arises from himself."

"Why would he say such things?"

"Because I convinced him I understand his problem and will help him."

"What could you possibly have said to do that?"

He remained silent, banking the 'thopter into the downwind leg for a landing at the guard complex on the roof of the Keep.

"I demand you tell me what you said!"

"I'm not sure you could take it."

"I'll be the judge of that! I command you to speak at once!"

"Permit me to land us first," he said. And not waiting for her permission, he turned onto the base leg, brought the wings into optimum lift, settled gently onto the bright orange pad atop the roof.

"Now," Alia said. "Speak."

"I told him that to endure oneself may be the hardest task in the universe."

She shook her head. "That's . . . that's . . ."

"A bitter pill," he said, watching the guards run toward them across the roof, taking up their escort positions.

"Bitter nonsense!"

"The greatest palatinate earl and the lowliest stipendiary serf share the same problem. You cannot hire a mentat or any other intellect to solve it for you. There's no writ of inquest or calling of witnesses to provide answers. No servant—or disciple—can dress the wound. You dress it yourself or continue bleeding for all to see."

She whirled away from him, realizing in the instant of action what this betrayed about her own feelings. Without wile of voice or witch-wrought trickery, he had reached into her psyche once more. How did he do this?

"What have you told him to do?" she whispered.

"I told him to judge, to impose order."

Alia stared out at the guard, marking how patiently they waited—how orderly. "To dispense justice," she murmured.

"Not that!" he snapped. "I suggested that he judge, no more, guided by one principle, perhaps . . ."

"And that?"

"To keep his friends and destroy his enemies."

"To judge unjustly, then."

"What is justice? Two forces collide. Each may have the right in his own sphere. And here's where an Emperor commands orderly solutions. Those collisions he cannot prevent—he solves."

"How?"

"In the simplest way: he decides."

"Keeping his friends and destroying his enemies."

"Isn't that stability? People want order, this kind or some other. They sit in the prison of their hungers and see that war has become the sport of the rich. That's a dangerous form of sophistication. It's disorderly."

"I will suggest to my brother that you are much too dangerous and must be destroyed," she said, turning to face him.

"A solution I've already suggested," he said.

"And that's why you are dangerous," she said, measuring out her words. "You've mastered your passions."

"That is *not* why I'm dangerous." Before she could move, he leaned across, gripped her chin in one hand, planted his lips on hers.

It was a gentle kiss, brief. He pulled away and she stared at him with a shock leavened by glimpses of spasmodic grins on the faces of her guardsmen still standing at orderly attention outside.

Alia put a finger to her lips. There'd been such a sense of familiarity about that kiss. His lips had been flesh of a future she'd seen in some prescient byway. Breast heaving, she said: "I should have you flayed."

"Because I'm dangerous?"

"Because you presume too much!"

"I presume nothing. I take nothing which is not first offered to me. Be glad I did not take all that was offered." He opened his door, slid out. "Come along. We've dallied too long on a fool's errand." He strode toward the entrance dome beyond the pad.

Alia leaped out, ran to match his stride. "I'll tell him

everything you've said and everything you did," she said.

"Good." He held the door for her.

"He will order you executed," she said, slipping into the dome.

"Why? Because I took the kiss I wanted?" He followed her, his movement forcing her back. The door slid closed behind him.

"The kiss *you* wanted!" Outrage filled her.

"All right, Alia. The kiss you wanted, then." He started to move around her toward the drop field.

As though his movement had propelled her into heightened awareness, she realized his candor—the utter truthfulness of him. *The kiss I wanted,* she told herself. *True.*

"Your truthfulness, that's what's dangerous," she said, following him.

"You return to the ways of wisdom," he said, not breaking his stride. "A mentat could not've stated the matter more directly. Now: what is it you saw in the desert?"

She grabbed his arm, forcing him to a halt. He'd done it again: shocked her mind into sharpened awareness.

"I can't explain it," she said, "but I keep thinking of the Face Dancers. Why is that?"

"That is why your brother sent you to the desert," he said, nodding. "Tell him of this persistent thought."

"But why?" She shook her head. "Why Face Dancers?"

"There's a young woman dead out there," he said. "Perhaps no young woman is reported missing among the Fremen."

I think what a joy it is to be alive, and I wonder if I'll ever leap inward to the root of this flesh and know myself as once I was. The root is there. Whether any act of mine can find it, that remains tangled in the future. But all things a man can do are mine. Any act of mine may do it.

—The Ghola Speaks
Alia's Commentary

As he lay immersed in the screaming odor of the spice, staring inward through the oracular trance, Paul saw the moon become an elongated sphere. It rolled and twisted, hissing—the terrible hissing of a star being quenched in an infinite sea—down...down...down...like a ball thrown by a child.

It was gone.

This moon had not set. Realization engulfed him. It was gone: no moon. The earth quaked like an animal

131

shaking its skin. Terror swept over him.

Paul jerked upright on his pallet, eyes wide open, staring. Part of him looked outward, part inward. Outwardly, he saw the plasmeld grillwork which vented his private room, and he knew he lay beside a stonelike abyss of his Keep. Inwardly, he continued to see the moon fall.

Out! Out!

His grillwork of plasmeld looked onto the blazing light of noon across Arrakeen. Inward—there lay blackest night. A shower of sweet odors from a garden roof nibbled at his senses, but no floral perfume could roll back that fallen moon.

Paul swung his feet to the cold surface of the floor, peered through the grillwork. He could see directly across to the gentle arc of a footbridge constructed of crystal-stabilized gold and platinum. Fire jewels from far Cedon decorated the bridge. It led to the galleries of the inner city across a pool and fountain filled with waterflowers. If he stood, Paul knew, he could look down into petals as clean and red as fresh blood whirling, turning there—disks of ambient color tossed on an emerald freshet.

His eyes absorbed the scene without pulling him from spice thralldom.

That terrible vision of a lost moon.

The vision suggested a monstrous loss of individual security. Perhaps he'd seen his civilization fall, toppled by its own pretensions.

A moon...a moon...a falling moon.

It had taken a massive dose of the spice essence to penetrate the mud thrown up by the tarot. All it had shown him was a falling moon and the hateful way he'd known from the beginning. To buy an end for the Jihad, to silence the volcano of butchery, he must discredit himself.

Disengage...disengage...disengage...

Floral perfume from the garden roof reminded him of

Chani. He longed for her arms now, for the clinging arms of love and forgetfulness. But even Chani could not exorcise this vision. What would Chani say if he went to her with the statement that he had a particular death in mind? Knowing it to be inevitable, why not choose an aristocrat's death, ending life on a secret flourish, squandering any years that might have been? To die before coming to the end of willpower, was that not an aristocrat's choice?

He stood, crossed to the lapped opening in the grillwork, went out onto a balcony which looked upward to flowers and vines trailing from the garden. His mouth held the dryness of a desert march.

Moon . . . moon—where is that moon?

He thought of Alia's description, the young woman's body found in the dunes. A Fremen addicted to semuta! Everything fitted the hateful pattern.

You do not take from this universe, he thought. *It grants what it will.*

The remains of a conch shell from the seas of Mother Earth lay on a low table beside the balcony rail. He took its lustrous smoothness into his hands, tried to feel backward in Time. The pearl surface reflected glittering moons of light. He tore his gaze from it, peered upward past the garden to a sky become a conflagration—trails of rainbow dust shining in the silver sun.

My Fremen call themselves "Children of the Moon," he thought.

He put down the conch, strode along the balcony. Did that terrifying moon hold out hope of escape? He probed for meaning in the region of mystic communion. He felt weak, shaken, still gripped by the spice.

At the north end of his plasmeld chasm, he came in sight of the lower buildings of the government warren. Foot traffic thronged the roof walks. He felt that the people moved there like a frieze against a background of doors, walls, tile designs. The people were tiles! When he blinked, he could hold them frozen in his mind. A frieze.

A moon falls and is gone.

A feeling came over him that the city out there had been translated into an odd symbol for his universe. The buildings he could see had been erected on the plain where his Fremen had obliterated the Sardaukar legions. Ground once trampled by battles rang now to the rushing clamor of business.

Keeping to the balcony's outer edge, Paul strode around the corner. Now, his vista was a suburb where city structures lost themselves in rocks and the blowing sand of the desert. Alia's temple dominated the foreground; green and black hangings along its two-thousand-meter sides displayed the moon symbol of Muad'dib.

A falling moon.

Paul passed a hand across his forehead and eyes. The symbol-metropolis oppressed him. He despised his own thoughts. Such vacillation in another would have aroused his anger.

He loathed his city!

Rage rooted in boredom flickered and simmered deep within him, nurtured by decisions that couldn't be avoided. He knew which path his feet must follow. He'd seen it enough times, hadn't he? *Seen* it! Once . . . long ago, he'd thought of himself as an inventor of government. But the invention had fallen into old patterns. It was like some hideous contrivance with plastic memory. Shape it any way you wanted, but relax for a moment, and it snapped into the ancient forms. Forces at work beyond his reach in human breasts eluded and defied him.

Paul stared out across the rooftops. What treasures of untrammeled life lay beneath those roofs? He glimpsed leaf-green places, open plantings amidst the chalk-red and gold of the roofs. Green, the gift of Muad'dib and his water. Orchards and groves lay within his view—open plantings to rival those of fabled Lebanon.

"Muad'dib spends water like a madman," Fremen said.

Paul put his hands over his eyes.

The moon fell.

He dropped his hands, stared at his metropolis with clarified vision. Buildings took on an aura of monstrous imperial barbarity. They stood enormous and bright beneath the northern sun. Colossi! Every extravagance of architecture a demented history could produce lay within his view: terraces of mesa proportion, squares as large as some cities, parks, premises, bits of cultured wilderness.

Superb artistry abutted inexplicable prodigies of dismal tastlessness. Details impressed themselves upon him: a postern out of most ancient Baghdad...a dome dreamed in mythical Damascus...an arch from the low gravity of Atar...harmonious elevations and queer depths. All created an effect of unrivaled magnificence.

A moon! A moon! A moon!

Frustration tangled him. He felt the pressure of mass-unconscious, that burgeoning sweep of humankind across his universe. They rushed upon him with a force like a gigantic tidal bore. He sensed the vast migrations at work in human affairs: eddies, currents, gene flows. No dams of abstinence, no seizures of impotence nor maledictions could stop it.

Muad'dib's Jihad was less than an eye-blink in this larger movement. The Bene Gesserit swimming in this tide, that corporate entity trading in genes, was trapped in the torrent as he was. Visions of a falling moon must be measured against other legends, other visions in a universe where even the seemingly eternal stars waned, flickered, died...

What mattered a single moon in such a universe?

Far within his fortress citadel, so deep within that the sound sometimes lost itself in the flow of city noises, a ten-string rebaba tinkled with a song of the Jihad, a lament for a woman left behind on Arrakis:

> *Her hips are dunes curved by the wind,*
> *Her eyes shine like summer heat.*
> *Two braids of hair hang down her back—*
> *Rich with water rings, her hair!*

My hands remember her skin,
Fragrant as amber, flower-scented.
Eyelids tremble with memories...
I am stricken by love's white flame!

The song sickened him. A tune for stupid creatures lost in sentimentality! As well sing to the dune-impregnated corpse Alia had seen.

A figure moved in shadows of the balcony's grillwork. Paul whirled.

The ghola emerged into the sun's full glare. His metal eyes glittered.

"Is it Duncan Idaho or the man called Hayt?" Paul asked.

The ghola came to a stop two paces from him. "Which would my Lord prefer?"

The voice carried a soft ring of caution.

"Play the Zensunni," Paul said bitterly. *Meanings within meanings!* What could a Zensunni philosopher say or do to change one jot of the reality unrolling before them at this instant?

"My Lord is troubled."

Paul turned away, stared at the Shield Wall's distant scarp, saw wind-carved arches and buttresses, terrible mimicry of his city. Nature playing a joke on him! *See what I can build!* He recognized a slash in the distant massif, a place where sand spilled from a crevasse, and thought: *There! Right there, we fought Sardaukar!*

"What troubles my lord?" the ghola asked.

"A vision," Paul whispered.

"Ahhhhh, when the Tleilaxu first awakened me, I had visions. I was restless, lonely... not really knowing I was lonely. Not then. My visions revealed nothing! The Tleilaxu told me it was an intrusion of the flesh which men and gholas all suffer, a sickness, no more."

Paul turned, studied the ghola's eyes, those pitted, steely balls without expression. What visions did those eyes see?

"Duncan... Duncan..." Paul whispered.

"I am called Hayt."

"I saw a moon fall," Paul said. "It was gone, destroyed. I heard a great hissing. The earth shook."

"You are drunk on too much time," the ghola said.

"I ask for the Zensunni and get the mentat!" Paul said. "Very well! Play my vision through your logic, mentat. Analyze it and reduce it to mere words laid out for burial."

"Burial, indeed," the ghola said. "You run from death. You strain at the next instant, refuse to live here and now. Augury! What a crutch for an Emperor!"

Paul found himself fascinated by a well-remembered mole on the ghola's chin.

"Trying to live in this future," the ghola said, "do you give substance to such a future? Do you make it real?"

"If I go the way of my vision-future, I'll be alive *then*," Paul muttered. "What makes you think I want to live there?"

The ghola shrugged. "You asked me for a substantial answer."

"Where is there substance in a universe composed of events?" Paul asked. "Is there a final answer? Doesn't each solution produce new questions?"

"You've digested so much time you have delusions of immortality," the ghola said. "Even *your* Empire, my lord, must live its time and die."

"Don't parade smoke-blackened altars before me," Paul growled. "I've heard enough sad histories of gods and messiahs. Why should I need special powers to forecast ruins of my own like all those others? The lowliest servant of my kitchens could do this." He shook his head. "The moon fell!"

"You've not brought your mind to rest at its beginning," the ghola said.

"Is that how you destroy me?" Paul demanded. "Prevent me from collecting my thoughts?"

"Can you collect chaos?" the ghola asked. "We

Zensunni say: 'Not collecting, that is the ultimate gathering.' What can you gather without gathering yourself?"

"I'm deviled by a vision and you spew nonsense!" Paul raged. "What do you know of prescience?"

"I've seen the oracle at work," the ghola said. "I've seen those who seek signs and omens for their individual destiny. They fear what they seek."

"My falling moon is real," Paul whispered. He took a trembling breath. "It moves. It moves."

"Men always fear things which move by themselves," the ghola said. "You fear your own powers. Things fall into your head from nowhere. When they fall out, where do they go?"

"You comfort me with thorns," Paul growled.

An inner illumination came over the ghola's face. For a moment, he became pure Duncan Idaho. "I give you what comfort I can," he said.

Paul wondered at that momentary spasm. Had the ghola felt grief which his mind rejected? Had Hayt put down a vision of his own?

"My moon has a name," Paul whispered.

He let the vision flow over him then. Though his whole being shrieked, no sound escaped him. He was afraid to speak, fearful that his voice might betray him. The air of this terrifying future was thick with Chani's absence. Flesh that had cried in ecstasy, eyes that had burned him with their desire, the voice that had charmed him because it played no tricks of subtle control—all gone, back into the water and the sand.

Slowly, Paul turned away, looked out at the present and the plaza before Alia's temple. Three shaven-headed pilgrims entered from the processional avenue. They wore grimy yellow robes and hurried with their heads bent against the afternoon's wind. One walked with a limp, dragging his left foot. They beat their way against the wind, rounded a corner and were gone from his sight.

Just as his moon would go, they were gone. Still, his

vision lay before him. Its terrible purpose gave him no choice.

The flesh surrenders itself, he thought. *Eternity takes back its own. Our bodies stirred these waters briefly, danced with a certain intoxication before the love of life and self, dealt with a few strange ideas, then submitted to the instruments of Time. What can we say of this? I occurred. I am not ... yet, I occurred.*

> *"You do not beg the sun for mercy."*
> —Maud'dib's Travail
>   from The Stilgar Commentary

One moment of incompetence can be fatal, the Reverend Mother Gaius Helen Mohiam reminded herself.

She hobbled along, apparently unconcerned, within a ring of Fremen guards. One of those behind her, she knew, was a deaf-mute immune to any wiles of Voice. No doubt he'd been charged to kill her at the slightest provocation.

Why had Paul summoned her? she wondered. Was he about to pass sentence? She remembered the day long ago when she'd tested him . . . the child kwisatz haderach. He was a deep one.

Damn his mother for all eternity! It was her fault the

Bene Gesserit had lost their hold on this gene line.

Silence surged along the vaulted passages ahead of her entourage. She sensed the word being passed. Paul would hear the silence. He'd know of her coming before it was announced. She didn't delude herself with ideas that her powers exceeded his.

Damn him!

She begrudged the burdens age had imposed on her: the aching joints, responses not as quick as once they'd been, muscles not as elastic as the whipcords of her youth. A long day lay behind her and a long life. She'd spent this day with the Dune Tarot in a fruitless search for some clue to her own fate. But the cards were sluggish.

The guards herded her around a corner into another of the seemingly endless vaulted passages. Triangular meta-glass windows on her left gave a view upward to trellised vines and indigo flowers in deep shadows cast by the afternoon sun. Tiles lay underfoot—figures of water creatures from exotic planets. Water reminders everywhere. Wealth . . . riches.

Robed figures passed across another hall in front of her, cast covert glances at the Reverend Mother. Recognition was obvious in their manner—and tension.

She kept her attention on the sharp hairline of the guard immediately in front: young flesh, pink creases at the uniform collar.

The immensity of this ighir citadel began to impress her. Passages . . . passages . . . They passed an open doorway from which emerged the sound of timbur and flute playing soft, elder music. A glance showed her blue-in-blue Fremen eyes staring from the room. She sensed in them the ferment of legendary revolts stirring in wild genes.

There lay the measure of her personal burden, she knew. A Bene Gesserit could not escape awareness of the genes and their possibilities. She was touched by a feeling of loss: that stubborn fool of an Atreides! How could he deny the jewels of posterity within his loins? A kwisatz haderach! Born out of this time, true, but real—as real as his abomination of a sister ... and there lay a dangerous unknown. A wild Reverend Mother spawned without Bene Gesserit inhibitions, holding no loyalty to orderly development of the genes. She shared her brother's powers, no doubt—and more.

The size of the citadel began to oppress her. Would the passages never end? The place reeked of terrifying physical power. No planet, no civilization in all human history had ever before seen such man-made immensity. A dozen ancient cities could be hidden in its walls!

They passed oval doors with winking lights. She recognized them for Ixian handiwork: pneumatic transport orifices. Why was she being marched all this distance, then? The answer began to shape itself in her mind: to oppress her in preparation for this audience with the Emperor.

A small clue, but it joined other subtle indications—the relative suppression and selection of words by her escort, the traces of primitive shyness in their eyes when they called her *Reverend Mother*, the cold and bland, essentially odorless nature of these halls—all combined to reveal much that a Bene Gesserit could interpret.

Paul wanted something from her!

She concealed a feeling of elation. A bargaining lever existed. It remained only to find the nature of that lever and test its strength. Some levers had moved things greater than this citadel. A finger's touch had been known to topple civilizations.

The Reverend Mother reminded herself then of Scytale's assessment: *When a creature has developed into one thing, he will choose death rather than change into his opposite.*

The passages through which she was being escorted grew larger by subtle stages—tricks of arching, graduated amplification of pillared supports, displacement of the triangular windows by larger, oblong shapes. Ahead of her, finally, loomed double doors centered in the far wall of a tall antechamber. She sensed that the doors were *very* large, and was forced to suppress a gasp as her trained awareness measured out the true proportions. The doorway stood at least eighty meters high, half that in width.

As she approached with her escort, the doors swung inward—an immense and silent movement of hidden machinery. She recognized more Ixian handiwork. Through that towering doorway she marched with her guards into the Grand Reception Hall of the Emperor Paul Atreides—"Muad'dib, before whom all people are dwarfed." Now, she saw the effect of that popular saying at work.

As she advanced toward Paul on the distant throne, the Reverend Mother found herself more impressed by the architectural subtleties of her surroundings than she was by the immensities. The space was large: it could've housed the entire citadel of any ruler in human history. The open sweep of the room said much about hidden structural forces balanced with nicety. Trusses and supporting beams behind these walls and the faraway domed ceiling must surpass anything ever before attempted. Everything spoke of engineering genius.

Without seeming to do so, the hall grew smaller at its far end, refusing to dwarf Paul on his throne centered on a dais. An untrained awareness, shocked by surrounding proportions, would see him at first as many times larger than his actual size. Colors played upon the unprotected psyche: Paul's green throne had been cut from a single Hagar emerald. It suggested growing things and, out of the Fremen mythos, reflected the mourning color. It whispered that here sat he who could make you mourn—life and death in one symbol, a clever stress of opposites. Behind the throne, draperies cascaded in burnt orange, curried gold of Dune earth, and cinnamon flecks of melange. To a trained eye, the symbolism was obvious, but it contained hammer blows to beat down the uninitiated.

Time played its role here.

The Reverend Mother measured the minutes required to approach the Imperial Presence at her hobbling pace. You had time to be cowed. Any tendency toward resentment would be squeezed out of you by the unbridled power which focused down upon your person. You might start the long march toward that throne as a human of dignity, but you ended the march as a gnat.

Aides and attendants stood around the Emperor in a curiously ordered sequence—attentive household guardsmen along the draped back wall, that abomination, Alia, two steps below Paul and on his left hand; Stilgar, the Imperial lackey, on the step directly below Alia; and on the right, one step up from the floor of the hall, a solitary figure: the fleshly revenant of Duncan Idaho, the ghola. She marked older Fremen among the guardsmen, bearded Naibs with stillsuit scars on their noses, sheathed crysknives at their waists, a few maula pistols, even some lasguns. Those most be trusted men, she thought, to carry lasguns in Paul's presence when he obviously wore a shield generator. She could see the shimmering of its field around him. One burst of a lasgun into that field and the entire citadel would be a hole in the ground.

Her guard stopped ten paces from the foot of the dais, parted to open an unobstructed view of the Emperor. She noted now the absence of Chani and Irulan, wondered at it. He held no important audience without them, so it was said.

Paul nodded to her, silent, measuring.

Immediately, she decided to take the offensive, said: "So, the great Paul Atreides deigns to see the one he banished."

Paul smiled wryly, thinking: *She knows I want something from her.* That knowledge had been inevitable, she being who she was. He recognized her powers. The Bene Gesserit didn't become Reverend Mothers by chance.

"Shall we dispense with fencing?" he asked.

Would it be this easy? she wondered. And she said:
"Name the thing you want."

Stilgar stirred, cast a sharp glance at Paul. The
Imperial lackey didn't like her tone.

"Stilgar wants me to send you away," Paul said.

"Not kill me?" she asked. "I would've expected
something more direct from a Fremen Naib."

Stilgar scowled, said: "Often, I must speak otherwise
than I think. That is called diplomacy."

"Then let us dispense with diplomacy as well," she said.
"Was it necessary to have me walk all that distance. I am
an old woman."

"You had to be shown how callous I can be," Paul said.
"That way, you'll appreciate magnanimity."

"You dare such gaucheries with a Bene Gesserit?" she
asked.

"Gross actions carry their own messages," Paul said.

She hesitated, weighed his words. So—he might yet
dispense with her . . . grossly, obviously, if she . . . if she
what?

"Say what it is you want from me," she muttered.

Alia glanced at her brother, nodded toward the
draperies behind the throne. She knew Paul's reasoning in
this, but disliked it all the same. Call it *wild prophecy*: She
felt pregnant with reluctance to take part in this
bargaining.

"You must be careful how you speak to me, old
woman," Paul said.

He called me old woman when he was a stripling, the
Reverend Mother thought. *Does he remind me now of my
hand in his past? The decision I made then, must I remake
it here?* She felt the weight of decision, a physical thing
that set her knees to trembling. Muscles cried their
fatigue.

"It was a long walk," Paul said, "and I can see that
you're tired. We will retire to my private chamber behind
the throne. You may sit there." He gave a hand-signal to
Stilgar, arose.

Stilgar and the ghola converged on her, helped her up the steps, followed Paul through a passage concealed by the draperies. She realized then why he had greeted her in the hall: a dumb-show for the guards and Naibs. He feared them, then. And now—now, he displayed kindly benevolence, daring such wiles on a Bene Gesserit. Or was it daring? She sensed another presence behind, glanced back to see Alia following. The younger woman's eyes held a brooding, baleful cast. The Reverend Mother shuddered.

The private chamber at the end of the passage was a twenty-meter cube of plasmeld, yellow glowglobes for light, the deep orange hangings of a desert stilltent around the walls. It contained divans, soft cushions, a faint odor of melange, crystal water flagons on a low table. It felt cramped, tiny after the outer hall.

Paul seated her on a divan, stood over her, studying the ancient face—steely teeth, eyes that hid more than they revealed, deeply wrinkled skin. He indicated a water flagon. She shook her head, dislodging a wisp of gray hair.

In a low voice, Paul said: "I wish to bargain with you for the life of my beloved."

Stilgar cleared his throat.

Alia fingered the handle of the crysknife sheathed at her neck.

The ghola remained at the door, face impassive, metal eyes pointed at the air above the Reverend Mother's head.

"Have you had a vision of my hand in her death?" the Reverend Mother asked. She kept her attention on the ghola, oddly disturbed by him. Why should she feel threatened by the ghola? He was a tool of the conspiracy.

"I know what it is you want from me," Paul said, avoiding her question.

Then he only suspects, she thought. The Reverend Mother looked down at the tips of her shoes exposed by a fold of her robe. Black...black...shoes and robe showed marks of her confinement: stains, wrinkles. She lifted her chin, met an angry glare in Paul's eyes. Elation surged through her, but she hid the emotion behind pursed lips, slitted eyelids.

"What coin do you offer?" she asked.

"You may have my seed, but not my person," Paul said. "Irulan banished and inseminated by artificial—"

"You dare!" the Reverend Mother flared, stiffening.

Stilgar took a half step forward.

Disconcertingly, the ghola smiled. And now Alia was studying him.

"We'll not discuss the things your Sisterhood forbids," Paul said. "I will listen to no talk of sins, abominations or the beliefs left over from past Jihads. You may have my seed for your plans, but no child of Irulan's will sit on my throne."

"Your throne," she sneered.

"*My* throne."

"Then who will bear the Imperial heir?"

"Chani."

"She is barren."

"She is with child."

An involuntary indrawn breath exposed her shock. "You lie!" she snapped.

Paul held up a restraining hand as Stilgar surged forward.

"We've known for two days that she carries my child."

"But Irulan..."

"By artificial means only. That's my offer."

The Reverend Mother closed her eyes to hide his face. Damnation! To cast the genetic dice in such a way! Loathing boiled in her breast. The teaching of the Bene Gesserit, the lessons of the Butlerian Jihad—all proscribed such an act. One did not demean the highest aspirations of humankind. No machine could function in the way of a human mind. No word or deed could imply that men might be bred on the level of animals.

"Your decision," Paul said.

She shook her head. The genes, the precious Atreides

genes—only these were important. Need went deeper than proscription. For the Sisterhood, mating mingled more than sperm and ovum. One aimed to capture the psyche.

The Reverend Mother understood now the subtle depths of Paul's offer. He would make the Bene Gesserit party to an act which would bring down popular wrath...were it ever discovered. They could not admit such paternity if the Emperor denied it. This coin might save the Atreides genes for the Sisterhood, but it would never buy a throne.

She swept her gaze around the room, studying each face: Stilgar, passive and waiting now; the ghola frozen at some inward place; Alia watching the ghola...and Paul—wrath beneath a shallow veneer.

"This is your only offer?" she asked.

"My only offer."

She glanced at the ghola, caught by a brief movement of muscles across his cheeks. Emotion? "You, ghola," she said. "Should such an offer be made? Having been made, should it be accepted? Function as the mentat for us."

The metallic eyes turned to Paul.

"Answer as you will," Paul said.

The ghola returned his gleaming attention to the Reverend Mother, shocked her once more by smiling. "An offer is only as good as the real thing it buys," he said. "The exchange offered here is life-for-life, a high order of business."

Alia brushed a strand of coppery hair from her forehead, said: "And what else is hidden in this bargain?"

The Reverend Mother refused to look at Alia, but the words burned in her mind. Yes, far deeper implications lay here. The sister was an abomination, true, but there could be no denying her status as a Reverend Mother with all the title implied. Gaius Helen Mohiam felt herself in this instant to be not one single person, but all the others who sat like tiny congeries in her memory. They were alert, every Reverend Mother she had absorbed in becoming a Priestess of the Sisterhood. Alia would be standing in the same situation here.

"What else?" the ghola asked. "One wonders why the witches of the Bene Gesserit have not used Tleilaxu methods."

Gaius Helen Mohiam and all the Reverend Mothers within her shuddered. Yes, the Tleilaxu did loathsome things. If one let down the barriers to artificial insemination, was the next step a Tleilaxu one—controlled mutation?

Paul, observing the play of emotion around him, felt abruptly that he no longer knew these people. He could see only strangers. Even Alia was a stranger.

Alia said: "If we set the Atreides genes adrift in a Bene Gesserit river, who knows what may result?"

Gaius Helen Mohiam's head snapped around, and she met Alia's gaze. For a flashing instant, they were two Reverend Mothers together, communing on a single thought: *What lay behind any Tleilaxu action? The ghola was a Tleilaxu thing. Had he put this plan into Paul's mind? Would Paul attempt to bargain directly with the Bene Tleilax?*

She broke her gaze from Alia's, feeling her own ambivalence and inadequacies. The pitfall of Bene Gesserit training, she reminded herself, lay in the powers granted: such powers predisposed one to vanity and pride. But power deluded those who used it. One tended to believe power could overcome any barrier . . . including one's own ignorance.

Only one thing stood paramount here for the Bene Gesserit, she told herself. That was the pyramid of generations which had reached an apex in Paul Atreides . . . and in his abomination of a sister. A wrong choice here and the pyramid would have to be rebuilt . . . starting generations back in the parallel lines and with breeding specimens lacking the choicest characteristics.

Controlled mutation, she thought. *Did the Tleilaxu*

really practice it? How tempting! She shook her head, the better to rid it of such thoughts.

"You reject my proposal?" Paul asked.

"I'm thinking," she said.

And again, she looked at the sister. The optimum cross for this female Atreides had been lost... killed by Paul. Another possibility remained, however—one which would *cement* the desired characteristic into an offspring. Paul dared offer animal breeding to the Bene Gesserit! How much was he really prepared to pay for his Chani's life? Would he accept a cross with his own sister?

Sparring for time, the Reverend Mother said: "Tell me, oh flawless exemplar of all that's holy, has Irulan anything to say of your proposal?"

"Irulan will do what you tell her to do," Paul growled.

True enough, Mohiam thought. She firmed her jaw, offered a new gambit: "There are two Atreides."

Paul, sensing something of what lay in the old witch's mind, felt blood darken his face. "Careful what you suggest," he said.

"You'd just *use* Irulan to gain your own ends, eh?" she asked.

"Wasn't she trained to be used?" Paul asked.

And we trained her, that's what he's saying, Mohiam thought. *Well... Irulan's a divided coin. Was there another way to spend such a coin?*

"Will you put Chani's child on the throne?" the Reverend Mother asked.

"On *my* throne," Paul said. He glanced at Alia, wondering suddenly if she knew the divergent possibilities in this exchange. Alia stood with eyes closed, an odd stillness-of-person about her. With what inner force did she commune? Seeing his sister thus, Paul felt he'd been cast adrift. Alia stood on a shore that was receding from him.

The Reverend Mother made her decision, said: "This is too much for one person to decide. I must consult with my Council on Wallach. Will you permit a message?"

As though she needed my permission! Paul thought.

He said: "Agreed, then. But don't delay too long. I will not sit idly by while you debate."

"Will you bargain with the Bene Tleilax?" the ghola asked, his voice a sharp intrusion.

Alia's eyes popped open and she stared at the ghola as though she'd been wakened by a dangerous intruder.

"I've made no such decision," Paul said. "What I will do is go into the desert as soon as it can be arranged. Our child will be born in sietch."

"A wise decision," Stilgar intoned.

Alia refused to look at Stilgar. It was a wrong decision. She could feel this in every cell. Paul *must* know it. Why had he fixed himself upon such a path?

"Have the Bene Tleilax offered their services?" Alia asked. She saw Mohiam hanging on the answer.

Paul shook his head. "No." He glanced at Stilgar. "Stil, arrange for the message to be sent to Wallach."

"At once, m'Lord."

Paul turned away, waited while Stilgar summoned guards, left with the old witch. He sensed Alia debating whether to confront him with more questions. She turned, instead, to the ghola.

"Mentat," she said, "will the Tleilaxu bid for favor with my brother?"

The ghola shrugged.

Paul felt his attention wander. *The Tleilaxu? No . . . not in the way Alia meant.* Her question revealed, though, that she had not seen the alternatives here. Well . . . vision varied from sibyl to sibyl. Why not a variance from brother to sister? Wandering . . . wandering . . . He came back from each thought with a start to pick up shards of the nearby conversation.

". . . must know what the Tleilaxu . . ."

". . . the fullness of data is always . . ."

". . . healthy doubts where . . ."

Paul turned, looked at his sister, caught her attention. He knew she would see tears on his face and wonder at them. Let her wonder. Wondering was a kindness now. He glanced at the ghola, seeing only Duncan Idaho despite the metallic eyes. Sorrow and compassion warred in Paul. What might those metal eyes record?

There are many degrees of sight and many degrees of blindness, Paul thought. His mind turned to a paraphrase of the passage from the Orange Catholic Bible: *What senses do we lack that we cannot see another world all around us?*

Were those metal eyes another sense than sight?

Alia crossed to her brother, sensing his utter sadness. She touched a tear on his cheek with a Fremen gesture of awe, said: "We must not grieve for those dear to us before their passing."

"Before their passing," Paul whispered. "Tell me, little sister, what is *before?*"

"I've had a bellyful of the god and priest business! You think I don't see my own mythos? Consult your data once more, Hayt. I've insinuated my rites into the most elementary human acts. The people eat in the name of Muad'dib! They make love in my name, are born in my name—cross the street in my name. A roof beam cannot be raised in the lowliest hovel of far Gangishree without invoking the blessing of Muad'dib!"

—Book of Diatribes
from The Hayt Chronicle

"You risk much leaving your post and coming to me here at this time," Edric said, glaring through the walls of his tank at the Face Dancer.

"How weak and narrow is your thinking," Scytale said. "Who is it who comes to visit you?"

Edric hesitated, observing the hulk shape, heavy

155

eyelids, blunt face. It was early in the day and Edric's metabolism had not yet cycled from night repose into full melange consumption.

"This is not the shape which walked the streets?" Edric asked.

"One would not look twice at some of the figures I have been today," Scytale said.

The chameleon thinks a change of shape will hide him from anything, Edric thought with rare insight. And he wondered if his presence in the conspiracy truly hid them from all oracular powers. The Emperor's sister, now...

Edric shook his head, stirring the orange gas of his tank, said: "Why are you here?"

"The gift must be prodded to swifter action," Scytale said.

"That cannot be done."

"A way must be found," Scytale insisted.

"Why?"

"Things are not to my liking. The Emperor is trying to split us. Already he has made his bid to the Bene Gesserit."

"Oh, *that.*"

"That! You must prod the ghola to..."

"You fashioned him, Tleilaxu," Edric said. "You know better than to ask this." He paused, moved closer to the transparent wall of his tank. "Or did you lie to us about this gift?"

"Lie?"

"You said the weapon was to be aimed and released, nothing more. Once the ghola was given we could not tamper."

"Any ghola can be disturbed," Scytale said. "You need do nothing more than question him about his original being."

"What will this do?"

"It will stir him to actions which will serve our purposes."

"He is a mentat with powers of logic and reason," Edric

objected. "He may guess what I'm doing . . . or the sister. If her attention is focused upon—"

"Do you hide us from the sibyl or don't you?" Scytale asked.

"I'm not afraid of oracles," Edric said. "I'm concerned with logic, with real spies, with the physical powers of the Imperium, with the control of the spice, with—"

"One can contemplate the Emperor and his powers comfortably if one remembers that all things are finite," Scytale said.

Oddly, the Steersman recoiled in agitation, threshing his limbs like some weird newt. Scytale fought a sense of loathing at the sight. The Guild Navigator wore his usual dark leotard bulging at the belt with various containers. Yet . . . he gave the impression of nakedness when he moved. It was the swimming, reaching movements, Scytale decided, and he was struck once more by the delicate linkages of their conspiracy. They were not a compatible group. That was weakness.

Edric's agitation subsided. He stared out at Scytale, vision colored by the orange gas which sustained him. What plot did the Face Dancer hold in reserve to save himself? Edric wondered. The Tleilaxu was not acting in a predictable fashion. Evil omen.

Something in the Navigator's voice and actions told Scytale that the Guildsman feared the sister more than the Emperor. This was an abrupt thought flashed on the screen of awareness. Disturbing. Had they overlooked something important about Alia? Would the ghola be sufficient weapon to destroy both?

"You know what is said of Alia?" Scytale asked, probing.

"What do you mean?" Again, the fish-man was agitated.

"Never have philosophy and culture had such a patroness," Scytale said. "Pleasure and beauty unite in—"

"What is enduring about beauty and pleasure?" Edric demanded. "We will destroy both Atreides. Culture! They dispense culture the better to rule. Beauty! They promote the beauty which enslaves. They create a literate ignorance—easiest thing of all. They leave nothing to chance. Chains! Everything they do forges chains, enslaves. But slaves always revolt."

"The sister may wed and produce offspring," Scytale said.

"Why do you speak of the sister?" Edric asked.

"The Emperor may choose a mate for her," Scytale said.

"Let him choose. Already, it is too late."

"Even you cannot invent the next moment," Scytale warned. "You are not a creator... any more than are the Atreides." He nodded. "We must not presume too much."

"We aren't the ones to flap our tongues about creation," Edric protested. "We aren't the rabble trying to make a messiah out of Muad'dib. What is this nonsense? Why are you raising such questions?"

"It's this planet," Scytale said. *"It* raises questions."

"Planets don't speak!"

"This one does."

"Oh?"

"It speaks of creation. Sand blowing in the night, that is creation."

"Sand blowing..."

"When you awaken, the first light shows you the new world—all fresh and ready for your tracks."

Untracked sand? Edric thought. *Creation?* He felt knotted with sudden anxiety. The confinement of his tank, the surrounding room, everything closed in upon him, constricted him.

Tracks in sand.

"You talk like a Fremen," Edric said.

"This is a Fremen thought and it's instructive," Scytale agreed. "They speak of Muad'dib's Jihad as leaving tracks in the universe in the same way that a Fremen tracks new sand. They've marked out a trail in men's lives."

"So?"

"Another night comes," Scytale said. "Winds blow."

"Yes," Edric said, "the Jihad is finite. Muad'dib has used his Jihad and—"

"He didn't use the Jihad," Scytale said. "The Jihad used him. I think he would've stopped it if he could."

"If he could? All he had to do was—"

"Oh, be still!" Scytale barked. "You can't stop a mental epidemic. It leaps from person to person across parsecs. It's overwhelmingly contagious. It strikes at the unprotected side, in the place where we lodge the fragments of other such plagues. Who can stop such a thing? Muad'dib hasn't the antidote. The thing has roots in chaos. Can orders reach there?"

"Have you been infected, then?" Edric asked. He turned slowly in the orange gas, wondering why Scytale's words carried such a tone of fear. Had the Face Dancer broken from the conspiracy? There was no way to peer into the future and examine this now. The future had become a muddy stream, clogged with prophets.

"We're all contaminated," Scytale said, and he reminded himself that Edric's intelligence had severe limits. How could this point be made that the Guildsman would understand it?

"But when we destroy him," Edric said, "the contag—"

"I should leave you in this ignorance," Scytale said. "But my duties will not permit it. Besides, it's dangerous to all of us."

Edric recoiled, steadied himself with a kick of one webbed foot which sent the orange gas whipping around his legs. "You speak strangely," he said.

"This whole thing is explosive," Scytale said in a calmer voice. "It's ready to shatter. When it goes, it will send bits of itself out through the centuries. Don't you see this?"

"We've dealt with religions before," Edric protested. "If this new—"

"It is *not* just a religion!" Scytale said, wondering what the Reverend Mother would say to this harsh education of their fellow conspirator. "Religious government is something else. Muad'dib has crowded his Qizarate in everywhere, displaced the old functions of government. But he has no permanent civil service, no interlocking embassies. He has bishoprics, islands of authority. At the center of each island is a man. Men learn how to gain and hold personal power. Men are jealous."

"When they're divided, we'll absorb them one by one," Edric said with a complacent smile. "Cut off the head and the body will fall to—"

"This body has two heads," Scytale said.

"The sister—who may wed."

"Who will certainly wed."

"I don't like your tone, Scytale."

"And I don't like your ignorance."

"What if she does wed? Will that shake our plans?"

"It will shake the universe."

"But they're not unique. I, myself, possess powers which—"

"You're an infant. You toddle where they stride."

"They are *not* unique!"

"You forget, Guildsman, that we once made a kwisatz haderach. This is a being filled by the spectacle of Time. It is a form of existence which cannot be threatened without enclosing yourself in the identical threat. Muad'dib knows we would attack his Chani. We must move faster than we have. You must get to the ghola, prod him as I have instructed."

"And if I do not?"

"We will feel the thunderbolt."

Oh, worm of many teeth,
Canst thou deny what has no cure?
The flesh and breath which lure thee
To the ground of all beginnings
Feed on monsters twisting in a door of fire!
Thou hast no robe in all thy attire
To cover intoxications of divinity
Or hide the burnings of desire!

—Wormsong
from the Dunebook

Paul had worked up a sweat on the practice floor using crysknife and short sword against the ghola. He stood now at a window looking down into the temple plaza, tried to imagine the scene with Chani at the clinic. She'd been taken ill at midmorning, the sixth week of her pregnancy. The medics were the best. They'd call when they had news.

Murky afternoon sandclouds darkened the sky over the plaza. Fremen called such weather "dirty air."

Would the medics never call? Each second struggled past, reluctant to enter his universe.

Waiting... waiting... The Bene Gesserit sent no word from Wallach. Deliberately delaying, of course.

Prescient vision had recorded these moments, but he shielded his awareness from the oracle, preferring the role here of a Timefish swimming not where he willed, but where the currents carried him. Destiny permitted no struggles now.

The ghola could be heard racking weapons, examining the equipment. Paul sighed, put a hand to his own belt, deactivated his shield. The tingling passage of its field ran down against his skin.

He'd face events when Chani came, Paul told himself. Time enough then to accept the fact that what he'd concealed from her had prolonged her life. Was it evil, he wondered, to prefer Chani to an heir? By what right did he make her choice for her? Foolish thoughts! Who could hesitate, given the alternatives—slave pits, torture, agonizing sorrow... and worse.

He heard the door open, Chani's footsteps.

Paul turned.

Murder sat on Chani's face. The wide Fremen belt which gathered the waist of her golden robe, the water rings worn as a necklace, one hand at her hip (never far from the knife), the trenchant stare which was her first inspection of any room—everything about her stood now only as a background for violence.

He opened his arms as she came to him, gathered her close.

"Someone," she rasped, speaking against his breast, "has been feeding me a contraceptive for a long time... before I began the new diet. There'll be problems with this birth because of it."

"But there are remedies?" he asked.

"Dangerous remedies. I know the source of that poison! I'll have her blood."

"My Sihaya," he whispered, holding her close to calm a sudden trembling. "You'll bear the heir we want. Isn't that enough?"

"My life burns faster," she said, pressing against him. "The birth now controls my life. The medics told me it goes at a terrible pace. I must eat and eat...and take more spice, as well...eat it, drink it. I'll kill her for this!"

Paul kissed her cheek. "No, my Sihaya. You'll kill no one." And he thought: *Irulan prolonged your life, beloved. For you, the time of birth is the time of death.*

He felt hidden grief drain his marrow then, empty his life into a black flask.

Chani pushed away from him. "She cannot be forgiven!"

"Who said anything about forgiving?"

"They why shouldn't I kill her?"

It was such a flat, Fremen question that Paul felt himself almost overcome by a hysterical desire to laugh. He covered it by saying: "It wouldn't help."

"You've *seen* that?"

Paul felt his belly tighten with vision-memory.

"What I've seen...what I've seen..." he muttered. Every aspect of surrounding events fitted a present which paralyzed him. He felt chained to a future which, exposed too often, had locked onto him like a greedy succubus. Tight dryness clogged his throat. Had he followed the witchcall of his own oracle, he wondered, until it'd spilled him into a merciless present?

"Tell me what you've *seen,*" Chani said.

"I can't."

"Why mustn't I kill her?"

"Because I ask it."

He watched her accept this. She did it the way sand accepted water: absorbing and concealing. Was there obedience beneath that hot, angry surface? he wondered.

And he realized then that life in the royal Keep had left Chani unchanged. She'd merely stopped here for a time, inhabited a way station on a journey with her man. Nothing of the desert had been taken from her.

Chani stepped away from him then, glanced at the ghola who stood waiting near the diamond circle of the practice door.

"You've been crossing blades with him?" she asked.

"And I'm better for it."

Her gaze went to the circle on the floor, back to the ghola's metallic eyes.

"I don't like it," she said.

"He's not intended to do me violence," Paul said.

"You've seen *that?*"

"I've not *seen* it!"

"Then how do you know?"

"Because he's more than ghola; he's Duncan Idaho."

"The Bene Tleilax made him."

"They made more than they intended."

She shook her head. A corner of her nezhoni scarf rubbed the collar of her robe. "How can you change the fact that he is ghola?"

"Hayt," Paul said, "are you the tool of my undoing?"

"If the substance of here and now is changed, the future is changed," the ghola said.

"That is no answer!" Chani objected.

Paul raised his voice: "How will I die, Hayt?"

Light glinted from the artificial eyes. "It is said, m'Lord, that you will die of money and power."

Chani stiffened. "How dare he speak thus to you?"

"The mentat is truthful," Paul said.

"Was Duncan Idaho a real friend?" she asked.

"He gave his life for me."

"It is sad," Chani whispered, "that a ghola cannot be restored to his original being."

"Would you convert me?" the ghola asked, directing his gaze to Chani.

"What does he mean?" Chani asked.

"To be converted is to be turned around," Paul said. "But there's no going back."

"Every man carries his own past with him," Hayt said.

"And every ghola?" Paul asked.

"In a way, m'Lord."

"Then what of that past in your secret flesh?" Paul asked.

Chani saw how the question disturbed the ghola. His movements quickened, hands clenched into fists. She glanced at Paul, wondering why he probed thus. Was there a way to restore this creature to the man he'd been?

"Has a ghola ever remembered his real past?" Chani asked.

"Many attempts have been made," Hayt said, his gaze fixed on the floor near his feet. "No ghola has ever been restored to his former being."

"But you long for this to happen," Paul said.

The blank surfaces of the ghola's eyes came up to center on Paul with a pressing intensity. "Yes!"

Voice soft, Paul said: "If there's a way . . ."

"This flesh," Hayt said, touching left hand to forehead in a curious saluting movement, "is not the flesh of my original birth. It is . . . reborn. Only the shape is familiar. A Face Dancer might do as well."

"Not as well," Paul said. "And you're not a Face Dancer."

"That is true, m'Lord."

"Whence comes your shape?"

"The genetic imprint of the original cells."

"Somewhere," Paul said, "there's a plastic something which remembers the shape of Duncan Idaho. It's said the ancients probed this region before the Butlerian Jihad. What's the extent of this memory, Hayt? What did it learn from the original?"

The ghola shrugged.

"What if he wasn't Idaho?" Chani asked.

"He was."

"Can you be certain?" she asked.

"He is Duncan in every aspect. I cannot imagine a force strong enough to hold that shape thus without any relaxation or any deviation."

"M'Lord!" Hayt objected. "Because we cannot imagine a thing, that doesn't exclude it from reality. There are things I must do as a ghola that I would not do as a man."

Keeping his attention on Chani, Paul said: "You see?" She nodded.

Paul turned away, fighting deep sadness. He crossed to the balcony windows, drew the draperies. Lights came on in the sudden gloom. He pulled the sash of his robe tight, listened for sounds behind him.

Nothing.

He turned. Chani stood as though entranced, her gaze centered on the ghola.

Hayt, Paul saw, had retreated to some inner chamber of his being—had gone back to the ghola place.

Chani turned at the sound of Paul's return. She still felt the thralldom of the instant Paul had precipitated. For a brief moment, the ghola had been an intense, vital human being. For that moment, he had been someone she did not fear—indeed, someone she liked and admired. Now, she understood Paul's purpose in this probing. He had wanted her to see the *man* in the ghola flesh.

She stared at Paul. "That man, was that Duncan Idaho?"

"That was Duncan Idaho. He is still there."

"Would *he* have allowed Irulan to go on living?" Chani asked.

The water didn't sink too deep, Paul thought. And he said: "If I commanded it."

"I don't understand," she said. "Shouldn't you be angry?"

"I am angry."

"You don't sound . . . angry. You sound sorrowful."

He closed his eyes. "Yes. That, too."

"You're my man," she said. "I know this, but suddenly I don't understand you."

Abruptly, Paul felt that he walked down a long cavern. His flesh moved—one foot and then another—but his thoughts went elsewhere. "I don't understand myself," he whispered. When he opened his eyes, he found that he had moved away from Chani.

She spoke from somewhere behind him. "Beloved, I'll not ask again what you've *seen*. I only know I'm to give you the heir we want."

He nodded, then: "I've known that from the beginning." He turned, studied her. Chani seemed very far away.

She drew herself up, placed a hand on her abdomen. "I'm hungry. The medics tell me I must eat three or four times what I ate before. I'm frightened, beloved. It goes too fast."

Too fast, he agreed. *This fetus knows the necessity for speed.*

The audacious nature of Muad'dib's actions may be seen in the fact that He knew from the beginning whither He was bound, yet not once did He step aside from that path. He put it clearly when He said: "I tell you that I come now to my time of testing when it will be shown that I am the Ultimate Servant." Thus He weaves all into One, that both friend and foe may worship Him. It is for this reason and this reason only that His Apostles prayed: "Lord, save us from the other paths which Muad'dib covered with the Waters of His Life." Those "other paths" may be imagined only with the deepest revulsion.

—from The Yiam-el-Din
(Book of Judgment)

The messenger was a young woman—her face, name and family known to Chani—which was how she'd penetrated Imperial Security.

Chani had done no more than identify her for a
Security Officer named Bannerjee, who then arranged the
meeting with Muad'dib. Bannerjee acted out of instinct
and the assurance that the young woman's father had
been a member of the Emperor's Death Commandos, the
dreaded Fedaykin, in the days before the Jihad.
Otherwise, he might have ignored her plea that her
message was intended only for the ears of Muad'dib.

She was, of course, screened and searched before the
meeting in Paul's private office. Even so, Bannerjee
accompanied her, hand on knife, other hand on her arm.

It was almost midday when they brought her into the
room—an odd space, mixture of desert-Fremen and
Family-Aristocrat. *Hiereg* hangings lined three walls:
delicate tapestries adorned with figures out of Fremen
mythology. A view screen covered the fourth wall, a
silver-gray surface behind an oval desk whose top held
only one object, a Fremen sandclock built into an *orrery*.
The orrery, a suspensor mechanism from Ix, carried both
moons of Arrakis in the classic Worm Trine aligned with
the sun.

Paul, standing beside the desk, glanced at Bannerjee.
The Security Officer was one of those who'd come up
through the Fremen Constabulary, winning his place on
brains and proven loyalty despite the smuggler ancestry
attested by his name. He was a solid figure, almost fat.
Wisps of black hair fell down over the dark, wet-
appearing skin of his forehead like the crest of an exotic
bird. His eyes were blue-blue and steady in a gaze which
could look upon happiness or atrocity without change of
expression. Both Chani and Stilgar trusted him. Paul
knew that if he told Bannerjee to throttle the girl
immediately, Bannerjee would do it.

"Sire, here is the messenger girl," Bannerjee said.
"M'Lady Chani said she sent word to you."

"Yes." Paul nodded curtly.

Oddly, the girl didn't look at him. Her attention
remained on the orrery. She was dark-skinned, of
medium height, her figure concealed beneath a robe

whose rich wine fabric and simple cut spoke of wealth. Her blue-black hair was held in a narrow band of material which matched the robe. The robe concealed her hands. Paul suspected that the hands were tightly clasped. It would be in character. Everything about her would be in character—including the robe: a last piece of finery saved for such a moment.

Paul motioned Bannerjee aside. He hesitated before obeying. Now, the girl moved—one step forward. When she moved there was grace. Still, her eyes avoided him.

Paul cleared his throat.

Now the girl lifted her gaze, the whiteless eyes widening with just the right shade of awe. She had an odd little face with delicate chin, a sense of reserve in the way she held her small mouth. The eyes appeared abnormally large above slanted cheeks. There was a cheerless air about her, something which said she seldom smiled. The corners of her eyes even held a faint yellow misting which could have been from dust irritation or the tracery of semuta.

Everything was in character.

"You asked to see me," Paul said.

The moment of supreme test for this girl-shape had come. Scytale had put on the shape, the mannerisms, the sex, the voice—everything his abilities could grasp and assume. But this was a female known to Muad'dib in the sietch days. She'd been a child, then, but she and Muad'dib shared common experiences. Certain areas of memory must be avoided delicately. It was the most exacting part Scytale had ever attempted.

"I am Otheym's Lichna of Berk al Dib."

The girl's voice came out small, but firm, giving name, father and pedigree.

Paul nodded. He saw how Chani had been fooled. The timbre of voice, everything reproduced with exactitude. Had it not been for his own Bene Gesserit training in voice and for the web of *dao* in which oracular vision enfolded him, this Face-Dancer disguise might have gulled even him.

Training exposed certain discrepancies: the girl was

older than her known years; too much control tuned the
vocal cords; set of neck and shoulders missed by a fraction
the subtle hauteur of Fremen poise. But there were
niceties, too: the rich robe had been patched to betray
actual status... and the features were beautifully exact.
They spoke a certain sympathy of this Face Dancer for
the role being played.

"Rest in my home, daughter of Otheym," Paul said in
formal Fremen greeting. "You are welcome as water after
a dry crossing."

The faintest of relaxations exposed the confidence this
apparent acceptance had conveyed.

"I bring a message," she said.

"A man's messenger is as himself," Paul said.

Scytale breathed softly. It went well, but now came the
crucial task: the Atreides must be guided onto that special
path. He must lose his Fremen concubine in circumstances where no other shared the blame. The failure must
belong only to the *omnipotent* Muad'dib. He had to be
led into an ultimate realization of his failure and thence to
acceptance of the Tleilaxu alternative.

"I am the smoke which banishes sleep in the night,"
Scytale said, employing a Fedaykin code phrase: *I bear
bad tidings.*

Paul fought to maintain calmness. He felt naked, his
soul abandoned in a groping-time concealed from every
vision. Powerful oracles hid this Face Dancer. Only the
edges of these moments were known to Paul. He knew
only what he could *not* do. He could not slay this Face
Dancer. That would precipitate the future which must be
avoided at all cost. Somehow, a way must be found to
reach into the darkness and change the terrifying pattern.

"Give me your message," Paul said.

Bannerjee moved to place himself where he could
watch the girl's face. She seemed to notice him for the first
time and her gaze went to the knife handle beneath the
Security Officer's hand.

"The innocent do not believe in evil," she said, looking
squarely at Bannerjee.

Ahhh, well done, Paul thought. It was what the real Lichna would've said. He felt a momentary pang for the real daughter of Otheym—dead now, a corpse in the sand. There was no time for such emotions, though. He scowled.

Bannerjee kept his attention on the girl.

"I was told to deliver my message in secret," she said.

"Why?" Bannerjee demanded, voice harsh, probing.

"Because it is my father's wish."

"This is my friend," Paul said. "Am I not a Fremen? Then my friend may hear anything I hear."

Scytale composed the girl-shape. Was this a true Fremen custom . . . or was it a test?

"The Emperor may make his own rules," Scytale said. "This is the message: My father wishes you to come to him, bringing Chani."

"Why must I bring Chani?"

"She is your woman and a Sayyadina. This is a Water matter, by the rules of our tribes. She must attest it that my father speaks according to the Fremen Way."

There truly are Fremen in the conspiracy, Paul thought. This moment fitted the shape of things to come for sure. And he had no alternative but to commit himself to this course.

"Of what will your father speak?" Paul asked.

"He will speak of a plot against you—a plot among the Fremen."

"Why doesn't he bring that message in person?" Bannerjee demanded.

She kept her gaze on Paul. "My father cannot come here. The plotters suspect him. He'd not survive the journey."

"Could he not divulge the plot to you?" Bannerjee asked. "How came he to risk his daughter on such a mission?"

"The details are locked in a distrans carrier that only Muad'dib may open," she said. "This much I know."

"Why not send the distrans, then?" Paul asked.

"It is a human distrans," she said.

"I'll go, then," Paul said. "But I'll go alone."

"Chani must come with you!"

"Chani is with child."

"When has a Fremen woman refused to . . ."

"My enemies fed her a subtle poison," Paul said. "It will be a difficult birth. Her health will not permit her to accompany me now."

Before Scytale could still them, strange emotions passed over the girl-features: frustration, anger. Scytale was reminded that every victim must have a way of escape—even such a one as Muad'dib. The conspiracy had not failed, though. This Atreides remained in the net. He was a creature who had developed firmly into one pattern. He'd destroy himself before changing into the opposite of that pattern. That had been the way with the Tleilaxu kwisatz haderach. It'd be the way with this one. And then . . . the ghola.

"Let me ask Chani to decide this," she said.

"I have decided it," Paul said. "You will accompany me in Chani's stead."

"It requires a Sayyadina of the Rite!"

"Are you not Chani's friend?"

Boxed! Scytale thought. *Does he suspect? No. He's being Fremen-cautious. And the contraceptive is a fact. Well—there are other ways.*

"My father told me I was not to return," Scytale said, "that I was to seek asylum with you. He said you'd not risk me."

Paul nodded. It was beautifully in character. He couldn't deny this asylum. She'd plead Fremen obedience to a father's command.

"I'll take Stilgar's wife, Harah," Paul said. "You'll tell us the way to your father."

"How do you know you can trust Stilgar's wife?"

"I know it."

"But I don't."

Paul pursed his lips, then: "Does your mother live?"

"My true mother has gone to Shai-hulud. My second

mother still lives and cares for my father. Why?"

"She's of Sietch Tabr?"

"Yes."

"I remember her," Paul said. "She will serve in Chani's place." He motioned to Bannerjee. "Have attendants take Otheym's Lichna to suitable quarters."

Bannerjee nodded. *Attendants.* The key word meant that this messenger must be put under special guard. He took her arm. She resisted.

"How will you go to my father?" she pleaded.

"You'll describe the way to Bannerjee," Paul said. "He is my friend."

"No! My father has commanded it! I cannot!"

"Bannerjee?" Paul said.

Bannerjee paused. Paul saw the man searching that encyclopedic memory which had helped bring him to his position of trust. "I know a guide who can take you to Otheym," Bannerjee said.

"Then I'll go alone," Paul said.

"Sire, if you..."

"Otheym wants it this way," Paul said, barely concealing the irony which consumed him.

"Sire, it's too dangerous," Bannerjee protested.

"Even an Emperor must accept some risks," Paul said. "The decision is made. Do as I've commanded."

Reluctantly, Bannerjee led the Face Dancer from the room.

Paul turned toward the blank screen behind his desk. He felt that he waited for the arrival of a rock on its blind journey from some height.

Should he tell Bannerjee about the messenger's true nature? he wondered. No! Such an incident hadn't been written on the screen of his vision. Any deviation here carried precipitate violence. A moment of fulcrum had to be found, a place where he could will himself out of the vision.

If such a moment existed...

No matter how exotic human civilization becomes, no matter the developments of life and society nor the complexity of the machine/human interface, there always come interludes of lonely power when the course of humankind, the very future of humankind, depends upon the relatively simple actions of single individuals.

> —from The Tleilaxu Godbuk

As he crossed over on the high footbridge from his Keep to the Qizarate Office Building, Paul added a limp to his walk. It was almost sunset and he walked through long shadows that helped conceal him, but sharp eyes still might detect something in his carriage that identified him. He wore a shield, but it was not activated, his aides having decided that the shimmer of it might arouse suspicions.

Paul glanced left. Strings of sandclouds lay across the

sunset like slatted shutters. The air was hiereg dry through his stillsuit filters.

He wasn't really alone out here, but the web of Security hadn't been this loose around him since he'd ceased walking the streets alone in the night. Ornithopters with night scanners drifted far overhead in seemingly random pattern, all of them tied to his movements through a transmitter concealed in his clothing. Picked men walked the streets below. Others had fanned out through the city after seeing the Emperor in his disguise—Fremen costume down to the stillsuit and *temag* desert boots, the darkened features. His cheeks had been distorted with plastene inserts. A catchtube ran down along his left jaw.

As he reached the opposite end of the bridge, Paul glanced back, noted a movement beside the stone lattice that concealed a balcony of his private quarters. Chani, no doubt. "Hunting for sand in the desert," she'd called this venture.

How little she understood the bitter choice. Selecting among agonies, he thought, made even lesser agonies near unbearable.

For a blurred, emotionally painful moment, he relived their parting. At the last instant, Chani had experienced a tau-glimpse of his feelings, but she had misinterpreted. She had thought his emotions were those experienced in the parting of loved ones when one entered the dangerous unknown.

Would that I did not know, he thought.

He had crossed the bridge now and entered the upper passageway through the office building. There were fixed glowglobes here and people hurrying on business. The Qizarate never slept. Paul found his attention caught by the signs above doorways, as though he were seeing them for the first time: *Speed Merchants. Wind Stills and Retorts. Prophetic Prospects. Tests of Faith. Religious Supply. Weaponry . . . Propagation of the Faith . . .*

A more honest label would've been *Propagation of the Bureaucracy,* he thought.

A type of religious civil servant had sprung up all through his universe. This new man of the Qizarate was more often a convert. He seldom displaced a Freman in the key posts, but he was filling all the interstices. He used melange as much to show he could afford it as for the geriatric benefits. He stood apart from his rulers— Emperor, Guild, Bene Gesserit, Landsraad, Family or Qizarate. His gods were Routine and Records. He was served by mentats and prodigious filing systems. Expediency was the first word in his catechism, although he gave proper lip-service to the precepts of the Butlerians. Machines could not be fashioned in the image of a man's mind, he said, but he betrayed by every action that he preferred machines to men, statistics to individuals, the faraway general view to the intimate personal touch requiring imagination and initiative.

As Paul emerged onto the ramp at the far side of the building, he heard the bells calling the Evening Rite at Alia's Fane.

There was an odd feeling of permanence about the bells.

The temple across the thronged square was new, its rituals of recent devising, but there was something about this setting in a desert sink at the edge of Arrakeen— something in the way wind-driven sand had begun to weather stones and plastene, something in the haphazard way buildings had gone up around the Fane. Everything conspired to produce the impression that this was a very old place full of traditions and mystery.

He was down into the press of people now— committed. The only guide his Security force could find had insisted it be done this way. Security hadn't liked Paul's ready agreement. Stilgar had liked it even less. And Chani had objected most of all.

The crowd around him, even while its members brushed against him, glanced his way unseeing and passed on, gave him a curious freedom of movement. It was the way they'd been conditioned to treat a Fremen, he knew.

He carried himself like a man of the inner desert. Such men were quick to anger.

As he moved into the quickening flow to the temple steps, the crush of people became even greater. Those all around could not help but press against him now, but he found himself the target for ritual apologies: "Your pardon, noble sir. I cannot prevent this discourtesy." "Pardon, sir; this crush of people is the worst I've ever seen." "I abase myself, holy citizen. A lout shoved me."

Paul ignored the words after the first few. There was no feeling in them except a kind of ritual fear. He found himself, instead, thinking that he had come a long way from his boyhood days in Caladan Castle. Where had he put his foot on the path that led to this journey across a crowded square on a planet so far from Caladan? Had he really put his foot on a path? He could not say he had acted at any point in his life for one specific reason. The motives and impinging forces had been complex—more complex possibly than any other set of goads in human history. He had the heady feeling here that he might still avoid the fate he could see so clearly along this path. But the crowd pushed him forward and he experienced the dizzy sense that he had lost his way, lost personal direction over his life.

The crowd flowed with him up the steps now into the temple portico. Voices grew hushed. The smell of fear grew stronger—acrid, sweaty.

Acolytes had already begun the service within the temple. Their plain chant dominated the other sounds—whispers, rustle of garments, shuffling feet, coughs—telling the story of the Far Places visited by the Priestess in her holy trance.

> "She rides the sandworm of space!
> She guides through all storms
> Into the land of gentle winds.
> Though we sleep by the snake's den,
> She guards our dreaming souls.
> Shunning the desert heat,
> She hides us in a cool hollow.

The gleaming of her white teeth
Guides us in the night.
By the braids of her hair
We are lifted up to heaven!
Sweet fragrance, flower-scented,
Surrounds us in her presence,"

Balak! Paul thought, thinking in Fremen. *Look out! She can be filled with angry passion, too.*

The temple portico was lined with tall, slender glow-tubes simulating candle flame. They flickered. The flickering stirred ancestral memories in Paul even while he knew that was the intent. This setting was an atavism, subtly contrived, effective. He hated his own hand in it.

The crowd flowed with him through tall metal doors into the gigantic nave, a gloomy place with the flickering lights far away overhead, a brilliantly illuminated altar at the far end. Behind the altar, a deceptively simple affair of black wood encrusted with sand patterns from the Fremen mythology, hidden lights played on the field of a pru-door to create a rainbow borealis. The seven rows of chanting acolytes ranked below that spectral curtain took on an eerie quality: black robes, white faces, mouths moving in unison.

Paul studied the pilgrims around him, suddenly envious of their intentness, their air of listening to truths he could not hear. It seemed to him that they gained something here which was denied to him, something mysteriously healing.

He tried to inch his way closer to the altar, was stopped by a hand on his arm. Paul whipped his gaze around, met the probing stare of an ancient Fremen—blue-blue eyes beneath overhanging brows, recognition in them. A name flashed into Paul's mind: Rasir, a companion from the sietch days.

In the press of the crowd, Paul knew he was completely vulnerable if Rasir planned violence.

The old man pressed close, one hand beneath a sand-grimed robe—grasping the hilt of a cryknife, no doubt. Paul set himself as best he could to resist attack.

The old man moved his head toward Paul's ear,
whispered: "We will go with the others."

It was the signal to identify his guide. Paul nodded.

Rasir drew back, faced the altar.

"She comes from the east," the acolytes chanted. "The
sun stands at her back. All things are exposed. In the full
glare of light—her eyes miss no thing, neither light nor
dark."

A wailing rebaba jarred across the voices, stilled them,
receded into silence. With an electric abruptness, the
crowd surged forward several meters. They were packed
into a tight mass of flesh now, the air heavy with their
breathing and the scent of spice.

"Shai-hulud writes on clean sand!" the acolytes
shouted.

Paul felt his own breath catch in unison with those
around him. A feminine chorus began singing faintly
from the shadows behind the shimmering pru-door:
"Alia...Alia...Alia..." It grew louder and louder, fell
to a sudden silence.

Again—voices beginning vesper-soft:

> "She stills all storms—
>   Her eyes kill our enemies,
>   And torment the unbelievers.
>   From the spires of Tuono
>   Where dawnlight strikes
>   And clear water runs,
>   You see her shadow.
>   In the shining summer heat
>   She serves us bread and milk—
>   Cool, fragrant with spices.
>   Her eyes melt our enemies,
>   Torment our oppressors
>   And pierce all mysteries.
>   She is Alia...Alia...Alia..."

Slowly, the voices trailed off.

Paul felt sickened. *What are we doing?* he asked

himself. Alia was a child witch, but she was growing older. And he thought: *Growing older is to grow more wicked.*

The collective mental atmosphere of the temple ate at his psyche. He could sense that element of himself which was one with those all around him, but the differences formed a deadly contradiction. He stood immersed, isolated in a personal sin which he could never expiate. The immensity of the universe outside the temple flooded his awareness. How could one man, one ritual, hope to knit such immensity into a garment fitted to all men?

Paul shuddered.

The universe opposed him at every step. It eluded his grasp, conceived countless disguises to delude him. That universe would never agree with any shape he gave it.

A profound hush spread through the temple.

Alia emerged from the darkness behind the shimmering rainbows. She wore a yellow robe trimmed in Atreides green—yellow for sunlight, green for the death which produced life. Paul experienced the sudden surprising thought that Alia had emerged here just for him, for him alone. He stared across the mob in the temple at his sister. She *was* his sister. He knew her ritual and its roots, but he had never before stood out here with the pilgrims, watched her through their eyes. Here, performing the mystery of this place, he saw that she partook of the universe which opposed him.

Acolytes brought her a golden chalice.

Alia raised the chalice.

With part of his awareness, Paul knew that the chalice contained the unaltered melange, the subtle poison, her sacrament of the oracle.

Her gaze on the chalice, Alia spoke. Her voice caressed the ears, flower sound, flowing and musical:

"In the beginning, we were empty," she said.

"Ignorant of all things," the chorus sang.

"We did not know the Power that abides in every place," Alia said.

"And in every Time," the chorus sang.

"Here is the Power," Alia said, raising the chalice slightly.

"It brings us joy," sang the chorus.

And it brings us distress, Paul thought.

"It awakens the soul," Alia said.

"It dispels all doubts," the chorus sang.

"In worlds, we perish," Alia said.

"In the Power, we survive," sang the chorus.

Alia put the chalice to her lips, drank.

To his astonishment, Paul found he was holding his breath like the meanest pilgrim of this mob. Despite every shred of personal knowledge about the experience Alia was undergoing, he had been caught in the tao-web. He felt himself remembering how that fiery poison coursed into the body. Memory unfolded the time-stopping when awareness became a mote which changed the poison. He reexperienced the awakening into timelessness where all things were possible. He *knew* Alia's present experience, yet he saw now that he did not know it. Mystery blinded the eyes.

Alia trembled, sank to her knees.

Paul exhaled with the enraptured pilgrims. He nodded. Part of the veil began to lift from him. Absorbed in the bliss of a vision, he had forgotten that each vision belonged to all those who were still on-the-way, still to become. In the vision, one passed through a darkness, unable to distinguish reality from insubstantial accident. One hungered for absolutes which could never be.

Hungering, one lost the present.

Alia swayed with the rapture of spice change.

Paul felt that some transcendental presence spoke to him, saying: "Look! See there! See what you've ignored?" In that instant, he thought he looked through other eyes, that he saw an imagery and rhythm in this place which no artist or poet could reproduce. It was vital and beautiful, a glaring light that exposed all power-gluttony... even his own.

Alia spoke. Her amplifed voice boomed across the nave.

"Luminous night," she cried.

A moan swept like a wave through the crush of pilgrims.

"Nothing hides in such a night!" Alia said. "What rare light is this darkness? You cannot fix your gaze upon it! Senses cannot record it. No words describe it." Her voice lowered. "The abyss remains. It is pregnant with all the things yet to be. Ahhhhh, what gentle violence!"

Paul felt that he waited for some private signal from his sister. It could be any action or word, something of wizardry and mystical processes, an outward streaming that would fit him like an arrow into a cosmic bow. This instant lay like quivering mercury in his awareness.

"There will be sadness," Alia intoned. "I remind you that all things are but a beginning, forever beginning. Worlds wait to be conquered. Some within the sound of my voice will attain exalted destinies. You will sneer at the past, forgetting what I tell you now: within all differences there is unity."

Paul suppressed a cry of disappointment as Alia lowered her head. She had not said the thing he waited to hear. His body felt like a dry shell, a husk abandoned by some desert insect.

Others must feel something similar, he thought. He sensed the restlessness about him. Abruptly, a woman in the mob, someone far down in the nave to Paul's left, cried out, a wordless noise of anguish.

Alia lifted her head and Paul had the giddy sensation that the distance between them collapsed, that he stared directly into her glazed eyes only inches away from her.

"Who summons me?" Alia asked.

"I do," the woman cried. "I do, Alia. Oh, Alia, help me. They say my son was killed on Muritan. Is he gone? Will I never see my son again . . . never?"

"You try to walk backward in the sand," Alia intoned.

"Nothing is lost. Everything returns later, but you may not recognize the changed form that returns."

"Alia, I don't understand!" the woman wailed.

"You live in the air but you do not see it," Alia said, sharpness in her voice. "Are you a lizard? Your voice has the Fremen accent. Does a Fremen try to bring back the dead? What do we need from our dead except their water?"

Down in the center of the nave, a man in a rich red cloak lifted both hands, the sleeves falling to expose white-clad arms. "Alia," he shouted, "I have had a business proposal. Should I accept?"

"You come here like a beggar," Alia said. "You look for the golden bowl but you will find only a dagger."

"I have been asked to kill a man!" a voice shouted from off to the right—a deep voice with sietch tones. "Should I accept? Accepting, would I succeed?"

"Beginning and end are a single thing," Alia snapped. "Have I not told you this before? You didn't come here to ask that question. What is it you cannot believe that you must come here and cry out against it?"

"She's in a fierce mood tonight," a woman near Paul muttered. "Have you ever seen her this angry?"

She knows I'm out here, Paul thought. *Did she see something in the vision that angered her? Is she raging at me?*

"Alia," a man directly in front of Paul called. "Tell these businessmen and faint-hearts how long your brother will rule!"

"I permit you to look around that corner by yourself," Alia snarled. "You carry your prejudice in your mouth! It is because my brother rides the worm of chaos that you have roof and water!"

With a fierce gesture, clutching her robe, Alia whirled away, strode through the shimmering ribbons of light, was lost in the darkness behind.

Immediately, the acolytes took up the closing chant, but their rhythm was off. Obviously, they'd been caught by the unexpected ending of the rite. An incoherent mumbling arose on all sides of the crowd. Paul felt the stirring around him—restless, dissatisfied.

"It was that fool with his stupid question about business," a woman near Paul muttered. "The hypocrite!"

What had Alia seen? What track through the future?

Something had happened here tonight, souring the rite of the oracle. Usually, the crowd clamored for Alia to answer their pitiful questions. They came as beggars to the oracle, yes. He had heard them thus many times as he'd watched, hidden in the darkness behind the altar. What had been different about this night?

The old Fremen tugged Paul's sleeve, nodded toward the exit. The crowd already was beginning to push in that direction. Paul allowed himself to be pressed along with them, the guide's hand upon his sleeve. There was the feeling in him then that his body had become the manifestation of some power he could no longer control. He had become a non-being, a stillness which moved itself. At the core of the non-being, there he existed, allowing himself to be led through the streets of his city, following a track so familiar to his visions that it froze his heart with grief.

I should know what Alia saw, he thought. *I have seen it enough times myself. And she didn't cry out against it . . . she saw the alternatives, too.*

Production growth and income growth must not get out of step in my Empire. That is the substance of my command. There are to be no balance-of-payment difficulties between the different spheres of influence. And the reason for this is simply because I command it. I want to emphasize my authority in this area. I am the supreme energy-eater of this domain, and will remain so, alive or dead. My Government is the economy.

—Order in Council
The Emperor Paul Muad'dib

"I will leave you here," the old man said, taking his hand from Paul's sleeve. "It is on the right, second door from the far end. Go with Shai-hulud, Muad'dib . . . and remember when you were Usul."

Paul's guide slipped away into the darkness.

There would be Security men somewhere out there

waiting to grab the guide and take the man to a place of questioning, Paul knew. But Paul found himself hoping the old Fremen would escape.

There were stars overhead and the distant light of First Moon somewhere beyond the Shield Wall. But this place was not the open desert where a man could sight on a star to guide his course. The old man had brought him into one of the new suburbs; this much Paul recognized.

This street now was thick with sand blown in from encroaching dunes. A dim light glowed from a single public suspensor globe far down the street. It gave enough illumination to show that this was a dead-end street.

The air around him was thick with the smell of a reclamation still. The thing must be poorly capped for its fetid odors to escape, loosing a dangerously wasteful amount of moisture into the night air. How careless his people had grown, Paul thought. They were millionaires of water—forgetful of the days when a man on Arrakis could have been killed for just an eighth share of the water in his body.

Why am I hesitating? Paul wondered. *It is the second door from the far end. I knew that without being told. But this thing must be played out with precision. So ... I hesitate.*

The noise of an argument arose suddenly from the corner house on Paul's left. A woman there berated someone: the new wing of their house leaked dust, she complained. Did he think water fell from heaven? If dust came in, moisture got out.

Some remember, Paul thought.

He moved down the street and the quarrel faded away behind.

Water from heaven! he thought.

Some Fremen had seen that wonder on other worlds. He had seen it himself, had ordered it for Arrakis, but the memory of it felt like something that had occurred to another person. Rain, it was called. Abruptly, he recalled a rainstorm on his birthworld—clouds thick and gray in the sky of Caladan, an electric storm presence, moist air, the big wet drops drumming on skylights. It ran in rivulets off the eaves. Storm drains took the water away to a river which ran muddy and turgid past the Family orchards . . . trees there with their barren branches glistening wetly.

Paul's foot caught in a low drift of sand across the street. For an instant, he felt mud clinging to the shoes of his childhood. Then he was back in the sand, in the dust-clotted, wind-muffled darkness with the Future hanging over him, taunting. He could feel the aridity of life around him like an accusation. *You did this!* They'd become a civilization of dry-eyed watchers and tale-tellers, people who solved all problems with power . . . and more power . . . and still more power—hating every erg of it.

Rough stones came underfoot. His vision remembered them. The dark rectangle of a doorway appeared on his right—black in black: Otheym's house, Fate's house, a place different from the ones around it only in the role Time had chosen for it. It was a strange place to be marked down in history.

The door opened to his knock. The gap revealed the dull green light of an atrium. A dwarf peered out, ancient face on a child's body, an apparition prescience had never seen.

"You've come then," the apparition said. The dwarf stepped aside, no awe in his manner, merely the gloating of a slow smile. "Come in! Come in!"

Paul hesitated. There'd been no dwarf in the vision, but all else remained identical. Visions could contain such disparities and still hold true to their original plunge into infinity. But the difference dared him to hope. He glanced back up the street at the creamy pearl glistening of his moon swimming out of jagged shadows. The moon haunted him. How did it fall?

"Come in," the dwarf insisted.

Paul entered, heard the door thud into its moisture

seals behind. The dwarf passed him, led the way, enormous feet slapping the floor, opened the delicate lattice gate into the roofed central courtyard, gestured. "They await, Sire."

Sire, Paul thought. *He knows me, then.*

Before Paul could explore this discovery, the dwarf slipped away down a side passage. Hope was a dervish wind whirling, dancing in Paul. He headed across the courtyard. It was a dark and gloomy place, the smell of sickness and defeat in it. He felt daunted by the atmosphere. Was it defeat to choose a lesser evil? he wondered. How far down this track had he come?

Light poured from a narrow doorway in the far wall. He put down the feeling of watchers and evil smells, entered the doorway into a small room. It was a barren place by Fremen standards with heireg hangings on only two walls. Opposite the door, a man sat on carmine cushions beneath the best hanging. A feminine figure hovered in shadows behind another doorway in a barren wall to the left.

Paul felt vision-trapped. This was the way it'd gone. Where was the dwarf? Where was the difference?

His senses absorbed the room in a single gestalten sweep. The place had received painstaking care despite its poor furnishings. Hooks and rods across the barren walls showed where hangings had been removed. Pilgrims paid enormous prices for authentic Fremen artifacts, Paul reminded himself. Rich pilgrims counted desert tapestries as treasures, true marks of a hajj.

Paul felt that the barren walls accused him with their fresh gypsum wash. The threadbare condition of the two remaining hangings amplified the sense of guilt.

A narrow shelf occupied the wall on his right. It held a row of portraits—mostly bearded Fremen, some in still-suits with their catchtubes dangling, some in Imperial uniforms posed against exotic offworld backgrounds. The most common scene was a seascape.

The Fremen on cushions cleared his throat, forcing

Paul to look at him. It was Otheym precisely as the vision
had revealed him: neck grown scrawny, a bird thing which
appeared too weak to support the large head. The face
was a lopsided ruin—networks of crisscrossed scars on
the left cheek below a drooping, wet eye, but clear skin on
the other side and a straight, blue-in-blue Fremen gaze. A
long kedge of a nose bisected the face.

Otheym's cushion sat in the center of a threadbare rug,
brown with maroon and gold threads. The cushion fabric
betrayed splotches of wear and patching, but every bit of
metal around the seated figure shone from polishing—the
portrait frames, shelf lip and brackets, the pedestal of a
low table on the right.

Paul nodded to the clear half of Otheym's face, said:
"Good luck to you and your dwelling place." It was the
greeting of an old friend and sietch mate.

"So I see you once more, Usul."

The voice speaking his tribal name whined with an old
man's quavering. The dull drooping eye on the ruined side
of the face moved above the parchment skin and scars.
Gray bristles stubbled that side and the jawline there hung
with scabrous peelings. Otheym's mouth twisted as he
spoke, the gap exposing silvery metal teeth.

"Muad'dib always answers the call of a Fedaykin,"
Paul said.

The woman in the doorway shadows moved, said: "So
Stilgar boasts."

She came forward into the light, an older version of the
Lichna which the Face Dancer had copied. Paul recalled
then that Otheym had married sisters. Her hair was gray,
nose grown witch-sharp. Weavers' calluses ran along her
forefingers and thumbs. A Fremen woman would've
displayed such marks proudly in the sietch days, but she
saw his attention on her hands, hid them under a fold of
her pale blue robe.

Paul remembered her name then—Dhuri. The shock
was he remembered her as a child, not as she'd been in his
vision of these moments. It was the whine that edged her

voice, Paul told himself. She'd whined even as a child.

"You see me here," Paul said. "Would I be here if Stilgar hadn't approved?" He turned toward Otheym. "I carry your water burden, Otheym. Command me."

This was the straight Fremen talk of sietch brothers.

Otheym produced a shaky nod, almost too much for that thin neck. He lifted a liver-marked left hand, pointed to the ruin of his face. "I caught the splitting disease on Tarahell, Usul," he wheezed. "Right after the victory when we'd all . . ." A fit of coughing stopped his voice.

"The tribe will collect his water soon," Dhuri said. She crossed to Otheym, propped pillows behind him, held his shoulder to steady him until the coughing passed. She wasn't really very old, Paul saw, but a look of lost hopes ringed her mouth, bitterness lay in her eyes.

"I'll summon doctors," Paul said.

Dhuri turned, hand on hip. "We've had medical men, as good as any you could summon." She sent an involuntary glance to the barren wall on her left.

And the medical men were costly, Paul thought.

He felt edgy, constrained by the vision but aware that minor differences had crept in. How could he exploit the differences? Time came out of its skein with subtle changes, but the background fabric held oppressive sameness. He knew with terrifying certainty that if he tried to break out of the enclosing pattern here, it'd become a thing of terrible violence. The power in this deceptively gentle flow of Time oppressed him.

"Say what you want of me," he growled.

"Couldn't it be that Otheym needed a friend to stand by him in this time?" Dhuri asked. "Does a Fedaykin have to consign his flesh to strangers?"

We shared Sietch Tabr, Paul reminded himself. *She has the right to berate me for apparent callousness.*

"What I can do I will do," Paul said.

Another fit of coughing shook Otheym. When it had passed, he gasped: "There's treachery, Usul. Fremen plot against you." His mouth worked then without sound.

Spittle escaped his lips. Dhuri wiped his mouth with a corner of her robe, and Paul saw how her face betrayed anger at such waste of moisture.

Frustrated rage threatened to overwhelm Paul then. *That Otheym should be spent thus! A Fedaykin deserved better.* But no choice remained—not for a Death Commando or his Emperor. They walked occam's razor in this room. The slightest misstep multiplied horrors—not just for themselves, but for all humankind, even for those who would destroy them.

Paul squeezed calmness into his mind, looked at Dhuri. The expression of terrible longing with which she gazed at Otheym strengthened Paul. *Chani must never look at me that way,* he told himself.

"Lichna spoke of a message," Paul said.

"My dwarf," Otheym wheezed. "I bought him on...on...on a world...I forget. He's a human distrans, a toy discarded by the Tleilaxu. He's recorded all the names...the traitors..."

Otheym fell silent, trembling.

"You speak of Lichna," Dhuri said. "When you arrived, we knew she'd reached you safely. If you're thinking of this new burden Otheym places upon you, Lichna is the sum of that burden. An even exchange, Usul: take the dwarf and go."

Paul suppressed a shudder, closed his eyes. *Lichna!* The real daughter had perished in the desert, a semuta-wracked body abandoned to the sand and the wind.

Opening his eyes, Paul said: "You could've come to me at any time for..."

"Otheym stayed away that he might be numbered among those who hate you, Usul," Dhuri said. "The house to the south of us at the end of the street, that is a gathering place for your foes. It's why we took this hovel."

"Then summon the dwarf and we'll leave," Paul said.

"You've not listened well," Dhuri said.

"You must take the dwarf to a safe place," Otheym

said, an odd strength in his voice. "He carries the only record of the traitors. No one suspects his talent. They think I keep him for amusement,"

"We cannot leave," Dhuri said. "Only you and the dwarf. It's known...how poor we are. We've said we're selling the dwarf. They'll take you for the buyer. It's your only chance."

Paul consulted his memory of the vision: in it, he'd left here with the names of the traitors, but never seeing how those names were carried. The dwarf obviously moved under the protection of another oracle. It occurred to Paul then that all creatures must carry some kind of destiny stamped out by purposes of varying strengths, by the fixation of training and disposition. From the moment the Jihad had chosen him, he'd felt himself hemmed in by the forces of a multitude. Their fixed purposes demanded and controlled his course. Any delusions of Free Will he harbored now must be merely the prisoner rattling his cage. His curse lay in the fact that he *saw* the cage. He *saw* it!

He listened now to the emptiness of this house: only the four of them in it—Dhuri, Otheym, the dwarf and himself. He inhaled the fear and tension of his companions, sensed the watchers—his own force hovering in 'thopters far overhead...and those others... next door.

I was wrong to hope, Paul thought. But thinking of hope brought him a twisted *sense* of hope, and he felt that he might yet seize his moment.

"Summon the dwarf," he said.

"Bijaz!" Dhuri called.

"You call me?" The dwarf stepped into the room from the courtyard, an alert expression of worry on his face.

"You have a new master, Bijaz," Dhuri said. She stared at Paul. "You may call him...Usul."

"Usul, that's the base of the pillar," Bijaz said, translating. "How can Usul be base when I'm the basest thing living?"

"He always speaks thus," Otheym apologized.

"I don't speak," Bijaz said. "I operate a machine called language. It creaks and groans, but is mine own."

A Tleilaxu toy, learned and alert, Paul thought. *The Bene Tleilax never threw away something this valuable.* He turned, studied the dwarf. Round melange eyes returned his stare.

"What other talents have you, Bijaz?" Paul asked.

"I know when we should leave," Bijaz said. "It's a talent few men have. There's a time for endings—and that's a good beginning. Let us begin to go, Usul."

Paul examined his vision memory: no dwarf, but the little man's words fitted the occasion.

"At the door, you called me Sire," Paul said. "You know me, then?"

"You've sired, Sire," Bijaz said, grinning. "You are much more than the base Usul. You're the Atreides Emperor, Paul Muad'dib. And you are my finger." He held up the index finger of his right hand.

"Bijaz!" Dhuri snapped. "You tempt fate."

"I tempt my finger," Bijaz protested, voice squeaking. He pointed at Usul. "I point at Usul. Is my finger not Usul himself? Or is it a reflection of something more base?" He brought the finger close to his eyes, examined it with a mocking grin, first one side then the other. "Ahhh, it's merely a finger, after all."

"He often rattles on thus," Dhuri said, worry in her voice. "I think it's why he was discarded by the Tleilaxu."

"I'll not be patronized," Bijaz said, "yet I have a new patron. How strange the workings of the finger." He peered at Dhuri and Otheym, eyes oddly bright. "A weak glue bound us, Otheym. A few tears and we part." The dwarf's big feet rasped on the floor as he whirled completely around, stopped facing Paul. "Ahhh, patron! I came the long way around to find you."

Paul nodded.

"You'll be kind, Usul?" Bijaz asked. "I'm a person, you know. Persons come in many shapes and sizes. This be but one of them. I'm weak of muscle, but strong of mouth; cheap to feed, but costly to fill. Empty me as you will, there's still more in me than men put there."

"We've no time for your stupid riddles," Dhuri growled. "You should be gone."

"I'm riddled with conundrums," Bijaz said, "but not all of them stupid. To be gone, Usul, is to be a bygone. Yes? Let us let bygones be bygones. Dhuri speaks truth, and I've the talent for hearing that, too."

"You've truthsense?" Paul asked, determined now to wait out the clockwork of his vision. Anything was better than shattering these moments and producing the new consequences. There remained things for Otheym to say lest Time be diverted into even more horrifying channels.

"I've *now*-sense," Bijaz said.

Paul noted that the dwarf had grown more nervous. Was the little man aware of things about to happen? Could Bijaz be his own oracle?

"Did you inquire of Lichna?" Otheym asked suddenly, peering up at Dhuri with his one good eye.

"Lichna is safe," Dhuri said.

Paul lowered his head, lest his expression betray the lie. *Safe!* Lichna was ashes in a secret grave.

"That's good then," Otheym said, taking Paul's lowered head for a nod of agreement. "One good thing among the evils, Usul. I don't like the world we're making, you know that? It was better when we were alone in the desert with only the Harkonnens for enemy."

"There's but a thin line between many an enemy and many a friend," Bijaz said. "Where that line stops, there's no beginning and no end. Let's end it, my friends." He moved to Paul's side, jittered from one foot to the other.

"What's *now*-sense?" Paul asked, dragging out these moments, goading the dwarf.

"Now!" Bijaz said, trembling. "Now! Now!" He tugged at Paul's robe. "Let us go now!"

"His mouth rattles, but there's no harm in him,"

Otheym said, affection in his voice, the one good eye staring at Bijaz.

"Even a rattle can signal departure," Bijaz said. "And so can tears. Let's be gone while there's time to begin."

"Bijaz, what do you fear?" Paul asked.

"I fear the spirit seeking me now," Bijaz muttered. Perspiration stood out on his forehead. His cheeks twitched. "I fear the one who thinks not and will have no body except mine—and that one gone back into itself! I fear the things I see and the things I do not see."

This dwarf does possess the power of prescience, Paul thought. Bijaz shared the terrifying oracle. Did he share the oracle's fate, as well? How potent was the dwarf's power? Did he have the little prescience of those who dabbled in the Dune Tarot? Or was it something greater? How much had he seen?

"Best you go," Dhuri said. "Bijaz is right."

"Every minute we linger," Bijaz said, "prolongs . . . prolongs the present!"

Every minute I linger defers my guilt, Paul thought. A worm's poisonous breath, its teeth dripping dust, had washed over him. It had happened long ago, but he inhaled the memory of it now—spice and bitterness. He could sense his own worm waiting—"the urn of the desert."

"These are troubled times," he said, addressing himself to Otheym's judgment of their world.

"Fremen know what to do in time of trouble," Dhuri said.

Otheym contributed a shaky nod.

Paul glanced at Dhuri. He'd not expected gratitude, would have been burdened by it more than he could bear, but Otheym's bitterness and the passionate resentment he saw in Dhuri's eyes shook his resolve. Was *anything* worth this price?

"Delay serves no purpose," Dhuri said.

"Do what you must, Usul," Otheym wheezed.

Paul sighed. The words of the vision had been spoken. "There'll be an accounting," he said, to complete it. Turning, he strode from the room, heard Bijaz foot-slapping behind.

"Bygones, bygones," Bijaz muttered as they went. "Let bygones fall where they may. This has been a dirty day."

The convoluted wording of legalisms grew up around the necessity to hide from ourselves the violence we intend toward each other. Between depriving a man of one hour from his life and depriving him of his life there exists only a difference of degree. You have done violence to him, consumed his energy. Elaborate euphemisms may conceal your intent to kill, but behind any use of power over another the ultimate assumption remains: "I feed on your energy."

> —Addenda to Orders in Council
> The Emperor Paul Muad'dib

First Moon stood high over the city as Paul, his shield activated and shimmering around him, emerged from the cul-de-sac. A wind off the massif whirled sand and dust down the narrow street, causing Bijaz to blink and shield his eyes.

"We must hurry," the dwarf muttered. "Hurry! Hurry!"

"You sense danger?" Paul asked, probing.

"I *know* danger!"

An abrupt sense of peril very near was followed almost immediately by a figure joining them out of a doorway.

Bijaz crouched and whimpered.

It was only Stilgar moving like a war machine, head thrust forward, feet striking the street solidly.

Swiftly, Paul explained the value of the dwarf, handed Bijaz over to Stilgar. The pace of the vision moved here with great rapidity. Stilgar sped away with Bijaz. Security Guards enveloped Paul. Orders were given to send men down the street toward the house beyond Otheym's. The men hurried to obey, shadows among shadows.

More sacrifices, Paul thought.

"We want live prisoners," one of the guard officers hissed.

The sound was a vision-echo in Paul's ears. It went with solid precision here—vision/reality, tick for tick. Ornithopters drifted down across the moon.

The night was full of Imperial troopers attacking.

A soft hiss grew out of the other sounds, climbed to a roar while they still heard the sibilance. It picked up a terra-cotta glow that hid the stars, engulfed the moon.

Paul, knowing that sound and glow from the earliest nightmare glimpses of his vision, felt an odd sense of fulfillment. It went the way it must.

"Stone burner!" someone screamed.

"Stone burner!" The cry was all around him. "Stone burner . . . stone burner . . ."

Because it was required of him, Paul threw a protective arm across his face, dove for the low lip of a curb. It already was too late, of course.

Where Otheym's house had been there stood now a pillar of fire, a blinding jet roaring at the heavens. It gave off a dirty brilliance which threw into sharp relief every ballet movement of the fighting and fleeing men, the tipping retreat of ornithopters.

For every member of this frantic throng it was too late. The ground grew hot beneath Paul. He heard the sound of running stop. Men threw themselves down all around him, every one of them aware that there was no point in running. The first damage had been done; and now they must wait out the extent of the stone burner's potency. The things's radiation, which no man could outrun, already had penetrated their flesh. The peculiar result of stone-burner radiation already was at work in them. What else this weapon might do now lay in the planning of the men who had used it, the men who had defied the Great Convention to use it.

"God's . . . a stone burner," someone whimpered. "I . . . don't . . . want . . . to . . . be . . . blind."

"Who does?" The harsh voice of a trooper far down the street.

"The Tleilaxu will sell many eyes here," someone near Paul growled. "Now, shut up and wait!"

They waited.

Paul remained silent, thinking what this weapon implied. Too much fuel in it and it'd cut its way into the planet's core. Dune's molten level lay deep, but the more dangerous for that. Such pressures released and out of control might split a planet, scattering lifeless bits and pieces through space.

"I think it's dying down a bit," someone said.

"It's just digging deeper," Paul cautioned. "Stay put, all of you. Stilgar will be sending help."

"Stilgar got away?"

"Stilgar got away."

"The ground's hot," someone complained.

"They dared use atomics!" a trooper near Paul protested.

"The sound's diminishing," someone down the street said.

Paul ignored the words, concentrated on his fingertips against the street. He could feel the rolling-rumbling of the thing—deep . . . deep . . .

"My eyes!" someone cried. "I can't see!"

Someone closer to it than I was, Paul thought. He still could see to the end of the cul-de-sac when he lifted his head, although there was a mistiness across the scene. A red-yellow glow filled the area where Otheym's house and its neighbor had been. Pieces of adjoining buildings made dark patterns as they crumbled into the glowing pit.

Paul climbed to his feet. He felt the stone burner die, silence beneath him. His body was wet with perspiration against the stillsuit's slickness—too much for the suit to accommodate. The air he drew into his lungs carried the heat and sulfur stench of the burner.

As he looked at the troopers beginning to stand up around him, the mist on Paul's eyes faded into darkness. He summoned up his oracular vision of these moments, then, turned and strode along the track that Time had carved for him, fitting himself into the vision so tightly that it could not escape. He felt himself grow aware of this place as a multitudinous possession, reality welded to prediction.

Moans and groans of his troopers arose all around him as the men realized their blindness.

"Hold fast!" Paul shouted. "Help is coming!" And, as the complaints persisted, he said: "This is Muad'dib! I command you to hold fast! Help comes!"

Silence.

Then, true to his vision, a nearby guardsman said: "Is it truly the Emperor? Which of you can see? Tell me."

"None of us has eyes," Paul said. "They have taken my eyes, as well, but not my vision. I can *see* you standing there, a dirty wall within touching distance on your left. Now wait bravely. Stilgar comes with our friends."

The thwock-thwock of many 'thopters grew louder all around. There was the sound of hurrying feet. Paul *watched* his friends come, matching their sounds to his oracular vision.

"Stilgar!" Paul shouted, waving an arm. "Over here!"

"Thanks to Shai-hulud," Stilgar cried, running up to Paul. "You're not . . ." In the sudden silence, Paul's vision showed him Stilgar staring with an expression of agony at the ruined eyes of his friend and Emperor. "Oh, m'Lord," Stilgar groaned. "Usul...Usul...Usul..."

"What of the stone burner?" one of the newcomers shouted.

"It's ended," Paul said, raising his voice. He gestured. "Get up there now and rescue the ones who were closest to it. Put up barriers. Lively now!" He turned back to Stilgar.

"Do you *see*, m'Lord?" Stilgar asked, wonder in his tone. "How can you see?"

For answer, Paul put a finger out to touch Stilgar's cheek above the stillsuit mouthcap, felt tears. "You need give no moisture to me, old friend," Paul said. "I am not dead."

"But your eyes!"

"They've blinded my body, but not my vision," Paul said. "Ah, Stil, I live in an apocalyptic dream. My steps fit into it so precisely that I fear most of all I will grow bored reliving the thing so exactly."

"Usul, I don't, I don't..."

"Don't try to understand it. Accept it. I am in the world beyond this world here. For me, they are the same. I need no hand to guide me. I see every movement all around me. I see every expression of your face. I have no eyes, yet I see."

Stilgar shook his head sharply. "Sire, we must conceal your affliction from—"

"We hide it from no man," Paul said.

"But the law..."

"We live by the Atreides Law now, Stil. The Fremen Law that the blind should be abandoned in the desert applies only to the blind. I am not blind. I live in the cycle of being where the war of good and evil has its arena. We are at a turning point in the succession of ages and we have our parts to play."

In a sudden stillness, Paul heard one of the wounded being led past him. "It was terrible," the man groaned, "a great fury of fire."

"None of these men shall be taken into the desert,"

Paul said. "You hear me, Stil?"

"I hear you, m'Lord."

"They are to be fitted with new eyes at my expense."

"It will be done, m'Lord."

Paul, hearing the awe grow in Stilgar's voice, said: "I will be at the Command 'thopter. Take charge here."

"Yes, m'Lord."

Paul stepped around Stilgar, strode down the street. His vision told him every movement, every irregularity beneath his feet, every face he encountered. He gave orders as he moved, pointing to men of his personal entourage, calling out names, summoning to himself the ones who represented the intimate apparatus of government. He could feel the terror grow behind him, the fearful whispers.

"His eyes!"

"But he looked right at you, called you by name!"

At the Command 'thopter, he deactivated his personal shield, reached into the machine and took the microphone from the hand of a startled communications officer, issued a swift string of orders, thrust the microphone back into the officer's hand. Turning, Paul summoned a weapons specialist, one of the eager and brilliant new breed who remembered sietch life only dimly.

"They used a stone burner," Paul said.

After the briefest pause, the man said: "So I was told, Sire."

"You know what that means, of course."

"The fuel could only have been atomic."

Paul nodded, thinking of how this man's mind must be racing. Atomics. The Great Convention prohibited such weapons. Discovery of the perpetrator would bring down the combined retributive assault of the Great Houses. Old feuds would be forgotten, discarded in the face of this threat and the ancient fears it aroused.

"It cannot have been manufactured without leaving some traces," Paul said. "You will assemble the proper equipment and search out the place where the stone burner was made."

"At once, Sire." With one last fearful glance, the man sped away.

"M'Lord," the communications officer ventured from behind him. "Your eyes..."

Paul turned, reached into the 'thopter, returned the command set to his personal band. "Call Chani," he ordered. "Tell her... tell her I am alive and will be with her soon."

Now the forces gather, Paul thought. And he noted how strong was the smell of fear in the perspiration all around.

He has gone from Alia,
The womb of heaven!
Holy, holy, holy!
Fire-sand leagues
Confront our Lord.
He can see
Without eyes!
A demon upon him!
Holy, holy, holy
Equation:
He solved for
Martyrdom!

—The Moon Falls Down
Songs of Muad'dib

After seven days of radiating fevered activity, the Keep
took on an unnatural quiet. On this morning, there were

people about, but they spoke in whispers, heads close together, and they walked softly. Some scurried with an oddly furtive gait. The sight of a guard detail coming in from the forecourt drew questioning looks and frowns at the noise which the newcomers brought with their tramping about and stacking of weapons. The newcomers caught the mood of the interior, though, and began moving in that furtive way.

Talk of the stone burner still floated around: "He said the fire had blue-green in it and a smell out of hell."

"Elpa is a fool! He says he'll commit suicide rather than take Tleilaxu eyes."

"I don't like talk of eyes."

"Muad'dib passed me and called me by name!"

"How does *He* see without eyes?"

"People are leaving, had you heard? There's great fear. The Naibs say they'll go to Sietch Makab for a Grand Council."

"What've they done with the Panegyrist?"

"I saw them take him into the chamber where the Naibs are meeting. Imagine Korba a prisoner!"

Chani had arisen early, awakened by a stillness in the Keep. Awakening, she'd found Paul sitting beside her, his eyeless sockets aimed at some formless place beyond the far wall of their bedchamber. What the stone burner had done with its peculiar affinity for eye tissue, all that ruined flesh had been removed. Injections and unguents had saved the stronger flesh around the sockets, but she felt that the radiation had gone deeper.

Ravenous hunger seized her as she sat up. She fed on the food kept by the bedside—spicebread, a heavy cheese.

Paul gestured at the food. "Beloved, there was no way to spare you this. Believe me."

Chani stilled a fit of trembling when he aimed those empty sockets at her. She'd given up asking him to explain. He spoke so oddly: *"I was baptized in sand and it cost me the knack of believing. Who trades in faiths anymore? Who'll buy? Who'll sell?"*

What could he mean by such words?

He refused even to consider Tleilaxu eyes, although he bought them with a lavish hand for the men who'd shared his affliction.

Hunger satisfied, Chani slipped from bed, glanced back at Paul, noted his tiredness. Grim lines framed his mouth. The dark hair stood up, mussed from a sleep that hadn't healed. He appeared so saturnine and remote. The back and forth of waking and sleeping did nothing to change this. She forced herself to turn away, whispered: "My love...my love..."

He leaned over, pulled her back into the bed, kissed her cheeks. "Soon we'll go back to our desert," he whispered. "Only a few things remain to be done here."

She trembled at the finality in his voice.

He tightened his arms around her, murmured: "Don't fear me, my Sihaya. Forget mystery and accept love. There's no mystery about love. It comes from life. Can't you feel that?"

"Yes."

She put a palm against his chest, counting his heartbeats. His love cried out to the Fremen spirit in her—torrential, outpouring, savage. A magnetic power enveloped her.

"I promise you a thing, beloved," he said. "A child of ours will rule such an empire that mine will fade in comparison. Such achievements of living and art and sublime—"

"We're here now!" she protested, fighting a dry sob. "And...I feel we have so little...time."

"We have eternity, beloved."

"*You* may have eternity. I have only now."

"But this *is* eternity." He stroked her forehead.

She pressed against him, lips on his neck. The pressure agitated the life in her womb. She felt it stir.

Paul felt it, too. He put a hand on her abdomen, said: "Ahh, little ruler of the universe, wait your time. This moment is mine."

She wondered then why he always spoke of the life within her as singular. Hadn't the medics told him? She searched back in her own memory, curious that the subject had never arisen between them. Surely, he must know she carried twins. She hesitated on the point of raising this question. He *must* know. He knew everything. He knew all the things that were herself. His hands, his mouth—all of him knew her.

Presently, she said: "Yes, love. This is forever . . . this is real." And she closed her eyes tightly lest sight of his dark sockets stretch her soul from paradise to hell. No matter the *rihani* magic in which he'd enciphered their lives, his flesh remained real, his caresses could not be denied.

When they arose to dress for the day, she said: "If the people only knew your love . . ."

But his mood had changed. "You can't build politics on love," he said. "People aren't concerned with love; it's too disordered. They prefer despotism. Too much freedom breeds chaos. We can't have that, can we? And how do you make despotism lovable?"

"You're not a despot!" she protested, tying her scarf. "Your laws are just."

"Ahh, laws," he said. He crossed to the window, pulled back the draperies as though he could look out. "What's law? Control? Law filters chaos and what drips through? Serenity? Law—our highest ideal and our basest nature. Don't look too closely at the law. Do, and you'll find the rationalized interpretations, the legal casuistry, the precedents of convenience. You'll find the serenity, which is just another word for death."

Chani's mouth drew into a tight line. She couldn't deny his wisdom and sagacity, but these moods frightened her. He turned upon himself and she sensed internal wars. It was as though he took the Fremen maxim, *"Never to forgive—never to forget,"* and whipped his own flesh with it.

She crossed to his side, stared past him at an angle. The growing heat of the day had begun pulling the north wind out of these protected latitudes. The wind painted a false sky full of ochre plumes and sheets of crystal, strange designs in rushing gold and red. High and cold, the wind broke against the Shield Wall with fountains of dust.

Paul felt Chani's warmth beside him. Momentarily, he lowered a curtain of forgetfulness across his vision. He might just be standing here with his eyes closed. Time refused to stand still for him, though. He inhaled darkness—starless, tearless. His affliction dissolved substance until all that remained was astonishment at the way sounds condensed his universe. Everything around him leaned on his lonely sense of hearing, falling back only when he touched objects: the drapery, Chani's hand . . . He caught himself listening for Chani's breaths.

Where was the insecurity of things that were only probable? he asked himself. His mind carried such a burden of mutilated memories. For every instant of reality there existed countless projections, things fated never to be. An invisible self within him remembered the false pasts, their burden threatening at times to overwhelm the present.

Chani leaned against his arm.

He felt his body through her touch: dead flesh carried by time eddies. He reeked of memories that had glimpsed eternity. To see eternity was to be exposed to eternity's whims, oppressed by endless dimensions. The oracle's false immortality demanded retribution: Past and Future became simultaneous.

Once more, the vision arose from its black pit, locked onto him. It was his eyes. It moved his muscles. It guided him into the next moment, the next hour, the next day . . . until he felt himself to be always *there!*

"It's time we were going," Chani said. "The Council . . ."

"Alia will be there to stand in my place."

"Does she know what to do?"

"She knows."

Alia's day began with a guard squadron swarming into

the parade yard below her quarters. She stared down at a scene of frantic confusion, clamorous and intimidating babble. The scene became intelligible only when she recognized the prisoner they'd brought: Korba, the Panegyrist.

She made her morning toilet, moving occasionally to the window, keeping watch on the progress of impatience down there. Her gaze kept straying to Korba. She tried to remember him as the rough and bearded commander of the third wave in the battle of Arrakeen. It was impossible. Korba had become an immaculate fop dressed now in a Parato silk robe of exquisite cut. It lay open to the waist, revealing a beautifully laundered ruff and embroidered undercoat set with green gems. A purple belt gathered the waist. The sleeves poking through the robe's armhole slits had been tailored into rivulet ridges of dark green and black velvet.

A few Naibs had come out to observe the treatment accorded a fellow Fremen. They'd brought on the clamor, exciting Korba to protest his innocence. Alia moved her gaze across the Fremen faces, trying to recapture memories of the original men. The present blotted out the past. They'd all become hedonists, samplers of pleasures most men couldn't even imagine.

Their uneasy glances, she saw, strayed often to the doorway into the chamber where they would meet. They were thinking of Muad'dib's blind-sight, a new manifestation of mysterious powers. By their law, a blind man should be abandoned in the desert, his water given up to Shai-hulud. But eyeless Muad'dib saw them. They disliked buildings, too, and felt vulnerable in space built above the ground. Give them a proper cave cut from rock, then they could relax—but not here, not with this new Muad'dib waiting *inside*.

As she turned to go down to the meeting, she saw the letter where she'd left it on a table by the door: the latest message from their mother. Despite the special reverence held for Caladan as the place of Paul's birth, the Lady Jessica had emphasized her refusal to make her planet a stop on the hajj.

"No doubt my son is an epochal figure of history," she'd written, "but I cannot see this as an excuse for submitting to a rabble invasion."

Alia touched the letter, experienced an odd sensation of mutual contact. This paper had been in her mother's hands. Such an archaic device, the letter—but personal in a way no recording could achieve. Written in the Atreides Battle Tongue, it represented an almost invulnerable privacy of communication.

Thinking of her mother afflicted Alia with the usual inward blurring. The spice change that had mixed the psyches of mother and daughter forced her at times to think of Paul as a son to whom she had given birth. The capsule-complex of oneness could present her own father as a lover. Ghost shadows cavorted in her mind, people of possibility.

Alia reviewed the letter as she walked down the ramp to the antechamber where her guard amazons waited.

"You produce a deadly paradox," Jessica had written. "Government cannot be religious and self-assertive at the same time. Religious experience needs a spontaneity which laws inevitably suppress. And you cannot govern without laws. Your laws eventually must replace morality, replace conscience, replace even the religion by which you think to govern. Sacred ritual must spring from praise and holy yearnings which hammer out a significant morality. Government, on the other hand, is a cultural organism particularly attractive to doubts, questions and contentions. I see the day coming when ceremony must take the place of faith and symbolism replaces morality."

The smell of spice-coffee greeted Alia in the antechamber. Four guard amazons in green watchrobes came to attention as she entered. They fell into step behind her, striding firmly in the bravado of their youth, eyes alert for trouble. They had zealot faces untouched by awe. They radiated that special Fremen quality of violence: they could kill casually with no sense of guilt.

In this, I am different, Alia thought. *The Atreides name has enough dirt on it without that.*

Word preceded her. A waiting page darted off as she entered the lower hall, running to summon the full guard detail. The hall stretched out windowless and gloomy, illuminated only by a few subdued glowglobes. Abruptly, the doors to the parade yard opened wide at the far end to admit a glaring shaft of daylight. The guard with Korba in their midst wavered into view from the outside with the light behind them.

"Where is Stilgar?" Alia demanded.

"Already inside," one of her amazons said.

Alia led the way into the chamber. It was one of the Keep's more pretentious meeting places. A high balcony with rows of soft seats occupied one side. Across from the balcony, orange draperies had been pulled back from tall windows. Bright sunlight poured through from an open space with a garden and a fountain. At the near end of the chamber on her right stood a dais with a single massive chair.

Moving to the chair, Alia glanced back and up, saw the gallery filled with Naibs.

Household guardsmen packed the open space beneath the gallery, Stilgar moving among them with a quiet word here, a command there. He gave no sign that he'd seen Alia enter.

Korba was brought in, seated at a low table with cushions beside it on the chamber floor below the dais. Despite his finery, the Panegyrist gave the appearance now of a surly, sleepy old man huddled up in his robes as against the outer cold. Two guardsmen took up positions behind him.

Stilgar approached the dais as Alia seated herself.

"Where is Muad'dib?" he asked.

"My brother has delegated me to preside as Reverend Mother," Alia said.

Hearing this, the Naibs in the gallery began raising their voices in protest.

"Silence!" Alia commanded. In the abrupt quiet, she said: "Is it not Fremen law that a Reverend Mother presides when life and death are at issue?"

As the gravity of her statement penetrated, stillness came over the Naibs, but Alia marked angry stares across the rows of faces. She named them in her mind for discussion in Council—Hobars, Rajifiri, Tasmin, Saajid, Umbu, Legg...The names carried pieces of Dune in them: Umbu Sietch, Tasmin Sink, Hobars Gap...

She turned her attention to Korba.

Observing her attention, Korba lifted his chin, said: "I protest my innocence."

"Stilgar, read the charges," Alia said.

Stilgar produced a brown spicepaper scroll, stepped forward. He began reading, a solemn flourish in his voice as though to hidden rhythms. He gave the words an incisive quality, clear and full of probity:

"...that you did conspire with traitors to accomplish the destruction of our Lord and Emperor; that you did meet in vile secrecy with diverse enemies of the realm; that you..."

Korba kept shaking his head with a look of pained anger.

Alia listened broodingly, chin planted on her left fist, head cocked to that side, the other arm extended along the chair arm. Bits of the formal procedure began dropping out of her awareness, screened by her own feelings of disquiet.

"...venerable tradition...support of the legions and all Fremen everywhere...violence met with violence according to the Law...majesty of the Imperial Person...forfeit all rights to..."

It was nonsense, she thought. Nonsense! All of

it—nonsense . . . nonsense . . . nonsense . . .

Stilgar finished: "Thus the issue is brought to judgment."

In the immediate silence, Korba rocked forward, hands gripping his knees, veined neck stretched as though he were preparing to leap. His tongue flicked between his teeth as he spoke.

"Not by word or deed have I been traitor to my Fremen vows! I demand to confront my accuser!"

A simple enough protest, Alia thought.

And she saw that it had produced a considerable effect on the Naibs. They knew Korba. He was one of them. To become a Naib, he'd proved his Fremen courage and caution. Not brilliant, Korba, but reliable. Not one to lead a Jihad, perhaps, but a good choice as supply officer. Not a crusader, but one who cherished the old Fremen virtues: *The Tribe is paramount.*

Otheym's bitter words as Paul had recited them swept through Alia's mind. She scanned the gallery. Any of those men might see himself in Korba's place—some for good reason. But an innocent Naib was as dangerous as a guilty one here.

Korba felt it, too. "Who accuses me?" he demanded. "I have a Fremen right to confront my accuser."

"Perhaps you accuse yourself," Alia said.

Before he could mask it, mystical terror lay briefly on Korba's face. It was there for anyone to read: *With her powers, Alia had but to accuse him herself, saying she brought the evidence from the shadow region, the* alam al-mythal.

"Our enemies have Fremen allies," Alia pressed. "Water traps have been destroyed, qanats blasted, plantings poisoned and storage basins plundered . . ."

"And now—they've stolen a worm from the desert, taken it to another world!"

The voice of this intrusion was known to all of them—Muad'dib. Paul came through the doorway from the hall, pressed through the guard ranks and crossed to

Alia's side. Chani, accompanying him, remained on the sidelines.

"M'Lord," Stilgar said, refusing to look at Paul's face.

Paul aimed his empty sockets at the gallery, then down to Korba. "What, Korba—no words of praise?"

Muttering could be heard in the gallery. It grew louder, isolated words and phrases audible: "...law for the blind...Fremen way...in the desert...who breaks..."

"Who says I'm blind?" Paul demanded. He faced the gallery. "You, Rajifiri? I see you're wearing gold today, and that blue shirt beneath it which still has dust on it from the streets. You always were untidy."

Rajifiri made a warding gesture, three fingers against evil.

"Point those fingers at yourself!" Paul shouted. "We know where the evil is!" He turned back to Korba. "There's guilt on your face, Korba."

"Not my guilt! I may've associated with the guilty, but no..." He broke off, shot a frightened look at the gallery.

Taking her cue from Paul, Alia arose, stepped down to the floor of the chamber, advanced to the edge of Korba's table. From a range of less than a meter, she stared down at him, silent and intimidating.

Korba cowered under the burden of eyes. He fidgeted, shot anxious glances at the gallery.

"Whose eyes do you seek up there?" Paul asked.

"You cannot see!" Korba blurted.

Paul put down a momentary feeling of pity for Korba. The man lay trapped in the vision's snare as securely as any of those present. He played a part, no more.

"I don't need eyes to see you," Paul said. And he began describing Korba, every movement, every twitch, every alarmed and pleading look at the gallery.

Desperation grew in Korba.

Watching him, Alia saw he might break any second. Someone in the gallery must realize how near he was to breaking, she thought. Who? She studied the faces of the Naibs, noting small betrayals in the masked faces

... angers, fears, uncertainties ... guilts.

Paul felt silent.

Korba mustered a pitiful air of pomposity to plead: "Who accuses me?"

"Otheym accuses you," Alia said.

"But Otheym's dead!" Korba protested.

"How did you know that?" Paul asked. "Through your spy system? Oh, yes! We know about your spies and couriers. We know who brought the stone burner here from Tarahell."

"It was for the defense of the Qizarate!" Korba blurted.

"Is that how it got into traitorous hands?" Paul asked.

"It was stolen and we ..." Korba fell silent, swallowed. His gaze darted left and right. "Everyone knows I've been the voice of love for Muad'dib." He stared at the gallery. "How can a dead man accuse a Fremen?"

"Otheym's voice isn't dead," Alia said. She stopped as Paul touched her arm.

"Otheym sent us his voice," Paul said. "It gives the names, the acts of treachery, the meeting places and the times. Do you miss certain faces in the Council of Naibs, Korba? Where are Merkur and Fash? Keke the Lame isn't with us today. And Takim, where is he?"

Korba shook his head from side to side.

"They've fled Arrakis with the stolen worm," Paul said. "Even if I freed you now, Korba, Shai-hulud would have your water for your part in this. Why don't I free you, Korba? Think of all those men whose eyes were taken, the men who cannot see as I see. They have families and friends, Korba. Where could you hide from them?"

"It was an accident," Korba pleaded. "Anyway, they're getting Tleilaxu ..." Again, he subsided.

"Who knows what bondage goes with metal eyes?" Paul asked.

The Naibs in their gallery began exchanging whispered comments, speaking behind raised hands. They gazed coldly at Korba now.

"Defense of the Qizarate," Paul murmured, returning

to Korba's plea. "A device which either destroys a planet or produces J-rays to blind those too near it. Which effect, Korba, did you conceive as a defense? Does the Qizarate rely on stopping the eyes of all observers?"

"It was a curiosity, m'Lord," Korba pleaded. "We knew the Old Law said that only Families could possess atomics, but the Qizarate obeyed ... obeyed ..."

"Obeyed you," Paul said. "A curiosity, indeed."

"Even if it's only the voice of my accuser, you must face me with it!" Korba said. "A Fremen has rights."

"He speaks truth, Sire," Stilgar said.

Alia glanced sharply at Stilgar.

"The law is the law," Stilgar said, sensing Alia's protest. He began quoting Fremen Law, interspersing his own comments on how the Law pertained.

Alia experienced the odd sensation she was hearing Stilgar's words before he spoke them. How could he be this credulous? Stilgar had never appeared more official and conservative, more intent on adhering to the Dune Code. His chin was outthrust, aggressive. His mouth chopped. Was there really nothing in him but this outrageous pomposity?

"Korba is a Fremen and must be judged by Fremen Law," Stilgar concluded.

Alia turned away, looked out at the day shadows dropping down the wall across from the garden. She felt drained by frustration. They'd dragged this thing along well into midmorning. Now, what? Korba had relaxed. The Panegyrist's manner said he'd suffered an unjust attack, that everything he'd done had been for love of Muad'dib. She glanced at Korba, surprised a look of sly self-importance sliding across his face.

He might almost have received a message, she thought. He acted the part of a man who'd heard friends shout: *"Hold fast! Help is on its way!"*

For an instant, they'd held this thing in their hands—the information out of the dwarf, the clues that others were in the plot, the names of informants. But the

critical moment had flown. *Stilgar? Surely not Stilgar.*
She turned, stared at the old Fremen.

Stilgar met her gaze without flinching.

"Thank you, Stil," Paul said. "for reminding us of the
Law."

Stilgar inclined his head. He moved close, shaped silent
words in a way he knew both Paul and Alia could read. *I'll
wring him dry and then take care of the matter.*

Paul nodded, signaled the guardsmen behind Korba.

"Remove Korba to a maximum security cell," Paul
said. "No visitors except counsel. As counsel, I appoint
Stilgar."

"Let me choose my own counsel!" Korba shouted.

Paul whirled. "You deny the fairness and judgment of
Stilgar?"

"Oh, no, m'Lord, but..."

"Take him away!" Paul barked.

The guardsmen lifted Korba off the cushions, herded
him out.

With new mutterings, the Naibs began quitting their
gallery. Attendants came from beneath the gallery,
crossed to the windows and drew the orange draperies.
Orange gloom took over the chamber.

"Paul," Alia said.

"When we precipitate violence," Paul said. "it'll be
when we have full control of it. Thank you, Stil; you
played your part well. Alia, I'm certain, has identified the
Naibs who were with him. They couldn't help giving
themselves away."

"You cooked this up between you?" Alia demanded.

"Had I ordered Korba slain out of hand, the Naibs
would have understood," Paul said. "But this formal
procedure without strict adherence to Fremen Law—they
felt their own rights threatened. Which Naibs were with
him, Alia?"

"Rajifiri for certain," she said, voice low. "And Saajid,
but..."

"Give Stilgar the complete list," Paul said.

Alia swallowed in a dry throat, sharing the general fear of Paul in this moment. She knew how he moved among them without eyes, but the delicacy of it daunted her. To see their forms in the air of his vision! She sensed her person shimmering for him in a sidereal time whose accord with reality depended entirely on his words and actions. He held them all in the palm of his vision!

"It's past time for your morning audience, Sire," Stilgar said. "Many people—curious... afraid..."

"Are you afraid, Stil?"

It was barely a whisper: "Yes."

"You're my friend and have nothing to fear from me," Paul said.

Stilgar swallowed. "Yes, m'Lord."

"Alia, take the morning audience," Paul said. "Stilgar, give the signal."

Stilgar obeyed.

A flurry of movement erupted at the great doors. A crowd was pressed back from the shadowy room to permit entrance of officials. Many things began happening all at once: the household guard elbowing and shoving back the press of Supplicants, garishly robed Pleaders trying to break through, shouts, curses. Pleaders waved the papers of their calling. The Clerk of the Assemblage strode ahead of them through the opening cleared by the guard. He carried the List of Preferences, those who'd be permitted to approach the Throne. The Clerk, a wiry Fremen named Tecrube, carried himself with weary cynicism, flaunting his shaven head, clumped whiskers.

Alia moved to intercept him, giving Paul time to slip away with Chani through the private passage behind the dais. She experienced a momentary distrust of Tecrube at the prying curiosity in the stare he sent after Paul.

"I speak for my brother today," she said. "Have the Supplicants approach one at a time."

"Yes, m'Lady." He turned to arrange his throng.

"I can remember a time when you wouldn't have mistaken your brother's purpose here," Stilgar said.

"I was distracted," she said. "There's been a dramatic change in you, Stil. What is it?"

Stilgar drew himself up, shocked. One changed, of course. But dramatically? This was a particular view of himself that he'd never encountered. Drama was a questionable thing. Imported entertainers of dubious loyalty and more dubious virtue were dramatic. Enemies of the Empire employed drama in their attempts to sway the fickle populace. Korba had slipped away from Fremen virtues to employ drama for the Qizarate. And he'd die for that.

"You're being perverse," Stilgar said. "Do you distrust me?"

The distress in his voice softened her expression, but not her tone. "You *know* I don't distrust you. I've always agreed with my brother that once matters were in Stilgar's hands we could safely forget them."

"Then why do you say I've...changed?"

"You're preparing to disobey my brother," she said. "I can read it in you. I only hope it doesn't destroy you both."

The first of the Pleaders and Supplicants were approaching now. She turned away before Stilgar could respond. His face, though, was filled with the things she'd sensed in her mother's letter—the replacement of morality and conscience with law.

"You produce a deadly paradox."

Tibana was an apologist for Socratic Christianity, probably a native of IV Anbus who lived between the eight and ninth centuries before Corrino, likely in the second reign of Dalamak. Of his writings, only a portion survives from which this fragment is taken: "The hearts of all men dwell in the same wilderness."

—from The Dunebuk of Irulan

"You are Bijaz," the ghola said, entering the small chamber where the dwarf was held under guard. "I am called Hayt."

A strong contingent of the household guard had come in with the ghola to take over the evening watch. Sand carried by the sunset wind had stung their cheeks while they crossed the outer yard, made them blink and hurry. They could be heard in the passage outside now exchanging the banter and ritual of their tasks.

"You are not Hayt," the dwarf said. "You are Duncan Idaho. I was there when they put your dead flesh into the tank and I was there when they removed it, alive and ready for training."

The ghola swallowed in a throat suddenly dry. The bright glowglobes of the chamber lost their yellowness in the room's green hangings. The light showed beads of perspiration on the dwarf's forehead. Bijaz seemed a creature of odd integrity, as though the purpose fashioned into him by the Tleilaxu were projected out through his skin. There was power beneath the dwarf's mask of cowardice and frivolity.

"Muad'dib has charged me to question you to determine what it is the Tleilaxu intend you to do here," Hayt said.

"Tleilaxu, Tleilaxu," the dwarf sang. "I am the Tleilaxu, you dolt! For that matter, so are you."

Hayt stared at the dwarf. Bijaz radiated a charismatic alertness that made the observer think of ancient idols.

"You hear that guard outside?" Hayt asked. "If I gave them the order, they'd strangle you."

"Hai! Hai!" Bijaz cried. "What a callous lout you've become. And you said you came seeking truth."

Hayt found he didn't like the look of secret repose beneath the dwarf's expression. "Perhaps I only seek the future," he said.

"Well spoken," Bijaz said. "Now we know each other. When two thieves meet they need no introduction."

"So we're thieves," Hayt said. "What do we steal?"

"Not thieves, but dice," Bijaz said. "And you came here to read my spots. I, in turn, read yours. And lo! You have two faces!"

"Did you really see me go into the Tleilaxu tanks?" Hayt asked, fighting an odd reluctance to ask that question.

"Did I not say it?" Bijaz demanded. The dwarf bounced to his feet. "We had a terrific struggle with you. The flesh did not want to come back."

Hayt felt suddenly that he existed in a dream controlled by some other mind, and that he might momentarily forget this to become lost in the convolutions of that mind.

Bijaz tipped his head slyly to one side, walked all around the ghola, staring up at him. "Excitement kindles old patterns in you," Bijaz said. "You are the pursuer who doesn't want to find what he pursues."

"You're a weapon aimed at Muad'dib," Hayt said, swiveling to follow the dwarf. "What is it you're to do?"

"Nothing!" Bijaz said, stopping. "I give you a common answer to a common question."

"Then you were aimed at Alia," Hayt said. "Is she your target?"

"They call her Hawt, the Fish Monster, on the out-worlds," Bijaz said. "How is it I hear your blood boiling when you speak of her?"

"So they call her Hawt," the ghola said, studying Bijaz for any clue to his purpose. The dwarf made such odd responses.

"She is the virgin-harlot," Bijaz said. "She is vulgar, witty, knowledgeable to a depth that terrifies, cruel when she is most kind, unthinking while she thinks, and when she seeks to build she is as destructive as a coriolis storm."

"So you came here to speak out against Alia," Hayt said.

"Against her?" Bijaz sank to a cushion against the wall. "I came here to be captured by the magnetism of her physical beauty." He grinned, a saurian expression in the big-featured face.

"To attack Alia is to attack her brother," Hayt said.

"That is so clear it is difficult to see," Bijaz said. "In truth, Emperor and sister are one person back to back, one being half male and half female."

"That is a thing we've heard said by the Fremen of the deep desert," Hayt said. "And those are the ones who've revived the blood sacrifice to Shai-hulud. How is it you repeat their nonsense?"

"You dare say nonsense?" Bijaz demanded. "You, who are both man and mask? Ahh, but the dice cannot read their own spots. I forget this. And you are doubly confused because you serve the Atreides double-being. Your senses are not as close to the answer as your mind is."

"Do you preach that false ritual about Muad'dib to your guards?" Hayt asked, his voice low. He felt his mind being tangled by the dwarf's words.

"They preach to me!" Bijaz said. "And they pray. Why should they not? All of us should pray. Do we not live in the shadow of the most dangerous creation the universe has ever seen?"

"Dangerous creation..."

"Their own mother refuses to live on the same planet with them!"

"Why don't you answer me straight out?" Hayt demanded. "You know we have other ways of questioning you. We'll get our answers...one way or another."

"But I have answered you! Have I not said the myth is real? Am I the wind that carries death in its belly? No! I am words! Such words as the lightning which strikes from the sand in a dark sky. I have said: 'Blow out the lamp! Day is here!' And you keep saying: 'Give me a lamp so I can find the day.'"

"You play a dangerous game with me," Hayt said. "Did you think I could not understand these Zensunni ideas? You leave tracks as clear as those of a bird in mud."

Bijaz began to giggle.

"Why do you laugh?" Hayt demanded.

"Because I have teeth and wish I had not," Bijaz managed between giggles. "Having no teeth, I could not gnash them."

"And now I know your target," Hayt said. "You were aimed at me."

"And I've hit it right on!" Bijaz said. "You made such a big target, how could I miss?" He nodded as though to himself. "Now I will sing to you." He began to hum, a keening, whining monotonous theme, repeated over and over.

Hayt stiffened, experiencing odd pains that played up and down his spine. He stared at the face of the dwarf, seeing youthful eyes in an old face. The eyes were the center of a network of knobby white lines which ran to the hollows below his temples. Such a large head! Every feature focused on the pursed-up mouth from which that monotonous noise issued. The sound made Hayt think of ancient rituals, folk memories, old words and customs, half-forgotten meanings in lost mutterings. Something vital was happening here—a bloody play of ideas across Time. Elder ideas lay tangled in the dwarf's singing. It was like a blazing light in the distance, coming nearer and nearer, illuminating life across a span of centuries.

"What are you doing to me?" Hayt gasped.

"You are the instrument I was taught to play," Bijaz said. "I am playing you. Let me tell you the names of the other traitors among the Naibs. They are Bikouros and Cahueit. There is Djedida, who was secretary to Korba. There is Abumojandis, the aide to Bannerjee. Even now, one of them could be sinking a blade into your Muad'dib."

Hayt shook his head from side to side. He found it too difficult to talk.

"We are like brothers," Bijaz said, interrupting his monotonous hum once more. "We grew in the same tank: I first and then you."

Hayt's metal eyes inflicted him with a sudden burning pain. Flickering red haze surrounded everything he saw. He felt he had been cut away from every immediate sense except the pain, and he experienced his surroundings through a thin separation like windblown gauze. All had become accident, the chance involvement of inanimate matter. His own will was no more than a subtle, shifting thing. It lived without breath and was intelligible only as an inward illumination.

With a clarity born of desperation, he broke through

the gauze curtain with the lonely sense of sight. His attention focused like a blazing light under Bijaz. Hayt felt that his eyes cut through layers of the dwarf, seeing the little man as a hired intellect, and beneath that, a creature imprisoned by hungers and cravings which lay huddled in the eyes—layer after layer, until finally, there was only an entity-aspect being manipulated by symbols.

"We are upon a battleground," Bijaz said. "You may speak of it."

His voice freed by the command, Hayt said: "You cannot force me to slay Muad'dib."

"I have heard the Bene Gesserit say," Bijaz said, "that there is nothing firm, nothing balanced, nothing durable in all the universe—that nothing remains in its state, that each day, sometimes each hour, brings change."

Hayt shook his head dumbly from side to side.

"You believed the silly Emperor was the prize we sought," Bijaz said. "How little you understand our masters, the Tleilaxu. The Guild and Bene Gesserit believe we produce artifacts. In reality, we produce tools and services. Anything can be a tool—poverty, war. War is useful because it is effective in so many areas. It stimulates the metabolism. It enforces government. It diffuses genetic strains. It possesses a vitality such as nothing else in the universe. Only those who recognize the value of war and exercise it have any degree of self-determination."

In an oddly placid voice, Hayt said: "Strange thoughts coming from you, almost enough to make me believe in a vengeful Providence. What restitution was exacted to create you? It would make a fascinating story, doubtless with an even more extraordinary epilogue."

"Magnificent!" Bijaz chortled. "You attack—therefore you have willpower and exercise self-determination."

"You're trying to awaken violence in me," Hayt said in a panting voice.

Bijaz denied this with a shake of the head. "Awaken, yes; violence, no. You are a disciple of awareness by training, so you have said. I have an awareness to awaken in you, Duncan Idaho."

"Hayt!"

"Duncan Idaho. Killer extraordinary. Lover of many women. Swordsman soldier. Atreides field-hand on the field of battle. Duncan Idaho."

"The past cannot be awakened."

"Cannot?"

"It has never been done!"

"True, but our masters defy the idea that something cannot be done. Always, they seek the proper tool, the right application of effort, the services of the proper—"

"You hide your real purpose! You throw up a screen of words and they mean nothing!"

"There is a Duncan Idaho in you," Bijaz said. "It will submit to emotion or to dispassionate examination, but submit it will. This awareness will rise through a screen of suppression and selection out of the dark past which dogs your footsteps. It goads you even now while it holds you back. There exists that being within you upon which awareness must focus and which you will obey."

"The Tleilaxu think I'm still their slave, but I—"

"Quiet, slave!" Bijaz said in that whining voice.

Hayt found himself frozen in silence.

"Now we are down to bedrock," Bijaz said. "I know you feel it. And these are the power-words to manipulate you . . . I think they will have sufficient leverage."

Hayt felt the perspiration pouring down his cheeks, the trembling of his chest and arms, but he was powerless to move.

"One day," Bijaz said, "the Emperor will come to you. He will say: 'She is gone.' The grief mask will occupy his face. He will give water to the dead, as they call their tears hereabouts. And you will say, using my voice: 'Master! Oh, Master!'"

Hayt's jaw and throat ached with the locking of his muscles. He could only twist his head in a brief arc from side to side.

"You will say, 'I carry a message from Bijaz.'" The
dwarf grimaced. "Poor Bijaz, who has no mind . . . poor
Bijaz, a drum stuffed with messages, an essence for others
to use . . . pound on Bijaz and he produces a noise . . ."

Again, he grimaced. "You think me a hypocrite,
Duncan Idaho! I am not! I can grieve, too. But the time
has come to substitute swords for words."

A hiccup shook Hayt.

Bijaz giggled, then: "Ah, thank you, Duncan, thank
you. The demands of the body save us. As the Emperor
carries the blood of the Harkonnens in his veins, he will
do as we demand. He will turn into a spitting machine, a
biter of words that ring with a lovely noise to our
masters."

Hayt blinked, thinking how the dwarf appeared like an
alert little animal, a thing of spite and rare intelligence.
Harkonnen blood in the Atreides?

"You think of Beast Rabban, the vile Harkonnen, and
you glare," Bijaz said. "You are like the Fremen in this.
When words fail, the sword is always at hand, eh? You
think of the torture inflicted upon your family by the
Harkonnens. And, through his mother, your precious
Paul is a Harkonnen! You would not find it difficult to
slay a Harkonnen, now would you?"

Bitter frustration coursed through the ghola. Was it
anger? Why should this cause anger?

"Ohhh," Bijaz said, and: "Ahhhh, hah! Click-click.
There is more to the message. It is a trade the Tleilaxu
offer your precious Paul Atreides. Our masters will
restore his beloved. A sister to yourself—another ghola."

Hayt felt suddenly that he existed in a universe
occupied only by his own heartbeats.

"A ghola," Bijaz said. "It will be the flesh of his
beloved. She will bear his children. She will love only him.
We can even improve on the original if he so desires. Did
ever a man have greater opportunity to regain what he'd
lost? It is a bargain he will leap to strike."

Bijaz nodded, eyes drooping as though tiring. Then:

"He will be tempted . . . and in his distraction, you will move close. In the instant, you will strike! Two gholas, not one! That is what our masters demand!" The dwarf cleared his throat, nodded once more, said: "Speak."

"I will not do it," Hayt said.

"But Duncan Idaho would," Bijaz said. "It will be the moment of supreme vulnerability for this descendant of the Harkonnens. Do not forget this. You will suggest improvements to his beloved—perhaps a deathless heart, gentler emotions. You will offer asylum as you move close to him—a planet of his choice somewhere beyond the Imperium. Think of it! His beloved restored. No more need for tears, and a place of idyls to live out his years."

"A costly package," Hayt said, probing. "He'll ask the price."

"Tell him he must renounce his godhead and discredit The Qizarate. He must discredit himself, his sister."

"Nothing more?" Hayt asked, sneering.

"He must relinquish his CHOAM holdings, naturally."

"Naturally."

"And if you're not yet close enough to strike, speak of how much the Tleilaxu admire what he has taught them about the possibilities of religion. Tell him the Tleilaxu have a department of religious engineering, shaping religions to particular needs."

"How very clever," Hayt said.

"You think yourself free to sneer and disobey me," Bijaz said. He cocked his head slyly to one side. "Don't deny it . . ."

"They made you well, little animal," Hayt said.

"And you as well," the dwarf said. "You will tell him to hurry. Flesh decays and her flesh must be preserved in a cryological tank."

Hayt felt himself floundering, caught in a matrix of objects he could not recognize. The dwarf appeared so sure of himself! There had to be a flaw in the Tleilaxu logic. In making their ghola, they'd keyed him to the voice of Bijaz, but . . . But what? Logic / matrix / object . . . How easy it was to mistake clear reasoning for correct reasoning! Was Tleilaxu logic distorted?

Bijaz smiled, listened as though to a hidden voice. "Now, you will forget," he said. "When the moment comes, you will remember. He will say: 'She is gone.' Duncan Idaho will awaken then."

The dwarf clapped his hands together.

Hayt grunted, feeling that he had been interrupted in the middle of a thought . . . or perhaps in the middle of a sentence. What was it? Something about . . . targets?

"You think to confuse me and manipulate me," he said.

"How is that?" Bijaz asked.

"I am your target and you can't deny it," Hayt said.

"I would not think of denying it."

"What is it you'd try to do with me?"

"A kindness," Bijaz said. "A simple kindness."

The sequential nature of actual events is not illuminated with lengthy precision by the powers of prescience except under the most extraordinary circumstances. The oracle grasps incidents cut out of the historic chain. Eternity moves. It inflicts itself upon the oracle and the supplicant alike. Let Muad'dib's subjects doubt his majesty and his oracular visions. Let them deny his powers. Let them never doubt Eternity.

—The Dune Gospels

Hayt watched Alia emerge from her temple and cross the plaza. Her guard was bunched close, fierce expressions on their faces to mask the lines molded by good living and complacency.

A heliograph of 'thopter wings flashed in the bright afternoon sun above the temple, part of the Royal Guard with Muad'dib's fist-symbol on its fusilage.

Hayt returned his gaze to Alia. She looked out of place
here in the city, he thought. Her proper setting was the
desert—open, untrammeled space. An odd thing about
her came back to him as he watched her approach: Alia
appeared thoughtful only when she smiled. It was a trick
of the eyes, he decided, recalling a cameo memory of her
as she'd appeared at the reception for the Guild
Ambassador: haughty against a background of music and
brittle conversation among extravagant gowns and
uniforms. And Alia had been wearing white, dazzling, a
bright garment of chastity. He had looked down upon her
from a window as she crossed an inner garden with its
formal pond, its fluting fountains, fronds of pampas grass
and a white belvedere.

Entirely wrong...all wrong. She belonged in the
desert.

Hayt drew in a ragged breath. Alia had moved out of
his view then as she did now. He waited, clenching and
unclenching his fists. The interview with Bijaz had left
him uneasy.

He heard Alia's entourage pass outside the room where
he waited. She went into the Family quarters.

Now he tried to focus on the thing about her which
troubled him. The way she'd walked across the plaza?
Yes. She'd moved like a hunted creature fleeing some
predator. He stepped out onto the connecting balcony,
walked along it behind the plasmeld sunscreen, stopped
while still in concealing shadows. Alia stood at the
balustrade overlooking her temple.

He looked where she was looking—out over the city.
He saw rectangles, blocks of color, creeping movements
of life and sound. Structures gleamed, shimmered. Heat
patterns spiraled off the rooftops. There was a boy across
the way bouncing a ball in a cul-de-sac formed by a
buttressed massif at a corner of the temple. Back and
forth the ball went.

Alia, too, watched the ball. She felt a compelling
identity with that ball—back and forth...back and forth.

She sensed herself bouncing through corridors of Time.

The potion of melange she'd drained just before leaving the temple was the largest she'd ever attempted—a massive overdose. Even before beginning to take effect, it had terrified her.

Why did I do it? she asked herself.

"One made a choice between dangers. Was that it? This was the way to penetrate the fog spread over the future by that damnable Dune Tarot. A barrier existed. It must be breached. She had acted out of a necessity to see where it was her brother walked with his eyeless stride.

The familiar melange fugue state began creeping into her awareness. She took a deep breath, experienced a brittle form of calm, poised and selfless.

Possession of second sight has a tendency to make one a dangerous fatalist, she thought. Unfortunately, there existed no abstract leverage, no calculus of prescience. Visions of the future could not be manipulated as formulas. One had to enter them, risking life and sanity.

A figure moved from the harsh shadows of the adjoining balcony. The ghola! In her heightened awareness, Alia saw him with intense clarity—the dark, lively features dominated by those glistening metal eyes. He was a union of terrifying opposites, something put together in a shocking linear way. He was shadow and blazing light, a product of the process which had revived his dead flesh . . . and of something intensely pure . . . innocent.

He was innocence under siege!

"Have you been there all along, Duncan?" she asked.

"So I'm to be Duncan," he said. "Why?"

"Don't question me," she said.

And she thought, looking at him, that the Tleilaxu had left no corner of their ghola unfinished.

"Only gods can safely risk perfection," she said. "It's a dangerous thing for a man."

"Duncan died," he said, wishing she would not call him that. "I am Hayt."

She studied his artificial eyes, wondering what they

saw. Observed closely, they betrayed tiny black pock-
marks, little wells of darkness in the glittering metal.
Facets! The universe shimmered around her and lurched.
She steadied herself with a hand on the sun-warmed
surface of the balustrade. Ahhh, the melange moved
swiftly.

"Are you ill?" Hayt asked. He moved closer, the steely
eyes opened wide, staring.

Who spoke? she wondered. Was it Duncan Idaho? Was
it the mentat-ghola or the Zensunni philosopher? Or was
it a Tleilaxu pawn more dangerous than any Guild
Steersman? Her brother knew.

Again, she looked at the ghola. There was something
inactive about him now, a latent something. He was
saturated with waiting and with powers beyond their
common life.

"Out of my mother, I am like the Bene Gesserit," she
said. "Do you know that?"

"I know it."

"I use their powers, think as they think. Part of me
knows the sacred urgency of the breeding program . . . and
its products."

She blinked, feeling part of her awareness begin to
move freely in Time.

"It's said that the Bene Gesserit never let go," he said.
And he watched her closely, noting how white her
knuckles were where she gripped the edge of the balcony.

"Have I stumbled?" she asked.

He marked how deeply she breathed, with tension in
every movement, the glazed appearance of her eyes.

"When you stumble," he said, "you may regain your
balance by jumping beyond the thing that tripped you."

"The Bene Gesserit stumbled," she said. "Now they
wish to regain their balance by leaping beyond my
brother. They want Chani's baby . . . or mine."

"Are you with child?"

She struggled to fix herself in a timespace relationship
to this question. With child? When? Where?

"I see . . . my child," she whispered.

She moved away from the balcony's edge, turned her head to look at the ghola. He had a face of salt, bitter eyes—two circles of glistening lead . . . and, as he turned away from the light to follow her movement, blue shadows.

"What . . . do you see with such eyes?" she whispered.

"What other eyes see," he said.

His words rang in her ears, stretching her awareness. She felt that she reached across the universe—such a stretching . . . out . . . out. She lay intertwined with all Time.

"You've taken the spice, a large dose," he said.

"Why can't I see him?" she muttered. The womb of all creation held her captive. "Tell me, Duncan, why I cannot see him."

"Who can't you see?"

"I cannot see the father of my children. I'm lost in a Tarot fog. Help me."

Mentat logic offered its prime computation, and he said: "The Bene Gesserit want a mating between you and your brother. It would lock the genetic . . ."

A wail escaped her. "The egg in the flesh," she gasped. A sensation of chill swept over her, followed by intense heat. The unseen mate of her darkest dreams! Flesh of her flesh that the oracle could not reveal—would it come to that?

"Have you risked a dangerous dose of the spice?" he asked. Something within him fought to express the utmost terror at the thought that an Atreides woman might die, that Paul might face him with the knowledge that a female of the royal family had . . . gone.

"You don't know what it's like to hunt the future," she said. "Sometimes I glimpse myself . . . but I get in my own way. I cannot see through myself." She lowered her head, shook it from side to side.

"How much of the spice did you take?" he asked.

"Nature abhors prescience," she said, raising her head. "Did you know that, Duncan?"

He spoke softly, reasonably, as to a small child: "Tell

me how much of the spice you took." He took hold of her
shoulder with his left hand.

"Words are such gross machinery, so primitive and
ambiguous," she said. She pulled away from his hand.

"You must tell me," he said.

"Look at the Shield Wall," she commanded, pointing.
She sent her gaze along her own outstretched hand,
trembled as the landscape crumbled in an overwhelming
vision—a sandcastle destroyed by invisible waves. She
averted her eyes, was transfixed by the appearance of the
ghola's face. His features crawled, became aged, then
young . . . aged . . . young. He was life itself, assertive,
endless . . . She turned to flee, but he grabbed her left
wrist.

"I am going to summon a doctor," he said.

"No! You must let me have the vision! I have to know!"

"You are going inside now," he said.

She stared down at his hand. Where their flesh
touched, she felt an electric presence that both lured and
frightened her. She jerked free, gasped: "You can't hold
the whirlwind!"

"You must have medical help!" he snapped.

"Don't you understand?" she demanded. "My vision's
incomplete, just fragments. It flickers and jumps. I have
to remember the future. Can't you see that?"

"What is the future if you die?" he asked, forcing her
gently into the Family chambers.

"Words . . . words," she muttered. "I can't explain it.
One thing is the occasion of another thing, but there's no
cause . . . no effect. We can't leave the universe as it was.
Try as we may, there's a gap."

"Stretch out here," he commanded.

He is so dense! she thought.

Cool shadows enveloped her. She felt her own muscles
crawling like worms—a firm bed that she knew to be
insubstantial. Only space was permanent. Nothing else
had substance. The bed flowed with many bodies, all of
them her own. Time became a multiple sensation,

overloaded. It presented no single reaction for her to abstract. It was Time. It moved. The whole universe slipped backward, forward, sideways.

"It has no thing-aspect," she explained. "You can't get under it or around it. There's no place to get leverage."

There came a fluttering of people all around her. Many someones held her left hand. She looked at her own moving flesh, followed a twining arm out to a fluid mask of face: Duncan Idaho! His eyes were . . . wrong, but it was Duncan — child -man -adolescent - child -man -adolescent . . . Every line of his features betrayed concern for her.

"Duncan, don't be afraid," she whispered.

He squeezed her hand, nodded. "Be still," he said.

And he thought: *She must not die! She must not! No Atreides woman can die!* He shook his head sharply. Such thoughts defied mentat logic. Death was a necessity that life might continue.

The ghola loves me, Alia thought.

The thought became bedrock to which she might cling. He was a familiar face with a solid room behind him. She recognized one of the bedrooms in Paul's suite.

A fixed, immutable person did something with a tube in her throat. She fought against retching.

"We got her in time," a voice said, and she recognized the tones of a Family medic. "You should've called me sooner." There was suspicion in the medic's voice. She felt the tube slide out of her throat—a snake, a shimmering cord.

"The slapshot will make her sleep," the medic said. "I'll send one of her attendants to—"

"I will stay with her," the ghola said.

"That is not seemly!" the medic snapped.

"Stay . . . Duncan," Alia whispered.

He stroked her hand to tell her he'd heard.

"M'Lady," the medic said, "it'd be better if . . ."

"You do not tell me what is best," she rasped. Her throat ached with each syllable.

"M'Lady," the medic said, voice accusing, "*you* know

the dangers of consuming too much melange. I can only assume someone gave it to you without—"

"You are a fool," she rasped. "Would you deny me my visions? I knew what I took and why." She put a hand to her throat. "Leave us. At once!"

The medic pulled out of her field of vision, said: "I will send word to your brother."

She felt him leave, turned her attention to the ghola. The vision lay clearly in her awareness now, a culture medium in which the present grew outward. She sensed the ghola move in that play of Time, no longer cryptic, fixed now against a recognizable background.

He is the crucible, she thought. *He is danger and salvation.*

And she shuddered, knowing she saw the vision of her brother had seen. Unwanted tears burned her eyes. She shook her head sharply. No tears! They wasted moisture and, worse, distracted the harsh flow of vision. Paul must be stopped! Once, just once, she had bridged Time to place her voice where he would pass. But stress and mutability would not permit that here. The web of Time passed through her brother now like rays of light through a lens. He stood at the focus and he knew it. He had gathered all the lines to himself and would not permit them to escape or change.

"Why?" she muttered. "Is it hate? Does he strike out at Time itself because it hurt him? Is that it . . . hate?"

Thinking he heard her speak his name, the ghola said: "M'Lady?"

"If I could only burn this thing out of me!" she cried. "I didn't want to be different."

"Please, Alia," he murmured. "Let yourself sleep."

"I wanted to be able to laugh," she whispered. Tears slid down her cheeks. "But I'm sister to an Emperor who's worshipped as a god. People fear me. I never wanted to be feared."

He wiped the tears from her face.

"I don't want to be part of history," she whispered. "I

just want to be loved ... and to love."

"You are loved," he said.

"Ahhh, loyal, loyal Duncan," she said.

"Please, don't call me that," he pleaded.

"But you are," she said. "And loyalty is a valued commodity. It can be sold ... not bought, but sold."

"I don't like your cynicism," he said.

"Damn your logic! It's true!"

"Sleep," he said.

"Do you love me, Duncan?" she asked.

"Yes."

"Is that one of those lies," she asked, "one of the lies that are easier to believe than the truth? Why am I afraid to believe you?"

"You fear my differences as you fear your own."

"Be a man, not a mentat!" she snarled.

"I am a mentat and a man."

"Will you make me your woman, then?"

"I will do what love demands."

"And loyalty?"

"And loyalty."

"That's where you're dangerous," she said.

Her words disturbed him. No sign of the disturbance arose to his face, no muscle trembled—but she knew it. Vision-memory exposed the disturbance. She felt she had missed part of the vision, though, that she should remember something else from the future. There existed another perception which did not go precisely by the senses, a thing which fell into her head from nowhere the way prescience did. It lay in the Time shadows—infinitely painful.

Emotion! That was it—emotion! It had appeared in the vision, not directly, but as a product from which she could infer what lay behind. She had been possessed by emotion—a single constriction made up of fear, grief and love. They lay there in the vision, all collected into a single epidemic body, overpowering and primordial.

"Duncan, don't let me go," she whispered.

"Sleep," he said. "Don't fight it."

"I must . . . I must. He's the bait in his own trap. He's the servant of power and terror. Violence . . . deification is a prison enclosing him. He'll lose . . . everything. It'll tear him apart."

"You speak of Paul?"

"They drive him to destroy himself," she gasped, arching her back. "Too much weight, too much grief. They seduce him away from love." She sank back to the bed. "They're creating a universe where he won't permit himself to live."

"Who is doing this?"

"He is! Ohhh, you're so dense. He's part of the pattern. And it's too late . . . too late . . . too late . . ."

As she spoke, she felt her awareness descend, layer by layer. It came to rest directly behind her navel. Body and mind separated and merged in a storehouse of relic visions—moving, moving . . . She heard a fetal heartbeat, a child of the future. The melange still possessed her, then, setting her adrift in Time. She knew she had tasted the life of a child not yet conceived. One thing certain about this child—it would suffer the same awakening she had suffered. It would be an aware, thinking entity before birth.

*There exists a limit to the force even the most powerful
may apply without destroying themselves. Judging this
limit is the true artistry of government. Misuse of power is
the fatal sin. The law cannot be a tool of vengeance, never
a hostage, nor a fortification against the martyrs it has
created. You cannot threaten any individual and escape
the consequences.*

—Muad'dib on Law
The Stilgar Commentary

Chani stared out at the morning desert framed in the
fault cleft below Sietch Tabr. She wore no stillsuit, and
this made her feel unprotected here in the desert. The
sietch grotto's entrance lay hidden in the buttressed cliff
above and behind her.

The desert . . . the desert . . . She felt that the desert had
followed her wherever she had gone. Coming back to the

desert was not so much a homecoming as a turning around to see what had always been there.

A painful constriction surged through her abdomen. The birth would be soon. She fought down the pain, wanting this moment alone with her desert.

Dawn stillness gripped the land. Shadows fled among the dunes and terraces of the Shield Wall all around. Daylight lunged over the high scarp and plunged her up to her eyes in a bleak landscape stretching beneath a washed blue sky. The scene matched the feeling of dreadful cynicism which had tormented her since the moment she'd learned of Paul's blindness.

Why are we here? she wondered.

It was not a hajra, a journey of seeking. Paul sought nothing here except, perhaps, a place for her to give birth. He had summoned odd companions for this journey, she thought—Bijaz, the Tleilaxu dwarf; the ghola, Hayt, who might be Duncan Idaho's revenant; Edric, the Guild Steersman-Ambassador; Gaius Helen Mohiam, the Bene Gesserit Reverend Mother he so obviously hated; Lichna, Otheym's strange daughter, who seemed unable to move beyond the watchful eyes of guards; Stilgar, her uncle of the Naibs, and his favorite wife, Harah...and Irulan ...Alia...

The sound of wind through the rocks accompanied her thoughts. The desert day had become yellow on yellow, tan on tan, gray on gray.

Why such a strange mixture of companions?

"We have forgotten," Paul had said in response to her question, "that the word 'company' originally meant traveling companions. We are a company."

"But what value are they?"

"There!" he'd said, turning his frightful sockets toward her. "We've lost that clear, single-note of living. If it cannot be bottled, beaten, pointed or hoarded, we give it no value."

Hurt, she'd said: "That's not what I meant."

"Ahhh, dearest one," he'd said, soothing, "we are so

money-rich and so life-poor. I am evil, obstinate, stupid . . ."

"You are not!"

"That, too, is true. But my hands are blue with time. I think . . . I think I tried to invent life, not realizing it'd already been invented."

And he'd touched her abdomen to feel the new life there.

Remembering, she placed both hands over her abdomen and trembled, sorry that she'd asked Paul to bring her here.

The desert wind had stirred up evil odors from the fringe plantings which anchored the dunes at the cliff base. Fremen superstition gripped her: *evil odors, evil times.* She faced into the wind, saw a worm appear outside the plantings. It arose like the prow of a demon ship out of the dunes, threshed sand, smelled the water deadly to its kind, and fled beneath a long, burrowing mound.

She hated the water then, inspired by the worm's fear. Water, once the spirit-soul of Arrakis, had become a poison. Water brought pestilence. Only the desert was clean.

Below her, a Fremen work gang appeared. They climbed to the sietch's middle entrance, and she saw that they had muddy feet.

Fremen with muddy feet!

The children of the sietch began singing to the morning above her, their voices piping from the upper entrance. The voices made her feel time fleeing from her like hawks before the wind. She shuddered.

What storms did Paul *see* with his eyeless vision?

She sensed a vicious madman in him, someone weary of songs and polemics.

The sky, she noted, had become crystal gray filled with alabaster rays, bizarre designs etched across the heavens by windborne sand. A line of gleaming white in the south caught her attention. Eyes suddenly alerted, she interpreted the sign: White sky in the south: Shai-hulud's mouth. A storm came, big wind. She felt the warning breeze, a crystal blowing of sand against her cheeks. The incense of death came on the wind: odors of water flowing in qanats, sweating sand, flint. The water—that was why Shai-hulud sent his coriolis wind.

Hawks appeared in the cleft where she stood, seeking safety from the wind. They were brown as the rocks and with scarlet in their wings. She felt her spirit go out to them: they had a place to hide; she had none.

"M'Lady, the wind comes!"

She turned, saw the ghola calling to her outside the upper entrance to the sietch. Fremen fears gripped her. Clean death and the body's water claimed for the tribe, these she understood. But...something brought back from death...

Windblown sand whipped at her, reddened her cheeks. She glanced over her shoulder at the frightful band of dust across the sky. The desert beneath the storm had taken on a tawny, restless appearance as though dune waves beat on a tempest shore the way Paul had once described a sea. She hesitated, caught by a feeling of the desert's transience. Measured against eternity, this was no more than a caldron. Dune surf thundered against cliffs.

The storm out there had become a universal thing for her—all the animals hiding from it...nothing left of the desert but its own private sounds: blown sand scraping along rock, a wind-surge whistling, the gallop of a boulder tumbled suddenly from its hill—then! somewhere out of sight, a capsized worm thumping its idiot way aright and slithering off to its dry depths.

It was only a moment as her life measured time, but in that moment she felt this planet being swept away—cosmic dust, part of other waves.

"We must hurry," the ghola said from right beside her.

She sensed fear in him then, concern for her safety.

"It'll shred the flesh from your bones," he said, as though he needed to explain such a storm to *her*.

Her fear of him dispelled by his obvious concern, Chani allowed the ghola to help her up the rock stairway to the sietch. They entered the twisting baffle which protected the entrance. Attendants opened the moisture seals, closed them behind.

Sietch odors assaulted her nostrils. The place was a ferment of nasal memories—the warren closeness of bodies, rank esters of the reclamation stills, familiar food aromas, the flinty burning of machines at work ... and through it all, the omnipresent spice: melange everywhere.

She took a deep breath. "Home."

The ghola took his hand from her arm, stood aside, a patient figure now, almost as though turned off when not in use. Yet ... he watched.

Chani hesitated in the entrance chamber, puzzled by something she could not name. This was truly her home. As a child, she'd hunted scorpions here by glowglobe light. Something was changed, though ...

"Shouldn't you be going to your quarters, m'Lady?" the ghola asked.

As though ignited by his words, a rippling birth constriction seized her abdomen. She fought against revealing it.

"M'Lady?" the ghola said.

"Why is Paul afraid for me to bear our children?" she asked.

"It is a natural thing to fear for your safety," the ghola said.

She put a hand to her cheek where the sand had reddened it. "And he doesn't fear for the children?"

"M'Lady, he cannot think of a child without remembering that your firstborn was slain by the Sardaukar."

She studied the ghola—flat face, unreadable mechanical eyes. Was he truly Duncan Idaho, this creature? Was he friend to anyone? Had he spoken truthfully now?

"You should be with the medics," the ghola said.

Again, she heard the fear for her safety in his voice. She felt abruptly that her mind lay undefended, ready to be invaded by shocking perceptions.

"Hayt, I'm afraid," she whispered. "Where is my Usul?"

"Affairs of state detain him," the ghola said.

She nodded, thinking of the government apparatus which had accompanied them in a great flight of ornithopters. Abruptly, she realized what puzzled her about the sietch: outworld odors. The clerks and aides had brought their own perfumes into this environment, aromas of diet and clothing, of exotic toiletries. They were an undercurrent of odors here.

Chani shook herself, concealing an urge to bitter laughter. Even the smells changed in Muad'dib's presence!

"There were pressing matters which he could not defer," the ghola said, misreading her hesitation.

"Yes...yes, I understand. I came with that swarm, too."

Recalling the flight from Arrakeen, she admitted to herself now that she had not expected to survive it. Paul had insisted on piloting his own 'thopter. Eyeless, he had guided the machine here. After that experience, she knew nothing he did could surprise her.

Another pain fanned out through her abdomen.

The ghola saw her indrawn breath, the tightening of her cheeks, said: "Is it your time?"

"I...yes, it is."

"You must not delay," he said. He grasped her arm, hurried her down the hall.

She sensed panic in him, said: "There's time."

He seemed not to hear. "The Zensunni approach to birth," he said, urging her even faster, "is to wait without purpose in the state of highest tension. Do not compete with what is happening. To compete is to prepare for failure. Do not be trapped by the need to achieve anything. This way, you achieve everything."

While he spoke, they reached the entrance to her quarters. He thrust her through the hangings, cried out: "Harah! Harah! It is Chani's time. Summon the medics!"

His call brought attendants running. There was a great bustling of people in which Chani felt herself an isolated island of calm...until the next pain came.

Hayt, dismissed to the outer passage, took time to wonder at his own actions. He felt fixated at some point of time where all truths were only temporary. Panic lay beneath his actions, he realized. Panic centered not on the possibility that Chani might die, but that Paul should come to him afterward...filled with grief...his loved one...gone...gone...

Something cannot emerge from nothing, the ghola told himself. *From what does this panic emerge?*

He felt that his mentat faculties had been dulled, let out a long, shuddering breath. A psychic shadow passed over him. In the emotional darkness of it, he felt himself waiting for some absolute sound—the snap of a branch in a jungle.

A sigh shook him. Danger had passed without striking.

Slowly, marshaling his powers, shedding bits of inhibition, he sank into mentat awareness. He forced it —not the best way—but somehow necessary. Ghost shadows moved within him in place of people. He was a transshipping station for every datum he had ever encountered. His being was inhabited by creatures of possibility. They passed in review to be compared, judged.

Perspiration broke out on his forehead.

Thoughts with fuzzy edges feathered away into darkness—unknown. Infinite systems! A mentat could not function without realizing he worked in infinite systems. Fixed knowledge could not surround the infinite. *Everywhere* could not be brought into finite perspective. Instead, he must *become* the infinite— momentarily.

In one gestalten spasm, he had it, seeing Bijaz seated before him blazing from some inner fire.

Bijaz!

The dwarf had done something to him!

Hayt felt himself teetering on the lip of a deadly pit. He projected the mentat computation line forward, seeing what could develop out of his own actions.

"A compulsion!" he gasped. "I've been rigged with a compulsion!"

A blue-robed courier, passing as Hayt spoke, hesitated. "Did you say something, sirra?"

Not looking at him, the ghola nodded. "I said everything."

There was a man so wise,
He jumped into
A sandy place
And burnt out both his eyes!
And when he knew his eyes were gone,
He offered no complaint.
He summoned up a vision
And made himself a saint.

—Children's Verse
from History of Muad'dib

Paul stood in darkness outside the sietch. Oracular vision told him it was night, that moonlight silhouetted the shrine atop Chin Rock high on his left. This was a memory-saturated place, his first sietch, where he and Chani...

I must not think of Chani, he told himself.

The thinning cup of his vision told him of changes all around—a cluster of palms far down to the right, the black-silver line of a qanat carrying water through the dunes piled up by that morning's storm.

Water flowing in the desert! He recalled another kind of water flowing in a river of his birthworld, Caladan. He hadn't realized then the treasure of such a flow, even the murky slithering in a qanat across a desert basin. Treasure.

With a delicate cough, an aide came up from behind.

Paul held out his hands for a magnabord with a single sheet of metallic paper on it. He moved as sluggishly as the qanat's water. The vision flowed, but he found himself increasingly reluctant to move with it.

"Pardon, Sire," the aide said. "The Semboule Treaty—your signature?"

"I can read it!" Paul snapped. He scrawled "Atreides Imper." in the proper place, returned the board, thrusting it directly into the aide's outstretched hand, aware of the fear this inspired.

The man fled.

Paul turned away. *Ugly, barren land!* He imagined it sun-soaked and monstrous with heat, a place of sandslides and the drowned darkness of dust pools, blowdevils unreeling tiny dunes across the rocks, their narrow bellies full of ochre crystals. But it was a rich land, too: big, exploding out of narrow places with vistas of storm-trodden emptiness, rampart cliffs and tumbledown ridges.

All it required was water . . . and love.

Life changed those irascible wastes into shapes of grace and movement, he thought. That was the message of the desert. Contrast stunned him with realization. He wanted to turn to the aides massed in the sietch entrance, shout at them: If you need something to worship, then worship life—all life, every last crawling bit of it! We're all in this beauty together!

They wouldn't understand. In the desert, they were endlessly desert. Growing things performed no green ballet for them.

He clenched his fists at his sides, trying to halt the vision. He wanted to flee from his own mind. It was a beast come to devour him! Awareness lay in him, sodden, heavy with all the living it had sponged up, saturated with too many experiences.

Desperately, Paul squeezed his thoughts outward.

Stars!

Awareness turned over at the thought of all those stars above him—an infinite volume. A man must be half mad to imagine he could rule even a teardrop of that volume. He couldn't begin to imagine the number of subjects his Imperium claimed.

Subjects? Worshippers and enemies, more likely. Did any among them see beyond rigid beliefs? Where was one man who'd escaped the narrow destiny of his prejudices? Not even an Emperor escaped. He'd lived a take-everything life, tried to create a universe in his own image. But the exultant universe was breaking across him at last with its silent waves.

I spit on Dune! he thought. *I give it my moisture!*

This myth he'd made out of intricate movements and imagination, out of moonlight and love, out of prayers older than Adam, and gray cliffs and crimson shadows, laments and rivers of martyrs—what had it come to at last? When the waves receded, the shores of Time would spread out there clean, empty, shining with infinite grains of memory and little else. Was this the golden genesis of man?

Sand scuffed against rocks told him that the ghola had joined him.

"You've been avoiding me today, Duncan," Paul said.

"It's dangerous for you to call me that," the ghola said.

"I know."

"I . . . came to warn you, m'Lord."

"I know."

The story of the compulsion Bijaz had put on him poured from the ghola then.

"Do you know the nature of the compulsion?" Paul asked.

"Violence."

Paul felt himself arriving at a place which had claimed him from the beginning. He stood suspended. The Jihad had seized him, fixed him onto a glidepath from which the terrible gravity of the Future would never release him.

"There'll be no violence from Duncan," Paul whispered.

"But, Sire..."

"Tell me what you see around us," Paul said.

"M'Lord?"

"The desert—how is it tonight?"

"Don't you *see* it?"

"I have no eyes, Duncan."

"But..."

"I've only my vision," Paul said, "and wish I didn't have it. I'm dying of prescience, did you know that, Duncan?"

"Perhaps...what you fear won't happen," the ghola said.

"What? Deny my own oracle? How can I when I've seen it fulfilled thousands of time? People call it a power, a gift. It's an affliction! It won't let me leave my life where I found it!"

"M'Lord," the ghola muttered, "I...it isn't...young master, you don't...I..." He fell silent.

Paul sensed the ghola's confusion, said: "What'd you call me, Duncan?"

"What? What I...for a moment..."

"You called me 'young master.'"

"I did, yes."

"That's what Duncan always called me." Paul reached

out, touched the ghola's face. "Was that part of your Tleilaxu training?"

"No."

Paul lowered his hand. "What, then?"

"It came from . . . me."

"Do you serve two masters?"

"Perhaps."

"Free yourself from the ghola, Duncan."

"How?"

"You're human. Do a human thing."

"I'm a ghola!"

"But your flesh is human. Duncan's in there."

"*Something's* in there."

"I care not how you do it," Paul said, "but you'll do it."

"You've foreknowledge?"

"Foreknowledge be damned!" Paul turned away. His vision hurtled forward now, gaps in it, but it wasn't a thing to be stopped.

"M'Lord, if you've—"

"Quiet!" Paul held up a hand. "Did you hear that?"

"Hear what, m'Lord?"

Paul shook his head. Duncan hadn't heard it. Had he only imagined the sound? It'd been his tribal name called from the desert—far away and low: "Usul . . . Uuuusssssuuuullll . . ."

"What is it, m'Lord?"

Paul shook his head. He felt watched. Something out there in the night shadows knew he was here. Something? No—some*one*.

"It was mostly sweet," he whispered, "and you were the sweetest of all."

"What'd you say, m'Lord?"

"It's the future," Paul said.

That amorphous human universe out there had undergone a spurt of motion, dancing to the tune of his vision. It had struck a powerful note then. The ghost-echoes might endure.

"I don't understand, m'Lord," the ghola said.

"A Fremen dies when he's too long from the desert," Paul said. "They call it the 'water sickness.' Isn't that odd?"

"That's very odd."

Paul strained at memories, tried to recall the sound of Chani breathing beside him in the night. *Where is there comfort?* he wondered. All he could remember was Chani at breakfast the day they'd left for the desert. She'd been restless, irritable.

"Why do you wear that old jacket?" she'd demanded, eyeing the black uniform coat with its red hawk crest beneath his Fremen robes. "You're an Emperor!"

"Even an Emperor has his favorite clothing," he'd said.

For no reason he could explain, this had brought real tears to Chani's eyes—the second time in her life when Fremen inhibitions had been shattered.

Now, in the darkness, Paul rubbed his own cheeks, felt moisture there. *Who gives moisture to the dead?* he wondered. It was his own face, yet not his. The wind chilled the wet skin. A frail dream formed, broke. What was this swelling in his breast? Was it something he'd eaten? How bitter and plaintive was this other self, giving moisture to the dead. The wind bristled with sand. The skin, dry now, was his own. But whose was the quivering which remained?

They heard the wailing then, far away in the sietch depths. It grew louder . . . louder . . .

The ghola whirled at a sudden glare of light, someone flinging wide the entrance seals. In the light, he saw a man with a raffish grin—no! Not a grin, but a grimace of grief! It was a Fedaykin lieutenant named Tandis. Behind him came a press of many people, all fallen silent now that they saw Muad'dib.

"Chani . . ." Tandis said.

"Is dead," Paul whispered. "I heard her call."

He turned toward the sietch. He knew this place. It was a place where he could not hide. His onrushing vision illuminated the entire Fremen mob. He *saw* Tandis, felt the Fedaykin's grief, the fear and anger.

"She is gone," Paul said.

The ghola heard the words out of a blazing corona. They burned his chest, his backbone, the sockets of his metal eyes. He felt his right hand move toward the knife at his belt. His own thinking became strange, disjointed. He was a puppet held fast by strings reaching down from that awful corona. He moved to another's commands, to another's desires. The strings jerked his arms, his legs, his jaw. Sounds came squeezing out of his mouth, a terrifying repetitive noise—

"Hrrak! Hraak! Hraak!"

The knife came up to strike. In that instant, he grabbed his own voice, shaped rasping words: "Run! Young master, run!"

"We will not run," Paul said. "We'll move with dignity. We'll do what must be done."

The ghola's muscles locked. He shuddered, swayed.

"*. . . what must be done!*" The words rolled in his mind like a great fish surfacing. "*. . . what must be done!*" Ahhh, that had sounded like the old Duke, Paul's grandfather. The young master had some of the old man in him. "*. . . what must be done!*"

The words began to unfold in the ghola's consciousness. A sensation of living two lives simultaneously spread out through his awareness: Hayt/Idaho/Hayt/Idaho . . . He became a motionless chain of relative existence, singular, alone. Old memories flooded his mind. He marked them, adjusted them to new understandings, made a beginning at the integration of a new awareness. A new *persona* achieved a temporary form of internal tyranny. The masculating synthesis remained charged with potential disorder, but events pressed him to the temporary adjustment. The young master needed him.

It was done then. He knew himself as Duncan Idaho, remembering everything of Hayt as though it had been stored secretly in him and ignited by a flaming catalyst. The corona dissolved. He shed the Tleilaxu compulsions.

"Stay close to me, Duncan," Paul said. "I'll need to depend on you for many things." And, as Idaho continued to stand entranced: "Duncan!"

"Yes, I am Duncan."

"Of course you are! This was the moment when you came back. We'll go inside now."

Idaho fell into step beside Paul. It was like the old times, yet not like them. Now that he stood free of the Tleilaxu, he could appreciate what they had given him. Zensunni training permitted him to overcome the shock of events. The mentat accomplishment formed a counterbalance. He put off all fear, standing above the source. His entire consciousness looked outward from a position of infinite wonder: he had been dead; he was alive.

"Sire," the Fedaykin Tandis said as they approached him, "the woman, Lichna, says she must see you. I told her to wait."

"Thank you," Paul said. "The birth..."

"I spoke to the medics," Tandis said, falling into step. "They said you have two children, both of them alive and sound."

"Two?" Paul stumbled, caught himself on Idaho's arm.

"A boy and a girl," Tandis said. "I saw them. They're good Fremen babies."

"How... how did she die?" Paul whispered.

"M'Lord?" Tandis bent close.

"Chani?" Paul said.

"It was the birth, m'Lord," Tandis husked. "They said her body was drained by the speed of it. I don't understand, but that is what they said."

"Take me to her," Paul whispered.

"M'Lord?"

"Take me to her!"

"That's where we're going, m'Lord." Again, Tandis bent close to Paul. "Why does your ghola carry a bared knife?"

"Duncan, put away your knife," Paul said. "The time for violence is past."

As he spoke, Paul felt closer to the sound of his voice than to the mechanism which had created the sound. Two babies! The vision had contained but one. Yet, these moments went as the vision went. There was a person here who felt grief and anger. Someone. His own awareness lay in the grip of an awful treadmill, replaying his life from memory.

Two babies?

Again he stumbled. *Chani, Chani,* he thought. *There was no other way. Chani, beloved, believe me that this death was quicker for you . . . and kinder. They'd have held our children hostage, displayed you in a cage and slave pits, reviled you with the blame for my death. This way . . . this way we destroy them and save our children.*

Children?

Once more, he stumbled.

I permitted this, he thought. *I should feel guilty.*

The sound of noisy confusion filled the cavern ahead of them. It grew louder precisely as he remembered it growing louder. Yes, this was the pattern, the inexorable pattern, even with two children.

Chani is dead, he told himself.

At some faraway instant in a past which he had shared with others, this future had reached down to him. It had chivvied him and herded him into a chasm whose walls grew narrower and narrower. He could feel them closing in on him. This was the way the vision went.

Chani is dead. I should abandon myself to grief.

But that was *not* the way the vision went.

"Has Alia been summoned?" he asked.

"She is with Chani's friends," Tandis said.

Paul sensed the mob pressing back to give him passage. Their silence moved ahead of him like a wave. The noisy confusion began dying down. A sense of congested emotion filled the sietch. He wanted to remove the people from his vision, found it impossible. Every face turning to

follow him carried its special imprint. They were pitiless
with curiosity, those faces. They felt grief, yes, but he
understood the cruelty which drenched them. They were
watching the articulate become dumb, the wise become a
fool. Didn't the clown always appeal to cruelty?

This was more than a deathwatch, less than a wake.

Paul felt his soul begging for respite, but still the vision
moved him. *Just a little farther now,* he told himself.
Black, visionless dark awaited him just ahead. There lay
the place ripped out of the vision by grief and guilt, the
place where the moon fell.

He stumbled into it, would've fallen had Idaho not
taken his arm in a fierce grip, a solid presence knowing
how to share his grief in silence.

"Here is the place," Tandis said.

"Watch your step, Sire," Idaho said, helping him over
an entrance lip. Hangings brushed Paul's face. Idaho
pulled him to a halt. Paul felt the room then, a reflection
against his cheeks and ears. It was a rock-walled space
with the rock hidden behind tapestries.

"Where is Chani?" Paul whispered.

Harah's voice answered him: "She is right here, Usul."

Paul heaved a trembling sigh. He had feared her body
already had been removed to the stills where Fremen
reclaimed the water of the tribe. Was that the way the
vision went? He felt abandoned in his blindness.

"The children?" Paul asked.

"They are here, too, m'Lord," Idaho said.

"You have beautiful twins, Usul," Harah said, "a boy
and a girl. See? We have them here in a creche."

Two children, Paul thought wonderingly. The vision
had contained only a daughter. He cast himself adrift
from Idaho's arm, moved toward the place where Harah
had spoken, stumbled into a hard surface. His hands
explored it: the metaglass outlines of a creche.

Someone took his left arm. "Usul?" It was Harah. She
guided his hand into the creche. He felt soft-soft flesh. It
was so warm! He felt ribs, breathing.

"That is your son," Harah whispered. She moved his hand. "And this is your daughter." Her hand tightened on his. "Usul, are you truly blind now?"

He knew what she was thinking. *The blind must be abandoned in the desert.* Fremen tribes carried no dead weight.

"Take me to Chani," Paul said, ignoring her question.

Harah turned him, guided him to the left.

Paul felt himself accepting now the fact that Chani was dead. He had taken his place in a universe he did not want, wearing flesh that did not fit. Every breath he drew bruised his emotions. *Two children!* He wondered if he had committed himself to a passage where his vision would never return. It seemed unimportant.

"Where is my brother?"

It was Alia's voice behind him. He heard the rush of her, the overwhelming presence as she took his arm from Harah.

"I must speak to you!" Alia hissed.

"In a moment," Paul said.

"Now! It's about Lichna."

"I know," Paul said. "In a moment."

"You don't have a moment!"

"I have many moments."

"But Chani doesn't!"

"Be still!" he ordered. "Chani is dead." He put a hand across her mouth as she started to protest. "I order you to be still!" He felt her subside and removed his hand. "Describe what you see," he said.

"Paul!" Frustration and tears battled in her voice.

"Never mind," he said. And he forced himself to inner stillness, opened the eyes of his vision to this moment. Yes—it was still here. Chani's body lay on a pallet within a ring of light. Someone had straightened her white robe, smoothed it trying to hide the blood from the birth. No matter; he could not turn his awareness from the vision of her face: such a mirror of eternity in the still features!

He turned away, but the vision moved with him. She

was gone...never to return. The air, the universe, all
vacant—everywhere vacant. Was this the essence of his
penance? he wondered. He wanted tears, but they would
not come. Had he lived too long a Fremen? This death
demanded its moisture!

Nearby, a baby cried and was hushed. The sound
pulled a curtain on his vision. Paul welcomed the
darkness. *This is another world,* he thought. *Two
children.*

The thought came out of some lost oracular trance. He
tried to recapture the timeless mind-dilation of the
melange, but awareness fell short. No burst of the future
came into this new consciousness. He felt himself
rejecting the future—any future.

"Goodbye, my Sihaya," he whispered.

Alia's voice, harsh and demanding, came from
somewhere behind him. "I've brought Lichna!"

Paul turned. "That's not Lichna," he said. "That's a
Face Dancer. Lichna's dead."

"But hear what she says," Alia said.

Slowly, Paul moved toward his sister's voice.

"I'm not surprised to find you alive, Atreides." The
voice was like Lichna's, but with subtle differences, as
though the speaker used Lichna's vocal cords, but no
longer bothered to control them sufficiently. Paul found
himself struck by an odd note of honesty in the voice.

"Not surprised?" Paul asked.

"I am Scytale, a Tleilaxu of the Face Dancers, and I
would know a thing before we bargain. Is that a ghola I
see behind you, or Duncan Idaho?"

"It's Duncan Idaho," Paul said. "And I will not bargain
with you."

"I think you'll bargain," Scytale said.

"Duncan," Paul said, speaking over his shoulder, "will
you kill this Tleilaxu if I ask it?"

"Yes, m'Lord." There was the suppressed rage of a
berserker in Idaho's voice.

"Wait!" Alia said. "You don't know what you're
rejecting."

"But I do know," Paul said.

"So it's truly Duncan Idaho of the Atreides," Scytale said. "We found the lever! A ghola *can* regain his past." Paul heard footsteps. Someone brushed past him on the left. Scytale's voice came from behind him now. "What do you remember of your past, Duncan?"

"Everything. From my childhood on. I even remember you at the tank when they removed me from it," Idaho said.

"Wonderful," Scytale breathed. "Wonderful."

Paul heard the voice moving. *I need a vision,* he thought. Darkness frustrated him. Bene Gesserit training warned him of terrifying menace in Scytale, yet the creature remained a voice, a shadow of movement— entirely beyond him.

"Are these the Atreides babies?" Scytale asked.

"Harah!" Paul cried. "Get her away from there!"

"Stay where you are!" Scytale shouted. "All of you! I warn you, a Face Dancer can move faster than you suspect. My knife can have both these lives before you touch me."

Paul felt someone touch his right arm, then move off to the right.

"That's far enough, Alia," Scytale said.

"Alia," Paul said. "Don't."

"It's my fault," Alia groaned. "My fault!"

"Atreides," Scytale said, "shall we bargain now?"

Behind him, Paul heard a single hoarse curse. His throat constricted at the suppressed violence in Idaho's voice. Idaho must not break! Scytale would kill the babies!

"To strike a bargain, one requires a thing to sell," Scytale said. "Not so, Atreides? Will you have your Chani back? We can restore her to you. A ghola, Atreides. A ghola *with full memory!* But we must hurry. Call your friends to bring a cryologic tank to preserve the flesh."

To hear Chani's voice once more, Paul thought. *To feel her presence beside me. Ahhh, that's why they gave me Idaho as a ghola, to let me discover how much the re-creation is like the original. But now—full restoration... at their price. I'd be a Tleilaxu tool forevermore. And Chani... chained to the same fate by a threat to our children, exposed once more to the Qizarate's plotting...*

"What pressures would you use to restore Chani's memory to her?" Paul asked, fighting to keep his voice calm. "Would you condition her to... to kill one of her own children?"

"We use whatever pressures we need," Scytale said. "What say you, Atreides?"

"Alia," Paul said, "bargain with this *thing*. I cannot bargain with what I cannot see."

"A wise choice," Scytale gloated. "Well, Alia, what do you offer me as your brother's agent?"

Paul lowered his head, bringing himself to stillness within stillness. He'd glimpsed something just then—like a vision, but not a vision. It had been a knife close to him. There!

"Give me a moment to think," Alia said.

"My knife is patient," Scytale said, "but Chani's flesh is not. Take a *reasonable* amount of time."

Paul felt himself blinking. It could not be... but it was! He felt eyes! Their vantage point was odd and they moved in an erratic way. *There!* The knife swam into his view. With a breath-stilling shock, Paul recognized the viewpoint. It was that of one of his children! He was seeing Scytale's knife hand from within the creche! It glittered only inches from him. Yes—and he could see himself across the room, as well—head down, standing quietly, a figure of no menace, ignored by the others in this room.

"To begin, you might assign us all your CHOAM holdings," Scytale suggested.

"All of them?" Alia protested.

"All."

Watching himself through the eyes in the creche, Paul slipped his cryskknife from its belt sheath. The movement produced a strange sensation of duality. He measured the distance, the angle. There'd be no second chance. He prepared his body then in the Bene Gesserit way, armed himself like a cocked spring for a single concentrated movement, a *prajna* thing requiring all his muscles balanced in one exquisite unity.

The crysknife leaped from his hand. The milky blur of it flashed into Scytale's right eye, jerked the Face Dancer's head back. Scytale threw both hands up and staggered backward against the wall. His knife clattered off the ceiling, to hit the floor. Scytale rebounded from the wall; he fell face forward, dead before he touched the floor.

Still through the eyes in the creche, Paul watched the faces in the room turn toward his eyeless figure, read the combined shock. Then Alia rushed to the creche, bent over it and hid the view from him.

"Oh, they're safe," Alia said. "They're safe."

"M'Lord," Idaho whispered, "was *that* part of your vision?"

"No." He waved a hand in Idaho's direction. "Let it be."

"Forgive me, Paul," Alia said. "But when that creature said they could ... revive ..."

"There are some prices an Atreides cannot pay," Paul said. "You know that."

"I know," she sighed. "But I was tempted ..."

"Who was not tempted?" Paul asked.

He turned away from them, groped his way to a wall, leaned against it and tried to understand what he had done. *How? How? The eyes in the creche!* He felt poised on the brink of terrifying revelation.

"My eyes, father."

The word-shapings shimmered before his sightless vision.

"My son!" Paul whispered, too low for any to hear. "You're ... aware."

Yes, father. Look!

Paul sagged against the wall in a spasm of dizziness. He felt that he'd been upended and drained. His own life whipped past him. He saw his father. He *was* his father. And the grandfather, and the grandfathers before that. His awareness tumbled through a mind-shattering corridor of his whole male line.

"How?" he asked silently.

Faint word-shapings appeared, faded and were gone, as though the strain was too great. Paul wiped saliva from the corner of his mouth. He remembered the awakening of Alia in the Lady Jessica's womb. But there had been no Water of Life, no overdose of melange this time ... or had there? Had Chani's hunger been for that? Or was this somehow the genetic product of his line, foreseen by the Reverend Mother Gaius Helen Mohiam?

Paul felt himself in the creche then, with Alia cooing over him. Her hands soothed him. Her face loomed, a giant thing directly over him. She turned him then and he saw his creche companion—a girl with that bony-ribbed look of strength which came from a desert heritage. She had a full head of tawny red hair. As he stared, she opened her eyes. Those eyes! Chani peered out of her eyes ... and the Lady Jessica. A multitude peered out of those eyes.

"Look at that," Alia said. "They're staring at each other."

"Babies can't focus at this age," Harah said.

"I could," Alia said.

Slowly, Paul felt himself being disengaged from that endless awareness. He was back at his own wailing wall then, leaning against it. Idaho shook his shoulder gently.

"M'Lord?"

"Let my son be called Leto for my father," Paul said, straightening.

"At the time of naming," Harah said, "I will stand beside you as a friend of the mother and give that name."

"And my daughter," Paul said. "Let her be called Ghanima."

"Usul!" Harah objected. "Ghanima's an ill-omened name."

"It saved your life," Paul said. "What matter that Alia

made fun of you with that name? My daughter is Ghanima, a spoil of war."

Paul heard wheels squeak behind him then—the pallet with Chani's body being moved. The chant of the Water Rite began.

"Hal yawm!" Harah said. "I must leave now if I am to be the observer of the holy truth and stand beside my friend for the last time. Her water belongs to the tribe."

"Her water belongs to the tribe," Paul murmured. He heard Harah leave. He groped outward and found Idaho's sleeve. "Take me to my quarters, Duncan."

Inside his quarters, he shook himself free gently. It was a time to be alone. But before Idaho could leave there was a disturbance at the door.

"Master!" It was Bijaz calling from the doorway.

"Duncan," Paul said, "let him come two paces forward. Kill him if he comes farther."

"Ayyah," Idaho said.

"Duncan is it?" Bijaz asked. "Is it *truly* Duncan Idaho?"

"It is," Idaho said. "I remember."

"Then Scytale's plan succeeded!"

"Scytale is dead," Paul said.

"But I am not and the plan is not," Bijaz said. "By the tank in which I grew! It can be done! I shall have my pasts—all of them. It needs only the right trigger."

"Trigger?" Paul asked.

"The compulsion to kill you," Idaho said, rage thick in his voice. "Mentat computation: They found that I thought of you as the son I never had. Rather than slay you, the true Duncan Idaho would take over the ghola body. But... it might have failed. Tell me, dwarf, if your plan had failed, if I'd killed him, what then?"

"Oh... then we'd have bargained with the sister to save her brother. But this way the bargaining is better."

Paul took a shuddering breath. He could hear the mourners moving down the last passage now toward the deep rooms and the water stills.

"It's not too late, m'Lord," Bijaz said. "Will you have your love back? We can restore her to you. A ghola, yes. But now—we hold out the full restoration. Shall we summon servants with a cryological tank, preserve the flesh of your beloved..."

It was harder now, Paul found. He had exhausted his powers in the first Tleilaxu temptation. And now all that was for nothing! To feel Chani's presence once more...

"Silence him," Paul told Idaho, speaking in Atreides battle tongue. He heard Idaho move toward the door.

"Master!" Bijaz squeaked.

"As you love me," Paul said, still in battle tongue, "do me this favor: Kill him before I succumb!"

"Noooooo..." Bijaz screamed.

The sound stopped abruptly with a frightened grunt.

"I did him the kindness," Idaho said.

Paul bent his head, listening. He no longer could hear the mourners. He thought of the ancient Fremen rite being performed now deep in the sietch, far down in the room of the death-still where the tribe recovered its water.

"There was no choice," Paul said. "You understand that, Duncan?"

"I understand."

"There are some things no one can bear. I meddled in all the possible futures I could create until, finally, they created me."

"M'Lord, you shouldn't..."

"There are problems in this universe for which there are no answers," Paul said. "Nothing. Nothing can be done."

As he spoke, Paul felt his link with the vision shatter. His mind cowered, overwhelmed by infinite possibilities. His lost vision became like the wind, blowing where it willed.

We say of Muad'dib that he has gone on a journey into that land where we walk without footprints.

—Preamble to the Qizarate Creed

There was a dike of water against the sand, an outer limit for the plantings of the sietch holding. A rock bridge came next and then the open desert beneath Idaho's feet. The promontory of Sietch Tabr dominated the night sky behind him. The light of both moons frosted its high rim. An orchard had been brought right down to the water.

Idaho paused on the desert side and stared back at flowered branches over silent water—reflections and reality—four moons. The stillsuit felt greasy against his skin. Wet flint odors invaded his nostrils past the filters. There was a malignant simpering to the wind through the orchard. He listened for night sounds. Kangaroo mice

inhabited the grass at the water verge; a hawk ow
bounced its droning call into the cliff shadows; th
wind-broken hiss of a sandfall came from the open bled

Idaho turned toward the sound.

He could see no movement out there on the moonli
dunes.

It was Tandis who had brought Paul this far. Then th
man had returned to tell his account. And Paul hae
walked out into the desert—like a Fremen.

"He was blind—truly blind," Tandis had said, a
though that explained it. "Before that, he had the visio
which he told to us . . . but . . ."

A shrug. Blind Fremen were abandoned in the desert
Muad'dib might be Emperor, but he was also Fremen
Had he not made provision that Fremen guard and rais
his children? He was Fremen.

It was a skeleton desert here, Idaho saw. Moon
silvered ribs of rock showed through the sand; then th
dunes began.

I should not have left him alone, not even for a minute
Idaho thought. *I knew what was in his mind.*

"He told me the future no longer needed his physica
presence," Tandis had reported. "When he left me, h
called back. 'Now I am free' were his words."

Damn them! Idaho thought.

The Fremen had refused to send 'thopters or searcher
of any kind. Rescue was against their ancient customs.

"There will be a worm for Muad'dib," they said. An
they began the chant for those committed to the desert
the ones whose water went to Shai-hulud: "Mother o
sand, father of Time, beginning of Life, grant hir
passage."

Idaho seated himself on a flat rock and stared at th
desert. The night out there was filled with camouflage
patterns. There was no way to tell where Paul had gone.

"Now I am free."

Idaho spoke the words aloud, surprised by the sound
of his own voice. For a time, he let his mind run.

emembering a day when he'd taken the child Paul to the
sea market on Caladan, the dazzling glare of a sun on
water, the sea's riches brought up dead, there to be sold.
Idaho remembered Gurney Halleck playing music of the
baliset for them—pleasure, laughter. Rhythms pranced in
his awareness, leading his mind like a thrall down
channels of remembered delight.

Gurney Halleck. Gurney would blame him for this
tragedy.

Memory music faded.

He recalled Paul's words: *"There are problems in this
universe for which there are no answers."*

Idaho began to wonder how Paul would die out there
in the desert. Quickly, killed by a worm? Slowly, in the
sun? Some of the Fremen back there in the sietch had said
Muad'dib would never die, that he had entered the
ruh-world where all possible futures existed, that he
would be present henceforth in the *alam al-mythal,*
wandering there endlessly even after his flesh had ceased
to be.

He'll die and I'm powerless to prevent it, Idaho
thought.

He began to realize that there might be a certain
fastidious courtesy in dying without a trace—no remains,
nothing, and an entire planet for a tomb.

Mentat, solve thyself, he thought.

Words intruded on his memory—the ritual words of
the Fedaykin lieutenant, posting a guard over Muad'dib's
children: "It shall be the solemn duty of the officer in
charge..."

The plodding, self-important language of government
enraged him. It had seduced the Fremen. It had seduced
everyone. A man, a great man, was dying out there, but
language plodded on...and on...and on...

What had happened, he wondered, to all the clean
meanings that screened out nonsense? Somewhere, in
some lost *where* which the Imperium had created, they'd
been walled off, sealed against chance rediscovery. His

mind quested for solutions, mentat fashion. Patterns of knowledge glistened there. Lorelei hair might shimmer thus, beckoning... beckoning the enchanted seaman into emerald caverns...

With an abrupt start, Idaho drew back from catatonic forgetfulness.

So! he thought. *Rather than face my failure, I would disappear within myself!*

The instant of that almost-plunge remained in his memory. Examining it, he felt his life stretch out as long as the existence of the universe. Real flesh lay condensed, finite in its emerald cavern of awareness, but infinite life had shared his being.

Idaho stood up, feeling cleansed by the desert. Sand was beginning to chatter in the wind, pecking at the surfaces of leaves in the orchard behind him. There was the dry and abrasive smell of dust in the night air. His robe whipped to the pulse of a sudden gust.

Somewhere far out in the bled, Idaho realized, a mother storm raged, lifting vortices of winding dust in hissing violence—a giant worm of sand powerful enough to cut flesh from bones.

He will become one with the desert, Idaho thought. *The desert will fulfill him.*

It was a Zensunni thought washing through his mind like clear water. Paul would go on marching out there, he knew. An Atreides would not give himself up completely to destiny, not even in the full awareness of the inevitable.

A touch of prescience came over Idaho then, and he saw that people of the future would speak of Paul in terms of seas. Despite a life soaked in dust, water would follow him. "His flesh foundered," they would say, "but he swam on."

Behind Idaho, a man cleared his throat.

Idaho turned to discern the figure of Stilgar standing on the bridge over the qanat.

"He will not be found," Stilgar said. "Yet all men will find him."

"The desert takes him—and deifies him," Idaho said. "Yet he was an interloper here. He brought an alien chemistry to this planet—water."

"The desert imposes its own rhythms," Stilgar said. "We welcomed him, called him our Mahdi, our Muad'dib, and gave him his secret name, Base of the Pillar: Usul."

"Still he was not born a Fremen."

"And that does not change the fact that we claimed him . . . and have claimed him finally." Stilgar put a hand on Idaho's shoulder. "All men are interlopers, old friend."

"You're a deep one, aren't you, Stil?"

"Deep enough. I can see how we clutter the universe with our migrations. Muad'dib gave us something uncluttered. Men will remember his Jihad for that, at least."

"He won't give up to the desert," Idaho said. "He's blind, but he won't give up. He's a man of honor and principle. He was Atreides-trained."

"And his water will be poured on the sand," Stilgar said. "Come." He pulled gently at Idaho's arm. "Alia is back and is asking for you."

"She was with you at Sietch Makab?"

"Yes—she helped whip those soft Naibs into line. They take her orders now . . . as I do."

"What orders?"

"She commanded the execution of the traitors."

"Oh." Idaho suppressed a feeling of verigo as he looked up at the promontory. "Which traitors?"

"The Guildsman, the Reverend Mother Mohiam, Korba . . . a few others."

"You slew a Reverend Mother?"

"I did. Muad'dib left word that it should not be done." He shrugged. "But I disobeyed him, as Alia knew I would."

Idaho stared again into the desert, feeling himself become whole, one person capable of seeing the pattern of what Paul had created. *Judgment strategy,* the Atreides called it in their training manuals. *People are subordinate to government, but the ruled influence the rulers.* Did the ruled have any concept, he wondered, of what they had helped create here?

"Alia . . ." Stilgar said, clearing his throat. He sounded embarrassed. "She needs the comfort of your presence."

"And she is the government," Idaho murmured.

"A regency, no more."

"Fortune passes everywhere, as her father often said," Idaho muttered.

"We make our bargain with the future," Stilgar said. "Will you come now? We need you back there." Again, he sounded embarrassed. "She is . . . distraught. She cries out against her brother one moment, mourns him the next."

"Presently," Idaho promised. He heard Stilgar leave. He stood facing into the rising wind, letting the grains of sand rattle against the stillsuit.

Mentat awareness projected the outflowing patterns into the future. The possibilities dazzled him. Paul had set in motion a whirling vortex and nothing could stand in its path.

The Bene Tleilax and the Guild had overplayed their hands and had lost, were discredited. The Qizarate was shaken by the treason of Korba and others high within it. And Paul's final voluntary act, his ultimate acceptance of their customs, had ensured the loyalty of the Fremen to him and to his house. He was one of them forever now.

"Paul is gone!" Alia's voice was choked. She had come up almost silently to where Idaho stood and was now beside him. "He was a fool, Duncan!"

"Don't say that!" he snapped.

"The whole universe will say it before I'm through," she said.

"Why, for the love of heaven?"

"For the love of my brother, not of heaven."

Zensunni insight dilated his awareness. He could sense that there was no vision in her—had been none since Chani's death. "You practice an odd love," he said.

"Love? Duncan, he had but to step off the track! What matter that the rest of the universe would have come shattering down behind him? He'd have been safe . . . and Chani with him!"

"Then . . . why didn't he?"

"For the love of heaven," she whispered. Then, more loudly, she said: "Paul's entire life was a struggle to escape his Jihad and its deification. At least, he's free of it. He chose this!"

"Ah, yes—the oracle." Idaho shook his head in wonder. "Even Chani's death. His moon fell."

"He *was* a fool, wasn't he, Duncan?"

Idaho's throat tightened with suppressed grief.

"Such a fool!" Alia gasped her control breaking. "He'll live forever while we must die!"

"Alia, don't . . ."

"It's just grief," she said, voice low. "Just grief. Do you know what I must do for him? I must save the life of the Princess Irulan. That one! You should hear *her* grief. Wailing, giving moisture to the dead; she swears she loved him and knew it not. She reviles her Sisterhood, says she'll spend her life teaching Paul's children."

"You trust her?"

"She reeks of trustworthiness!"

"Ahhh," Idaho murmured. The final pattern unreeled before his awareness like a design on fabric. The defection of the Princess Irulan was the last step. It left the Bene Gesserit with no remaining lever against the Atreides heirs.

Alia began to sob, leaned against him, face pressed into his chest. "Ohhh, Duncan, Duncan! He's gone!"

Idaho put his lips against her hair. "Please," he whispered. He felt her grief mingling with his like two streams entering the same pool.

"I need you, Duncan," she sobbed. "Love me!"

"I do," he whispered.

She lifted her head, peered at the moon-frosted outline of his face. "I know, Duncan. Love knows love."

Her words sent a shudder through him, a feeling of estrangement from his old self. He had come out here looking for one thing and had found another. It was as though he'd lurched into a room full of familiar people only to realize too late that he knew none of them.

She pushed away from him, took his hand. "Will you come with me, Duncan?"

"Wherever you lead," he said.

She led him back across the qanat into the darkness at the base of the massif and its Place of Safety.

EPILOGUE

No bitter stench of funeral-still for Muad'dib.
No knell nor solemn rite to free the mind
From avaricious shadows.
He is the fool saint,
The golden stranger living forever
On the edge of reason.
Let your guard fall and he is there!
His crimson peace and sovereign pallor
Strike into our universe on prophetic webs
To the verge of a quiet glance—there!
Out of bristling star-jungles:
Mysterious, lethal, an oracle without eyes,
Catspaw of prophecy, whose voice never dies!
Shai-hulud, he awaits thee upon a strand
Where couples walk and fix, eye to eye,
The delicious ennui of love.
He strides through the long cavern of time,
Scattering the fool-self of his dream.

—The Ghola's Hymn

FRANK HERBERT
...is science fiction

___THE BOOK OF FRANK HERBERT	04527-7 – $2.25
___CHILDREN OF DUNE	06174-4 – $2.95
___DESTINATION: VOID	05537-X – $2.75
___THE DOSADI EXPERIMENT	05514-0 – $2.75
___DUNE	05471-3 – $2.95
___DUNE MESSIAH	06173-6 – $2.95
___THE EYES OF HEISENBERG	05098-X – $2.25
___THE GODMAKERS	05516-7 – $2.50
___THE JESUS INCIDENT	05517-5 – $2.75
Frank Herbert and Bill Ransom	
___THE SANTAROGA BARRIER	05944-8 – $2.50
___SOUL CATCHER	05945-6 – $2.50
___WHIPPING STAR	05515-9 – $2.50
___THE WORLDS OF FRANK HERBERT	05297-4 – $2.25

Available at your local bookstore or return this form to:

**Berkley Book Mailing Service
P.O. Box 690
Rockville Centre, NY 11570**

Please send me the above titles. I am enclosing $_____
(Please add 50¢ per copy to cover postage and handling). Send check or money order—no cash or C.O.D.'s. Allow six weeks for delivery.

NAME_____

ADDRESS_____

CITY_____ STATE/ZIP_____ **49** D